AN UNHAPPY MEDIUM

Chief Langdon emerged from the front door and crouched to rub his fingers along the stoop. He stood and glared at Cass.

Cass turned and looked behind her. Nope, he was definitely looking at her. She braced herself as he walked toward her.

"Come with me, Cass." He gestured toward his patrol car.

Her mouth fell open. Her gaze shot to Tank, who wore a similarly shocked expression. Under other circumstances, it might have been comical. Now . . . not so much.

Chief Langdon took hold of Cass's arm and guided her gently toward the car. He turned her toward it and told her to put her hands on the roof. He began to pat her down.

"You're *frisking* me? This has to be some kind of joke." She tried to face him, but he stopped her.

"Chief, what's going on?" Tank finally found his voice.

Langdon ignored him, speaking instead to Cass. "I'm taking you in for questioning."

"What! Are you crazy? Why can't you question me here?"

"I'm taking you down to the station."

She huffed out a breath. "You were friends with my father, Otis. How can you do this?"

"You have the right to remain silent." He turned her to face him and caught her gaze. "I suggest you do." He guided her forward as she sputtered.

DEATH AT FIRST SIGHT

LENA GREGORY

First Edition: November 2016

Printed in the United States of America

BERKLEY PRIME CRIME
New York

BERKLEY PRIME CRIME
Published by Berkley
An imprint of Penguin Random House LLC
375 Hudson Street, New York, New York 10014

ISBN: 9780425282748

33614057762055

1 3 5 7 9 10 8 6 4 2

Book design by Kelly Lipovich

Greg, Elaina, Nicky, and Logan, you are my world.
Thank you for believing in me!

Acknowledgments

This book would not have been possible without the support and encouragement of my husband, Greg. We've built a wonderful life together, and I can't wait to see where our journey will lead next. I'd like to say a big thank-you to my children, Elaina, Nicky, and Logan, for their understanding and help while I spent long nights at the computer. My husband and children are truly the loves of my life. I also have to thank my best friend, Renee, for all of her support, long conversations, and reading many rough drafts. I still wouldn't know how to use Word without her help. I'd like to thank my sister, Debby, and my dad, who are probably my biggest fans and have read every word I've ever written. To my agent, Dawn Dowdle, thank you for believing in me and for being there in the middle of the night every time I have a question. Words cannot express my gratitude to Julie Mianecki for giving me this opportunity and for her wonderful advice and assistance in polishing this manuscript.

{1}

Cass sucked in a breath, the gasp audible in the silence of the small room. *Oh no . . .* The walls pressed in on her, loomed over her, threatened to suffocate her. *This can't be happening again.*

"Is everything all right?"

"Umm . . . sure." Darkness encroached, tunneling her vision. She forced it back, counted to ten, took deep breaths—anything to fight back the blackness. She struggled against the urge to push the glass ball away from her. "Sorry. I must have zoned out for a minute." She averted her gaze, hoping the other woman wouldn't catch the lie.

The woman's eyebrows drew together, a frown creasing her forehead. "Are you sure you didn't see anything bad?"

Cass forced a laugh as she shoved her chair back, stood, and moved away from the table. "Of course not. I told you I would only allow good spirits to enter." *Liar.*

Ellie Callahan shrugged. "So, what's the verdict?" Though she feigned indifference, eagerness lit her eyes.

"You know I can't give you specifics, Ellie." Impatience shortened Cass's temper, and she worked to soften her tone. She sighed and started to clean up. "Everything will work out. It's just going to take time." She wanted to tell her the truth—that her husband was a no-good, two-timing cheat who would never amount to anything, but she bit her tongue. It wouldn't change the fact that Ellie was going to go back to him, but it would hurt her. The young girl had been hurt enough. Besides, if the shadow that had slipped across Cass's vision was any indication, Ellie had bigger problems headed her way. Should she warn her? *Warn her about what?* Cass shook off a chill.

"Thank you so much, Cass." Ellie stood as well, lifted her bag from the back of the chair, and tucked it beneath her arm. Relief had relaxed Ellie's rigid posture and softened the scowl she usually wore, leaving her with a vulnerable appearance that tugged at Cass.

"No problem. Just do me a favor and don't tell your mother you were here."

Ellie blushed. "I'm sorry about Mom. She's kind of old-fashioned, and she doesn't understand . . . well . . . you know." She lowered her gaze to the crystal ball in the center of the table.

Cass nodded. "I know. It's okay."

Ellie held a twenty out to Cass.

"Don't worry about it. This one's on the house."

Ellie smiled and met Cass's gaze. "You sure?" She pushed her mousy brown hair back out of her face.

"Sure."

"Thank you." Ellie turned to go.

As she crossed the room, Cass fought the urge to call her back. What could she say? *Be careful?* Of what? The woman already had enough on her mind, her fragile nerves strung taut. A wandering husband, an overbearing mother—she didn't need any more.

As the door fell shut behind Ellie, Cass finally yanked the sash off her head, tumbling her long blond hair down her back, and reached up to massage her pounding temples. The constant throbbing kept time with the frantic beating of her heart, reminding her once again of the shadow that had crossed her vision. She shivered and dismissed the thought. She couldn't deal with this now. She was going to be late. Again.

The coin belt jangled as she slid it off and dropped it onto the table. She quickly discarded the flowing robe, hanging it over the velvet chair she'd just vacated, and pulled an oversized sweatshirt over her leggings and camisole.

After tossing the empty foam cups in the garbage, Cass pushed the remaining three chairs into place, returned the crystal ball to the shelf on the side wall, and ran a rag over the scarred wood table. That would have to be good enough for now.

The huge back window framed a perfect view of the bay, as well as the lighthouse that stood at the tip of the island, not far from her shop. A young couple crossed the beach, hand in hand, and climbed the two steps to Cass's back porch. Not local. She knew most of the locals by sight, if not personally. These two were tourists, for sure.

The wind chimes above the door tinkled as they entered the shop. *Great.* Just what she needed.

A quick glance at the clock above the door confirmed her fears. Three thirty. Ellie's reading had taken half an hour longer than expected. She'd have to hurry if she was going to make it to the theater on time. "May I help you?" She moved behind the counter and tossed the rag into a basket beneath the register.

"Hi." The man smiled and used his free hand to gesture toward the lighthouse while his companion looked on dreamily. "We were just over at the lighthouse, but there's no one around."

A blush stole over the young woman's cheeks as she giggled. When she lifted a hand to her mouth, her engagement ring caught the reflection of the late-afternoon sun.

"Nope. After Labor Day, the lighthouse is only open on weekends."

"Oh." Disappointment emanated from him.

"They have beautiful ceremonies, though. Well worth coming back out over the weekend if you want to book one."

The woman gasped. "How did you know we wanted to get married?"

Cass tapped the sign beside the register: PSYCHIC READINGS. "Sunset is the best time. Sometimes I sit out on the back porch and watch if I'm not too busy. Gorgeous."

"Wow. Are you really psychic?"

Not exactly. "That's what the sign says."

The woman's hand fluttered to her chest. "That is so cool. I've always wanted to go to a psychic."

Cass grinned. "I'll tell you what. I'm closing right now, but if you come back to talk to someone at the lighthouse over the weekend, come on in. I'll even give you a discount as an early wedding present."

"That'd be great. Thanks." They turned to go, but the woman stopped and turned back. "Do you do parties?"

"I do group readings."

She chewed her thumbnail. "We can't get back out this weekend, but if I come back next weekend with my bridesmaids, could you do a group reading for all of us together?"

"Sure." Cass rounded the counter and handed the woman a business card. "Just give me a call and we'll set something up. While you're out here, if you haven't already chosen a dress, Dreamweaver Designs is only a few doors down and has a beautiful line of beach wedding dresses." Maybe Bee would cut her some slack for being late if she sent him a customer. Another quick look at the clock. And then again, maybe not.

After locking the back door behind the couple, Cass grabbed her keys from the shelf behind the counter, slung her big leather tote bag over her shoulder, and headed for the front door. She turned the key in the lock of Mystical Musings and ran for the small, gravel parking lot. *Crap.* She stood frozen, staring at the empty lot. *Great.* How could she have forgotten she walked to the shop this morning? It had been such a beautiful fall day, and the walk along the beach from her house to the shop always relaxed her.

She heaved a sigh of resignation and started walking down the boardwalk. Bee would just have to start rehearsal without her.

She passed Dreamweaver Designs, only three doors down from Mystical Musings, and hesitated. Bee must have worked all night redesigning the front window display, which was typical for him. A black evening gown she'd never seen before was prominently displayed. Stunning. He'd really outdone himself this time. Maybe he'd let her wear that for the fashion show.

Of course, she'd have to lay off all the late-night fast food if she was going to wear the completely open back reflected in the mirror behind the display. As it was, she managed to stay slim only because she walked along the beach so often.

A shadow fell over her as someone rode past on a bike. *Ellie.* That disturbing darkness during her reading would undoubtedly haunt Cass all day. What was she going to do about warning Ellie? Doing nothing didn't sit right in her gut, and yet . . . What could she really do?

She hurried on her way, stepping off the boardwalk, crossing the narrow beach road, and heading toward the theater. She inhaled deeply. The cool, crisp air did little to relieve her headache but soothed her nerves a bit. This was her favorite time of year; the red, gold, and orange leaves creating a colorful backdrop for the island brought her such comfort. Her footsteps tapped a steady rhythm against the pavement, past the quaint shops, which dotted the beach road. As she headed toward the center of the island, old farmhouses lay scattered between small fields filled with corn, pumpkins, wildflowers, giving the entire landscape the look of a patchwork quilt—tranquil, comforting, and relaxing. A place you could snuggle down and enjoy the cozy feeling of being home.

Until the weekend, anyway, when crowds of tourists would flock to the tiny island that sat between the North and South Forks of Long Island. On Friday they'd come from New York City in droves, jamming up the expressway, filling the Long Island Rail Road cars, scrambling to reach Bay Island before ferry service stopped for the night.

She couldn't complain, though. Winter would come soon enough, and then she'd have to rely on her savings from the summer tourist season.

The acres slowly gave way to newer housing developments, and she stepped onto the sidewalk where it began. As she waited to cross Main Street, several passersby waved. She returned their greetings without much enthusiasm, though. She glanced at her watch, impatience warring with the throbbing in her head. The headache won out. She was already well over an hour late, but Bee would have to manage without her a few minutes longer.

When she reached the two small strips of white clapboard stores, which sat facing each other across Main Street and made up the "town" of Bay Island, she ran across the street and into the deli.

Habit had her scanning the small shop as she entered. Her gaze faltered when it landed on a stranger seated at one of the tables arranged in one corner of the shop. On the table in front of him was an open laptop, which he appeared to be totally engrossed in, with a coffee cup beside it. While strangers weren't unusual in town, especially at this time of year, there was something about this man that caught her attention.

She laughed at herself. It was most likely his devilish good looks. Dark, shaggy hair hung just past the collar of his leather jacket, giving him the bad boy look Cass had always found so attractive.

"Hey, Cass. How come you're not at the theater?"

Cass jumped, startled by the question and feeling a little

guilty about getting caught checking out a complete stranger. "I could ask you the same thing." Cass joined the line waiting for service.

Stephanie laughed. "I was there. I just ran out for coffee." She lifted a cup holder with three large to-go cups as proof.

"Is one of those for me?"

"Of course."

Stephanie's smile was contagious, and Cass grinned back. "You're a lifesaver." She took a step forward as the line inched up. "Hey, could you hang out a minute? I have to grab something for this headache, but I walked to the shop this morning and I'm already late and, well, you know . . ."

Good humor lit Stephanie's brown eyes. They both knew Bee's tantrum would be worse the later Cass got there.

"Yeah, I can wait. Of course, then we'll both be in trouble."

"You know what they say—misery loves company." Cass moved up again.

"What's the headache from?" Stephanie held one of the coffee cups out to Cass. "Here, maybe caffeine will help." At the sound of bells tinkling, Stephanie glanced past Cass toward the door that had just opened. Her smile faltered, and she tucked her frizzy brown hair behind her ear. She mumbled something under her breath, but Cass didn't quite catch it.

Cass turned to look over her shoulder and came face-to-face with an irate Marge Hawkins. *Uh-oh.*

The deep scowl and flushed cheeks were all the warning Cass needed to know Ellie hadn't kept her promise not to tell her mother she'd visited Cass for a reading. Oh well— that poor girl never could stand up to her mother.

"What did you tell my Ellie?" Marge pointed a finger and a wickedly sharp, bloodred nail within an inch of Cass's face.

Cass took a step back and bumped into the person in line in front of her.

"Hey!"

"Sorry." She didn't even turn at the indignant cry, hesitant to turn her back on Marge and her claws.

"We've been through this before, Ms. Hawkins. What I tell a client is confidential." Cass gripped her cup tightly and held her ground.

The irate woman huffed out a breath and moved even closer. Spittle sprayed from her mouth, and Cass had to resist the urge to reach up and wipe her face. "You listen to me, young lady. This is the last time I'm going to tell you to stay away from my daughter. I don't give a hoot about your fancy degree or your hocus-pocus. Just stay away from my Ellie. The next time I catch you near her, I'm calling Chief Langdon." She poked her claw into Cass's chest for good measure, then spun on her heel and strode out of the deli.

Cass heaved in a deep breath, struggling for control. The headache battered at her, and clamping her teeth so tightly together wasn't helping matters. Hot coffee trickled onto her hand, and she loosened her hold on the cup.

"Hmm . . . next time I say 'Don't look now' . . . you might want to listen." Stephanie's laughter seeped through Cass's rigid muscles, releasing some of the tension.

She reached up to massage the back of her neck. "Oh, is that what you said? Next time speak up a little." She laughed, but without any real humor. Sure, Cass had been publicly humiliated, but there wasn't much Marge could do to her.

Cass hadn't done anything wrong, and Ellie was a grown, *married* woman. That didn't stop the chill from racing up Cass's spine at the memory of the dark shadow that had crossed her vision while Ellie had been with her. *Ugh* . . . She was going to have to call Ellie and give her a warning. No way would she be able to sleep tonight if she didn't at least try to tell Ellie to be careful.

"Come on, move up." Stephanie took her arm and turned her toward the register. "If we don't get going soon, Bee's fit is going to make Marge's tantrum look tame."

As Cass turned, she glanced at the stranger. His slight smirk and deep blue eyes seemed to hold only curiosity, though he stared at her with an intensity that made her shiver. She allowed her gaze to linger for only a second or two, pulling away when heat began to creep up her cheeks.

2

"No. Wait. You're going to be wearing evening gowns and stiletto heels, not sneakers. You have to slow down. Start again." Bee turned as Cass and Stephanie entered the auditorium. "Okay, take a break." He waved his hands at the group of teenagers, who quickly dispersed, most pulling out cell phones and water bottles as they went. It was hard to believe these same kids, who were dressed in a various assortment of battered jeans, cutoff shorts, and flip-flops, would be the height of glamour in less than a month.

"Where have you two been?" Bee Maxwell strutted toward them, six feet of muscle packed between bleached blond hair and platform shoes—in full-on diva mode. He flung one end of a multicolored scarf around his neck.

Cass snatched one of the to-go cups from the holder in Stephanie's hand. "I come bearing gifts." She lifted the cup to him and batted her eyelashes.

"No fair." Stephanie feigned outrage, but a small smirk gave her away.

"I'm in more trouble than you."

Stephanie shrugged. "True."

Bee took the proffered cup. "Yeah, well, gift or no, I can't do this all by myself. And don't think batting those baby blues at me is going to get you off the hook. You promised you'd help." He gestured toward the stage behind him, perilously close to whining. "The girls could really use some pointers. Most of them have had no modeling experience. And the boys . . ." His hand fluttered to his chest. "Yikes."

"Take it easy on her," Stephanie said. "She just had a run-in with Marge."

Cass glanced at Stephanie, trying to silently relay her gratitude. Stephanie winked, and Cass returned her attention to Bee.

The indignation in Bee's eyes turned instantly to sympathy, just before they hardened. "That witch. I just got the letter today."

"What letter?"

"Isn't that what the run-in was about?" Bee opened his cup and blew delicately on his lukewarm coffee.

"No. I gave Ellie a reading today."

"Oh, that poor thing. I saw her husband in the hardware store, flirting with the new girl behind the counter. Hard to believe such a nice girl married such a jerk." Bee sipped from the cup, and his eyes fell closed. "Mmm . . . just what I needed. Okay, consider yourself forgiven." He waved a hand dismissively.

Stephanie huffed out a breath.

Cass grinned.

"So, anyway, I stopped at the post office on my way in and picked up the mail. I got yours, too, by the way." He paused. Sipped. Waited.

"Thank you for picking up my mail." Bee was one of her best friends, and Cass was used to his theatrics.

"Oh, no problem, dear. So, anyway"—he waved his free hand dramatically—"there was an official-looking letter from the board of directors, so I opened it." He stared at Cass.

"And?" A drumroll sounded in Cass's head, and she quelled the urge to roll her eyes.

"It said they're changing the date of the fashion show."

"What!" Coffee sloshed over the edge of her cup and spilled over her hand. She switched her cup to her other hand and shook off the mess. She and Stephanie fell into step on either side of Bee as he strode toward the stage. "What are you talking about? They can't do that."

"You're darn right, they can't. But they seem to think they can."

"What did the letter say? Where is it?"

Bee placed his coffee on the edge of the stage and dug through a large canvas satchel. "Here." He handed her an envelope.

She opened the letter and quickly scanned through the ridiculous excuses. "What are they talking about? Everyone knows Marge's theater group performs around the holidays."

"Finish reading." But Bee didn't give her a chance before launching into a tirade. "She says she gets first dibs on the theater, it's in her contract or some such drivel." He was perilously close to full-blown whining. "They can't do this to me, Cass. I've already sent out invitations and everything. I have a lot of time and money invested in this show."

"Don't worry, Bee." Cass grabbed napkins from her bag and wiped off her hand. It didn't help. The coffee had already dried, leaving her all sticky. "We'll work it out. You have a contract to use the building as well, so I doubt they can just change their minds about letting you use it." Of course, Marge was the president of the board of directors, so she could theoretically do whatever she wanted.

"I'm just telling you what the letter says, honey. They said she put in for the dates first, but there was an oversight. An oversight. Can you believe it? These people are going to ruin my entire career because of an *oversight*."

Bee was prone to dramatics, but this time he also happened to be right. His annual fashion show was a big event on Bay Island. It brought an influx of tourists for the entire weekend, at a time when the summer rush was dwindling. Plus, he'd begun to gain recognition for his designs, and a small group of buyers from New York City were expected to attend this year's event.

She stared at the offending letter still clutched in her hand. "So, what do you want to do?" She tried to concentrate on the letter, but the words didn't make sense. The full intensity of the headache had returned, slamming through her and jumbling the letters on the page. She rubbed her eyes.

"The letter says I have to go before the board next month to choose a different date."

"Next month? But the show is less than a month away." Cass gave up and tossed the letter onto the edge of the stage. She lowered her head, weaved her fingers into her hair, and squeezed.

"No kidding." Bee sipped his coffee. "You know what I need?"

Cass brushed at a coffee stain on her leggings. This day just kept getting better and better. "No. What?"

Bee could pout better than any kid she knew. He batted his thick, false eyelashes. "A donut."

She grinned. Donuts were Bee's answer to everything unpleasant. "Besides getting donuts, what are you going to do?"

"Well, we could do away with Marge." Bee smiled innocently.

The memory of the shadow intruded on Cass's thoughts, and she scowled at Bee. She was in no mood for his attempt at humor.

"What? The world would be a better place without that woman, anyway."

Cass continued to glare at him, without saying a word.

He shrugged. "Just sayin'." He returned to delicately sipping his coffee, but the gleam didn't leave his eyes.

Three hours and two donuts later, Cass helped Bee gather his things. "Are you going to keep running rehearsals?"

"Of course, dear. I'm having the show regardless." He gritted his teeth. "The buyers may not come if I change the date at the last minute." He shook his head and piled his sketches on the edge of the stage.

"I have to get going, Bee," Stephanie said.

He turned and kissed Stephanie's cheek. "Thanks, hon. I appreciate the help." He grinned. "And the donut run."

She laughed. "No problem. See you tomorrow. What time will you be here?"

"Around ten or eleven."

"See you then." She waved on her way out.

He glanced at Cass. "Can you come early tomorrow and work with the models?"

Cass hadn't modeled since she was a kid, but the little experience she had, along with twenty years of dance lessons, would be enough to give the kids what they needed. "I told them I'd meet them here in the morning and to bring shoes with heels."

"And you're going to draw up the stage design, right?"

"Yup." She'd have to come early and take a few measurements. "When is the runway going in?"

"It's scheduled for Monday. They have to take out a section of seats to make room. But now, who knows?" He shrugged and shook his head.

She'd have to try to do something to help. Maybe she'd try to contact some of the board members and see if she could find out what the real problem was. She squeezed his shoulder. "Don't worry too much, Bee. I have a feeling everything will work out."

"What kind of feeling?" He smiled. "A regular feeling, or a woo-woo feeling?" He wiggled his fingers.

"Just a feeling, Bee." She laughed.

Bee had made it very clear to everyone he didn't believe in *woo-woo*.

"Do you have the measurements for the runway?"

He dug through his bottomless bag, pulled out a small notepad, ripped off the top page, and handed it to her. "Here you go."

"Thanks." She looked over the measurements, folded the

paper, and stuck it in her pocket. "Stephanie is taking care of the flowers, right?"

He flipped to the back of the book and scanned his list. "Yes. The flowers, wine, and hors d'oeuvres."

Cass picked up the pile of sketches and shuffled through them. "Did the kids like the dresses?"

Bee's big brown eyes lit with joy. "They loved them."

Of course. The dresses were gorgeous, as always. "Is this the one Jess is going to wear?" she asked, pointing at a pale yellow garment.

"Yup. Her coloring will really make it pop, don't you think?"

"Definitely." The yellow would really stand out against Jess's dark tan. "Are you going to have her wear her hair up?"

"Absolutely. All those curls hanging down her back are wonderful, but we don't want them to hide the dress." Bee sifted through the pile and handed her a sketch of the back of the dress. A number of thin straps crisscrossed the otherwise open back in an elaborate design.

Her breath rushed out. "It's fabulous."

Bee beamed with pride as he put the sketches into his briefcase and snapped it closed. "It is, isn't it?" He slung the canvas satchel over his shoulder, lifted the briefcase, and glanced around.

"When did you make the black dress that's in your new display?" Cass fell into step beside him as he headed toward the door.

"I finished it last week, but I didn't get to do the window until last night."

"Well, it looks great. Any chance you'll let me wear it for the show?"

Bee harrumphed. "Only if you promise to change quickly. The black one comes in the next set after the red one you're modeling. And you'd have to put your hair up."

"Sure. No problem." Anything to wear that black dress. She stopped and waited for Bee to lock the door, then turned and stared at the parking lot. "Ugh . . . would you mind driving me home? I forgot I hitched a ride with Stephanie from the deli."

"I have to swing by the shop, anyway. I'll drop you off right after."

"Great. Thanks." She resisted the urge to brush the bottoms of her shoes off before sliding into Bee's immaculate black Trans Am, his pride and joy.

Cass's mind drifted as he drove, her thoughts turning to Ellie. It was too late to call now. She'd have to wait until morning, probably, but the phone call topped her mental to-do list. Once she warned Ellie to be careful, the nagging in her gut would probably go away. Of course, the chocolate donuts didn't help the heavy feeling in her stomach.

"I always get the creeps when I pass that house." Bee gestured out the window toward the old Madison Estate. Long since abandoned, the house sparked rumors of ghosts and strange happenings. It sat on a bluff, along the deserted stretch of road between the theater and the Bay Side Hotel, amid an overgrowth of encroaching brush and woods.

"We could stop in and say hello." She waggled her eyebrows when he pinned her with a glare.

Bee snorted but eyed her and lifted a brow as if he wasn't quite sure she was kidding. "Not in this lifetime, honey." He accelerated.

She laughed. "I was kidding, Bee."

"Yeah, well, I don't want you inviting any dead people into my car." He lovingly caressed the steering wheel. "Remember what happened last time I took you to the cemetery?"

"Oh please. That had nothing to do with me."

"Yeah, well. Whatever you did, it made my engine go all wonky. This baby didn't run right for months after that."

"I did not invite dead people into your car."

He scoffed. "Who knows? Maybe they just follow you around." He looked past her as if searching for some invisible ghost parade.

She bit back the urge to laugh. "Besides, you don't believe in that stuff. Remember?"

"Mmm . . . hmmm . . . but you never can be too careful."

She cracked the window open, the cool breeze whipping her hair around her face. The sea's briny scent invaded her lungs. The wooded area was one of the most beautiful on the island, especially in the fall with the leaves a full riot of color, and she wished it weren't already dark.

She tugged at the collar of her sweatshirt, suddenly feeling like she was suffocating, shadows running rampant through her mind.

Cass looked down. Trying to juggle her bag, a small wireless speaker for music, three dresses, and a cup of coffee, she punched the key fob button to lock the car door. She used the back of her wrist to swipe a few loose strands of hair back out of her face and dropped her keys into her bag as she crossed the small parking lot. Thoughts of Marge Hawkins had kept her up most of the night. How dare that cranky old . . .

Bee would be crushed if the show had to be rescheduled. He'd worked for years to build up his dress design business and the small shop on the boardwalk. Without the buyers attending the show, he'd miss a tremendous opportunity.

She reached the theater door, cursed, balanced the coffee cup between her arm and her chest, and struggled to dig the keys back out of her bag. *I can't even think straight this morning. How am I ever going to get through rehearsal?* She yanked the keys triumphantly from her bag and dropped the coffee cup, splashing its contents all over her feet and legs. "Ugh . . ."

She jammed the loose hair back behind her ear. Stepping over the puddle of coffee, she unlocked the door, walked in, and dumped all of her belongings on a long table in the entranceway.

This is all Marge's fault, she thought to herself. Between the run-in at the deli and the problem with Bee's show, the woman was grating on Cass's last nerve.

She turned, went back out to pick up the cup, and dropped it into the nearest wastebasket. Cass shoved her hands into her hair and squeezed. She released her hair and rubbed her eyes. Today was Saturday morning. They wouldn't be able to reach most of the board members until Monday morning anyway. They would simply run rehearsal today and then worry about everything else tomorrow.

With sort of a plan in mind, she heaved in a deep breath and collected her things. The thought of going for another cup of coffee flickered through her mind, but she quickly dismissed it. The models needed the extra time, and she'd promised Bee she'd have everything ready by the time he arrived.

As she walked toward the double doors of the theater, she ticked through each of the board members. There were eight all together. Marge was the president, so her opinions, no matter how warped or deranged, carried a lot of weight. Then there was her sidekick, the vice president, Chief of Police Otis Langdon, and . . . well . . . who was going to cross him? Cass massaged the bridge of her nose.

But wait . . . Hadn't one of the members retired and moved to Florida? Yes. A glimmer of hope surfaced. If they could find out who took Mary Harper's place, maybe they could find an ally. She sighed as she flipped on one row of house lights and started down the aisle. Things would work out. They always d—

She froze. Her heart stopped. A silhouette sat slumped in the pit. She squinted, trying to focus on the shadow. A nervous laugh bubbled out. "Hey. You scared me nearly to death." She started forward again, her hand pressed to her chest as if to keep her heart from jumping out. "You're early. Bee's not due in for another hour or so. He's not a morning person, if you know . . . what . . ."

Cass stopped. Something was wrong. Not much light found its way into the pit, leaving it bathed in shadows. She couldn't make out much of the figure, but what she could see seemed off. A head, cocked at an unnatural angle. She dropped the dresses and the speaker onto the nearest seat and crept closer. "Hello?"

A chill ran up her spine, goose bumps prickled her skin, and she held her breath as she fought the urge to turn and run. She changed course. Instead of heading toward the pit, she moved sideways toward the door, not daring to shift her gaze from whoever sat in the shadows. When she reached the door at the front of the auditorium, she wiped her sweaty palm on her pant leg and then felt along the wall for the light switch. She closed her eyes, hit the switch, let out her breath, and opened her eyes. The scream caught in her throat.

She gagged and slapped a hand over her mouth. *Oh no. Oh no. Oh no.* Indecision and stark terror held her frozen in place. She shook her head, as if she could clear the image from her mind, but it would be permanently etched there. She crept forward, one inch at a time. "Ms. Hawkins?" She forced the words past the lump in her throat. Another step.

"Mrs. Haw . . ." The scream finally tore free, and she turned and ran from the theater.

"Oh my . . ." She fumbled the bag from her shoulder and frantically dug for her phone. *Where the . . .* "Okay." She pulled the phone out and dropped the bag on the sidewalk. Tiny fingers of fear crawled up her spine. She glanced over her shoulder, scanned the parking lot, and searched the shadows crouched among the trees that surrounded the building. She sucked in a breath, but an iron vise gripped her chest, and she couldn't get enough air. Tremors shook her hands, and it took three tries before she managed to dial 911.

"Nine-one-one. What is your emergency?"

Cass pressed her back to the brick wall of the building, continuously searching the surrounding area. She sucked in a breath and fought to push the words past the lump of fear that had lodged in her throat. Was whoever killed Marge still lurking around?

"Nine-one-one. What is your emergency?"

She thought briefly about running around the building to her car, but fear paralyzed her. "At the theater. Marge Hawkins . . ."

"Hello?"

Cass's teeth started to chatter, and she clamped them tightly together.

"Hold on, honey," the woman on the line reassured her. "I'm sending someone over right now."

Sirens reached Cass's ears, and she sucked in a deep breath. She slid down to sit on the grass, with her back pressed against the wall. The shock that had had such a firm grip on her finally eased its hold. Help would be there any minute. She squeezed her eyes closed, but an image of Marge popped into her head.

The bruise that marred Marge's cheekbone beneath her right eye, the bright red mark on her neck . . . Odd. The mark on her forehead that could only be . . . Cass's eyes shot open, and she began to hyperventilate. An eddy of blackness crept into her peripheral vision. She dropped her head between her knees.

"Miss Donovan?"

Cass lifted her head. Chief of Police Otis Langdon was bent over her. *Great.* She wiped the tears from her cheeks and struggled to her feet.

Chief Langdon backed up and pulled his pants farther up around his considerable girth. "What's going on here?" He left his hands on his hips and glared at her from puffy, bloodshot eyes.

Cass sucked in a breath and let it out slowly. She held his gaze and tried to steady herself. "Marge Hawkins . . . in the theater . . ." A hiccup interrupted her, and the chief glanced over her shoulder and through the door she'd left open in her haste to flee. "In the pit . . ."

A scowl drew his thick, gray eyebrows down into a V, reminding Cass of two fat, gray caterpillars crossing paths. "So? What's the problem? She do somethin' to ya?"

Cass shook her head and forced a harsh whisper through her dry throat. "Sh . . . she . . . she's . . . dead."

Chief Langdon's frown deepened. "Wait here." He walked away, leaving Cass to panic in peace.

Of all the officers on the force, why did Langdon have to be the one to answer her call? Why couldn't Tank have come? She leaned forward and massaged her temples. Nothing would relieve the hammering of the stress headache. *Can this day even get any worse?*

A passing car caught her attention. The models would be arriving soon. She picked up her bag and phone and walked around the building, toward the parking lot, hoping to intercept the models before anyone went in. She glanced at her phone. *What?* How could that be possible? Only fifteen minutes had passed since she dropped her coffee.

"What did I tell you?" The irate voice stopped her in her tracks.

"I . . . uh . . ." She looked up from the phone and stared at Chief Langdon. His usually ruddy cheeks had gone an even deeper shade of purple.

"I don't want to hear it. I told you to stay put." He strode toward her, finger pointed at her face. "Did you touch anything in there?"

She quickly shook her head but then thought better of it. "Well . . . not by Ms. Hawkins, anyway. I had only started to walk over to see if she was all right, but then I realized she . . . wasn't." She forced down the bile creeping up the back of her throat.

Another car pulled into the lot, saving her from whatever he'd been about to say. Taylor Lawrence pulled up beside them and climbed out of the car.

Tank. A sigh of relief escaped Cass, prompting another scowl from Chief Langdon.

"Hey, Cass." Tank tipped his head toward Cass before turning his attention to Chief Langdon. "What's going on, Chief?"

"We got a dead body inside." Chief Langdon spared Cass a suspicious glare before walking away to talk into his radio.

For a brief minute she tried to hear what he was saying, then decided she didn't really care and turned her attention to Tank.

"You all right?" Tank put a massive hand on her shoulder and pulled her close for a hug. She wrapped her arms around him and enjoyed the brief illusion of safety. Tank was built like the vehicle he was nicknamed for, and being in his arms was like being wrapped up all nice and tight in a protective shell. Stephanie was a lucky woman. Not only was her husband built like a warrior, he had the personality of a teddy bear.

Tank grabbed both of her shoulders and set her back to study her expression. "Are you all right?"

She nodded and wiped tears from her face. "I'm all right, Tank. Thank you."

"Good, because Steph'll have my ass if I let anything happen to you." His grin filled his hardened, steel gray eyes with mischief, but then he sobered quickly. "What happened?"

Cass sniffed and took a deep breath. "Marge Hawkins is in the theater." She leaned past Tank to spy Chief Langdon pulling things from his trunk. "She's dead." Whispering made no sense. It wasn't like anyone was around to hear, but she couldn't seem to speak the words out loud. She'd never liked Ms. Hawkins, but finding a dead body . . . A shiver ran up her spine.

Tank blew out a breath with a whistle and turned. Chief Langdon was stringing crime scene tape around the perimeter of the building.

Cass followed his gaze. "Shouldn't you be doing something?"

"I am." Tank smiled and rubbed her arm. He let his hand fall when Chief Langdon approached.

"The crime scene unit will be here any minute. We'll go in with them."

Tank nodded. "Did you confirm, Chief?"

Langdon spared him a scathing glance. "Just keep an eye on your friend here. She's our only *witness*." The way he said *witness* made it sound more like *suspect*.

Sirens split the early-morning peace once again. More police cars, a crime scene van, and an ambulance all crowded into the small lot. Chaos ensued. Cass moved to stand beside her car, and Tank stuck to her side like glue.

"Can you tell me what happened when you got here, Cass?"

She shivered, the cool fall air nipping at her. "I went in and turned on the lights—well, some of them anyway—and I noticed someone sitting in the pit."

"The pit?"

A growing crowd had formed around the small theater. Some of the kids and their parents had begun to join the bedlam. "The seats down in the front of the stage where the musicians sit."

Tank nodded for her to continue as she scanned the growing sea of faces. Was the killer standing there watching? Another chill ran up her spine, but this one had nothing to do with the cold. "Um . . ."

Chief Langdon emerged from the front door and crouched to rub his fingers along the stoop. He stood and glared at Cass.

Cass turned and looked behind her. Nope, he was definitely looking at her. She braced herself as he walked toward her.

"Come with me, Cass." He gestured toward his patrol car.

Her mouth fell open. Her gaze shot to Tank, who wore a similarly shocked expression. Under other circumstances, it might have been comical. Now . . . not so much.

Chief Langdon took hold of Cass's arm and guided her gently toward the car. He turned her toward it and told her to put her hands on the roof. He began to pat her down.

"You're *frisking* me? This has to be some kind of joke." She tried to face him, but he stopped her.

"Chief, what's going on?" Tank finally found his voice.

Langdon ignored him, speaking instead to Cass. "I'm taking you in for questioning."

"What! Are you crazy? Why can't you question me here?"

"I'm taking you down to the station."

She huffed out a breath. "You were friends with my father, Otis. How can you do this?"

"You have the right to remain silent." He turned her to face him and caught her gaze. "I suggest you do." He guided her forward as she sputtered.

She looked for Tank, hoping he'd intervene, but he had already stepped away and was talking on the phone. She scanned the sea of faces watching her. Most of their stares had hardened from curiosity to anger.

Cass sighed. Such was the beauty of living in a small town. When she came home last year to bury her parents, the town had mourned with her. While making the final arrangements, the florist, whom she'd gone to high school with, had come around the counter to offer a hug and to cry with her. The funeral director's expression had been a grimace of true grief, rather than the grim but distant expression he usually would have deemed appropriate for such a somber occasion. The priest had concluded the ceremony with a hitch in his voice. That warmth had kept her on Bay Island after the funeral.

Now, that same sense of community hurt as the stares of accusation followed her. In a matter of minutes the entire town knew she was under suspicion. Marge had lived her whole life on Bay Island. Cass had returned only last year, after a seventeen-year hiatus.

As they rounded the side of the building, Cass saw Jay Callahan, Ellie's husband. A small smile tugged at the corners of his mouth. Cass sucked in a breath, but Jay turned and walked away, his smirk firmly in place.

She followed his progress through the crowd until her eyes met the hard, dark stare of the stranger from the deli. A deep scowl marred his features as his gaze met hers and held.

She must have slowed, because the chief tugged on her arm and leaned close. "I might not be able to arrest you, yet, but I can make your life miserable for a little while, and I'll definitely be watching you."

He guided her into his car, putting a hand on top of her head, his arm casting a shadow across her face. *A shadow? Ellie!* She searched for her as the chief pulled out through the crowd. Nothing. She'd tried to reach Ellie from Dreamweaver Designs last night, with no luck, even though it had been so late. Had that shadow during Ellie's reading been the death of her mother, or something more sinister? She had to find her.

4

"Thank you for picking me up, Steph."

"No problem." She rubbed a hand on Cass's arm but quickly returned her attention to the road ahead of her. "Tank called and said to come get you. I'm sorry it took so long. I don't know what the holdup was." She glanced over at Cass and grinned. "He said Chief Langdon was being an ass." Laughter danced in the other woman's eyes.

Chief Langdon had been friends with Cass's dad, and she and Steph had tormented him with their antics when they were kids. It had always been good-natured, until recently.

"When did Langdon get so . . . serious? I remember him being a little cranky sometimes, but I don't remember him being so mean."

Stephanie shrugged. "I don't know, really." She frowned. "Once you left for college, I didn't have much contact with him. Then, when you came back and opened the shop, he seemed . . . I don't know . . . weird, or something." Stephanie shook her head and stared straight ahead out the windshield, seemingly lost in her thoughts.

Stephanie had been her best friend growing up, but when Cass left, they'd fallen out of touch. When Cass came back home, seventeen years later, their friendship had resumed as if no time had passed. Stephanie had even accepted, with no questions asked, Cass's vague excuse for why she'd returned.

Cass hadn't yet been ready to explain why she'd given up her psychiatric practice to open a psychic shop on the boardwalk, or why she'd divorced her no-good, cheating ex-husband. She still wasn't ready to talk about it, and Stephanie didn't pry.

They pulled into Cass's driveway, and Stephanie shifted the car into park, jolting Cass from memories better left untouched. She stared out the window at her childhood home. The three-bedroom cottage sat right on the beach, down a ways from Mystical Musings and the boardwalk, on a quieter, more secluded stretch of beach, which was great in the summer. Now, though, the damp evening chill settled in her bones.

Bee sat on the porch swing, rocking slowly back and forth each time he shoved against the railing with his foot. Cass sighed and climbed out of the car. Stephanie followed her up the steps to the wide, wraparound porch.

Cass flopped back into an overstuffed chair she kept on the porch, closed her eyes, and waited for the inevitable bombardment of questions. It didn't come. She opened one eye.

Bee continued to rock back and forth, the creaking of the chain almost hypnotic. "Hey, there, beautiful."

A small smile tugged at Cass. "Hey."

Stephanie perched against the edge of the railing and stared out across Gardiners Bay. The gentle lapping of the small waves against the sand worked to soothe Cass's raw nerves as nothing else could. Grateful her friends understood her need for silence, Cass laid her head back against the seat.

Thanks to Chief Langdon, she'd lost a full day at Mystical Musings. That was the last thing she needed at this time of year. Weekends were the busiest times for tourists, and the season was quickly coming to a close. Losing a Saturday would hurt.

The setting sun peeking through the trees made shadows dance across the small patch of lawn and the wooden walkway that led to the beach. The deepening shadows on the porch made it almost impossible to make out—*shadows!*

"Ellie!" Cass jumped up from the chair, slamming her knee into a small table. "Ouch!"

Stephanie straightened from the rail and looked over her shoulder, but Bee continued his rhythmic rocking.

"What are you talking about? I don't see anyone." Stephanie squinted into the growing darkness.

"No, she's not here. I have to find her." The memory of the shadow passing over her wouldn't let Cass rest unless she checked on her.

"What's the big deal about finding Ellie?" Steph folded her arms across her chest, obviously not going anywhere without an explanation.

A sigh escaped before Cass could stop it. "All right. I gave Ellie a reading yesterday."

"Yeah, I heard." A grin split Stephanie's face, and Cass

couldn't help but cringe at the reminder of the run-in at the deli.

"Well, while I was reading her . . ." Cass swallowed past the lump in her throat. She wasn't really psychic, not in any traditional sense anyway, but the last time she'd encountered a shadow during a session, a death had followed as well. She looked up. Stephanie and Bee were staring wide-eyed, practically drooling with anticipation. "A shadow crossed over my vision, and everything started to get dark."

Stephanie frowned. "Has that ever happened before?"

Cass blew out a breath and looked directly into her friend's eyes. "Only once."

"Well, would you care to elaborate?" Bee finally stopped swinging and leaned forward, twisting his hands together, reminding Cass of an old woman fretting.

She shook her head. "No, not really."

Bee relented, albeit reluctantly, but Stephanie held her gaze a moment longer.

Cass held her breath. The last thing she wanted to get into right now was her failed psychiatric practice or the death of her patient. "Not right now, anyway. I'll tell you about it later, but right now I really need to find Ellie."

Bee shot to his feet. "Are you crazy? The sheriff already questioned you about her mother's . . . uh . . . well, you know."

Cass gave him a dirty look he probably couldn't see in the dark. "I have to check on her. If you two don't want to come, I'll do it myself." She hobbled down the steps, her knee throbbing.

"I said it was crazy, honey." Bee heaved himself off the

swing and tossed the end of his scarf around his neck. He smiled. "I didn't say we wouldn't come."

"Steph?"

Stephanie shrugged. "Oh, what the heck? Let's go." She started forward but stopped short. "But if Jay's car is there, I'm not stopping."

"No problem." Cass got back into the passenger seat with Bee in the back. He sat with his elbows resting on both front seats and his head poking between them. Apparently, his respect for her need for solitude had ended when they left the porch.

"So, what happened when you got to the police station? Did they put you in a cell?" He shivered. "Tell me *everything*."

"No, they didn't put me in a cell. They did fingerprint me, though, and put me in an interrogation room. You know, the ones with the one-way glass." She turned her head and grinned at him. "It was very *CSI*."

Bee laughed and clapped his hands together.

Stephanie harrumphed. "You two are taking this awfully lightly. Cass was questioned about a *murder*."

Bee waved off her concerns. "Eh, she obviously didn't kill the old battle-ax. Someone'll figure it out. Besides, there are probably plenty of people who'll be happier with Marge out of the picture."

"Well, still. I think you should take it a little more seriously."

Bee dropped back against the seat and sulked. Cass stared out the window as the scenery went by. Old houses, many built hundreds of years earlier, dotted the small residential neighborhood. It wasn't far to Ellie's house—you could cross the whole island in less than half an hour—and they pulled up in front of the small, cedar-shingled house a few minutes later. They all leaned forward to peer through the darkness. Not a single light was lit.

"Hmm . . ." Bee opened the car door.

"Where are you going?" Stephanie continued to stare at the house.

"I'm just gonna look around. That's what we came for, isn't it?"

Cass jumped out beside him. "Come on. We'll just peek in the front window. It looks pretty deserted."

"Yeah, what do you think they're doing? Sitting in there in the dark?" Bee walked up the front steps and peeked through the big picture window while Cass rang the bell and waited. Stephanie stood behind them.

"Where do you think she is?" Cass cupped both hands around her eyes in an effort to see into the living room. No use—the darkness just reflected her haggard image back at her.

Stephanie leaned over her shoulder. "I don't know, but she's usually here at this time of night. Jay likes his dinner on the table at exactly six, fifteen minutes after he walks in from work."

"That's true." Bee had given up trying to see in the window, and jiggled the door handle. Locked.

Cass thought back to the bruise on Marge's cheek. Had she had a run-in with her son-in-law? The scenario hardly seemed likely. Marge wasn't as mousy as her daughter. If it came down to a fight between Marge and Jay, Cass's money would have been on Marge. Jay was a bully, but also a wimp. Marge was made of steel.

"Come on. Let's run past Marge's house. Maybe Ellie's there." Cass started to walk away, but Stephanie stopped her.

"I'll drive past Marge's, but I'm not stopping under any circumstances, for any reason. Is that clear?"

Cass nodded, and Stephanie turned to Bee.

He grinned. "Crystal, honey."

Cass peered through Marge's large, dark bay window with Bee and Stephanie breathing heavily down her neck.

"Well?" Bee leaned even farther over her back.

Stephanie crowded even closer, nudging Bee out of the way. "Can you see anything?"

"Nothing. It's pitch bla—"

Bang!

Cass jumped back, knocking Bee over and slamming her head into Stephanie's chin. Bee struggled to his feet but succeeded only in getting tangled up with Stephanie and dragging her down in a heap with him. Cass tripped over them but managed to stay upright, barely, by grabbing hold of the porch railing.

"What was that?" Bee managed to wheeze out.

"I don't know. Something smashed against the inside of the window." Cass didn't dare take her gaze from the window while she tried to pull Stephanie and Bee to their feet. The three of them clung together as they backed off the porch and down the stairs, terrified to turn their backs on the house.

"Wh-wha-what do you think it was?" Bee's words were punctuated by the chattering of his teeth.

Cass shook her head. "No idea. Something's in there, though."

"You mean some*one*."

Cass shook her head. Stephanie was probably right, but who knew? They kept scooting backward until Cass's back hit the car. Stephanie ran around to get in, and Bee opened the back door, but Cass hesitated and continued to stare at the dark house.

"What are you doing? Get in the car." Stephanie's urgent whisper broke through the trance that had gripped Cass.

"We can't."

"What do you mean we can't? Are you out of your mind?" Bee's voice was always a bit high for a man, ranging from a tenor to an alto when needed, but now it bordered on soprano.

"What if someone's in trouble? Maybe it's Ellie." Cass stared at the window.

"And maybe it's whoever killed Marge." Stephanie jumped in the car and closed the door. She turned the key and rolled down the passenger window. "I'm outta here. Are you two coming or not?"

"No way I'm staying here in the dark with something lurking in that house. Maybe it's Marge's ghost." Bee hopped into the backseat but didn't close the door. "And if she's anywhere near as mean in the afterlife, I don't want any part of her."

Cass leaned over sideways, trying to talk into the window and keep an eye on the house at the same time. "What if whoever killed Marge is holding Ellie hostage in there?"

"What if they are? You want to go in and see?" She didn't

have to look at Stephanie to see the annoyance in the other woman's eyes. She could feel her gaze boring into her back.

"Why don't we just call the police?" Bee started punching buttons on his phone, and Cass finally tore her gaze from the house long enough to look at him.

"And tell them what, Bee? We were peeking in a dead woman's window, a woman I just so happen to be accused of murdering? How do you think that'll go over?"

He tossed the phone onto the seat next to him. "Okay, then. What do you suggest?" He turned to her, crossed one leg over the other, and folded his arms across his chest.

Cass shoved her hands into her hair and squeezed. *Ugh . . . Why don't we just get out of here?* But she couldn't. She released her hair and shot her gaze back to the house. She caught her lower lip between her teeth and scanned the dark property. No porch lights shone, and no streetlights cast their light far enough to push back the shadows enveloping the house. She looked up and down the deserted road.

"Let's go around back. We'll see if the door is open." The more she thought about it, the more she realized it was the only option. She couldn't leave knowing someone might be in trouble. And she couldn't call for help, given she was a suspect.

"Why don't I call Tank?" Stephanie looked so hopeful, Cass hated to burst her bubble.

"What do you think he'll say?" Cass stared at her and waited a beat. "Besides, he'll end up trying to help us and get into trouble."

Stephanie blew her hair off her forehead. "Fine."

The thought of Tank gave Cass an idea, though. "Hey, Steph, pop the trunk."

Stephanie did as asked, and Cass ran to the back of the car. Tank was fanatical about his wife's safety—Cass cringed at the thought of the danger she was placing his wife in right that minute—and he always kept emergency supplies in the trunk.

She dug through the trunk with Bee at her side. "Aha . . ." Cass pulled a tire iron from the meticulously organized provisions.

Bee pulled the first aid kit out triumphantly. "I'll just wait here with this."

"Put that down and come on. I want to get this over with and get out of here." Stephanie slammed the trunk closed the second Bee dropped the box.

Together, the three of them trudged around the house, careful to huddle close, with Cass in the lead, holding the tire iron at the ready. Cass searched the shadows flickering among the trees in the woods bordering three sides of the yard. They crept stealthily toward the house—at least as stealthily as two women and a better-than-six-foot man, built like a football player and wearing a women's scarf and platform shoes, could creep. When they reached the backyard, they climbed the three steps up to the deck. Bee and Stephanie stopped short, but Cass tiptoed to the door and tried the handle. Nothing. She paused and stared up at the window.

"Now what?"

Cass shrugged and looked around the yard. "I don't know." She spied a picnic table. *Hmm . . .* "Here, help me." They pulled the table over to the window, and Cass climbed on top and peered in.

"Anything?" Bee looked at her.

She shook her head and looked back at her friends.

"Good. Let's get out of here." Stephanie appeared to be looking everywhere at once as she started to walk away.

Cass reluctantly agreed. What else could they do? "Wait . . ."

Stephanie stopped and looked at her expectantly.

"Did you hear that?" The sound reached Cass again, soft, but definitely a scratching sound. She looked back through the window. A soft whine reached her ears. She glanced at Stephanie and Bee, and then she swung the tire iron. Shattering glass echoed loudly through the silence.

5

"Are you crazy?" Stephanie looked like she was about to have a heart attack, eyes wide, face beet red. "You can't break into Marge's house."

"There's someone crying in there. I heard it." Fear clutched Cass's throat, not for herself but for whoever—possibly Ellie—was crying inside the house.

Bee held one hand pressed tightly to his chest and fanned himself with the other. "You couldn't have just knocked on the door?"

Hmmm . . . Why didn't I think of that? Cass scowled at the offending weapon as if it had played some part in her momentary lack of judgment. She had no time to linger on the thought, though, because a terrible, high-pitched squeal tore through the now-broken window.

Cass dropped the tire iron, reached in through the hole, and unlocked the window.

"You're going in?" Bee's bushy brown eyebrows climbed all the way up beneath his bleached blond bangs.

"That's it. I'm outta here." Stephanie threw her hands in the air but made no move to walk away.

The scratching sound resumed, pulling Cass's attention from her friend's theatrics. "I'll be right back. Just give me one minute to make sure nobody's hurt in there."

"The only one that's gonna be hurt in there is you, if you get caught." Bee huffed, and climbed up onto the table beside her. He poked his head in the window, then clasped his hands together and bent over. "Here. Be careful, there's glass all over."

Cass put her foot in his hands, and he boosted her through the window.

"Hurry up. I'm not waiting out here more than one minute."

His words followed Cass into the dark kitchen, but she pretty much ignored him. There was no way in the world either of her friends would leave her in danger, no matter what happened. She didn't dare turn on a light. She crept silently through the dark, feeling her way so as not to crash into anything. Another squeal sounded from the other side of the closed kitchen door. "What the . . . ?"

She pushed the door open a little and poked her head through. Not that she could see anything in the dark. She pulled out her cell phone and pressed a button. Dim light emanated from it, illuminating an area about two inches in front of her. She pinpointed the source of the squeals easily enough. Frantic banging rattled a door off the small hallway. As best as she could judge, the noise was probably coming from the room at the front of the house, the one she'd been peeking into when something slammed into the window.

She tiptoed down the hallway, not really sure why, since whatever was behind that door was certainly making enough noise to mask her footsteps. When she reached the door, she took a deep breath and held it. She shoved her cell phone into her back pocket, gripped the knob, and turned it slowly. She pushed the door open an inch at a time.

The attack came out of nowhere. One minute she was stealthily pushing the door open, the next she was flat on her back in the hallway, a giant ball of fur planted firmly on her chest. The sound of someone screaming reached her ears. *Oh, wait. That's me screaming.* She clamped her teeth tightly together and struggled to get to her feet. *If this thing will just stop licking me.* She gripped the back of the dog's collar and tried to pull him off so she could stand. The hallway light snapped on, momentarily blinding her. She reached up to cover her eyes as the weight finally lifted from her chest.

"What are you doing?"

She sat up and squinted up into Bee's irate face.

"I . . . uh—"

"Never mind. Just get up and let's get out of here." Bee had the squirming dog gripped firmly by the collar with one hand, and he hauled Cass to her feet with the other. He propelled her none too gently toward the kitchen. "Steph's out there having an . . . episode." He tried to shove the giant fur ball back behind the door and close it.

"Wait. What are you doing?"

He lifted his gaze from the task at hand to glare at her. "I'm trying to get this thing back where it belongs so we can make our escape."

Bee struggled with the dog. Actually, it didn't even seem

to be a full-grown dog. It seemed more like a puppy, except it was massive. Its head and paws were enormous. Although its body hadn't caught up yet, the long fur standing on end made it seem sort of . . . proportionate.

"We can't leave it here." Cass started toward him.

"What?"

"You heard me. We can't leave it here. Who's going to take care of it?"

"I don't know. Maybe Ellie, or . . . a friend . . ."

They both knew it wasn't likely Marge had a friend to come over and take care of her puppy. While Marge was generally feared in the close-knit community, she was not liked.

Cass's mind raced. Actually, what was Marge even doing with a puppy? She wasn't exactly the maternal type.

"That's it. You've officially gone completely bonkers." Bee held his hands up in a gesture of surrender and stalked past her before disappearing into the kitchen.

"Hey, boy." Cass braced herself as the dog jumped up and planted his big paws against her stomach, knocking her back about two feet before she caught herself. "Down, boy."

She pushed him down and returned to the kitchen. A leash dangled from a hook beside the door, and two bowls sat in the corner beside a brand-new bag of food. She grabbed the food and shoved it through the window. Bee grumbled something incoherent and snatched the bag. Cass managed to clip the leash to the wiggling animal, but now what? She couldn't very well shove him through the window.

She sighed and opened the back door but then stopped short. Stephanie stood blocking her path, with her arms folded across her chest and her foot tapping indignantly. Her normally frizzy brown hair stood on end, giving her the appearance of someone who had just stuck her finger in a socket. Cass sucked in a breath, prepared for an argument, but Stephanie just turned and walked away toward the front of the house.

Cass followed silently. She glanced over at the dog, and he lowered his head and trudged along beside her. Bee pulled the picnic table back into place, threw the sack of food over his shoulder, and followed her to the car.

With Bee and Stephanie right on her heels Cass ushered the dog into her house. They hadn't spoken much on the drive home, each of them seemingly lost in their own thoughts.

"Well." Bee dropped the bag of dog food on the floor beside the door and rolled the shoulder he'd carried it over. "Now what?"

Stephanie rubbed her eyes but didn't offer any suggestions.

Cass shrugged. "I don't know."

"Maybe you should have thought of that before you went into Marge's." Stephanie glared at her, and Cass winced. A moment later, a wide grin spread across Stephanie's face. "Sure did bring back old times, though."

Laughter bubbled up as a flood of relief washed over Cass. Things with Stephanie were okay. "Remember the time we snuck into the boys' dorm and stole all their underwear?" She hadn't thought of that in years. It had been senior prank day and, on a dare, they'd raided the boys' dormitory at the college on the mainland during a football game. As proof of their success, they then wallpapered the high school gym with tighty-whities and boxers. Tears rolled down Cass's face, and she held her side in an effort to relieve the cramp settling there.

"You mean a reverse panty raid?" Bee looked appalled, which only made Stephanie and Cass laugh even harder.

"Langdon was *so* not amused." Stephanie could barely get the words out.

"Not as mad as he was the time we covered all the high school hallways with the leftover sod from the sod farm for homecoming. Ugh . . . The smell lingered for like a week and th—"

A loud howl interrupted their reminiscence.

All three of them turned. The dog stood at the front door, head tilted up, howling at the top of his lungs. The sound of tires crunching over the gravel driveway put a halt to their borderline hysterical laughter. Cass pulled the curtain at the front widow aside and peeked through. A pang of guilt shot through her as she glanced at Stephanie. "Uh . . . oh."

"Langdon?"

Cass shook her head. "No." She swallowed hard. "Worse."

Awareness crept into Stephanie's eyes, and she sighed when a loud pounding sounded against the door.

Cass bit her lip and waited, unsure what to do. "Quick, go out the back."

"Her car's parked out front." Bee scowled at the closed door.

"I'll say I borrowed it."

Stephanie sighed, resignation obvious in the slump of her slender shoulders. "Just let him in."

"Are you sure?"

Stephanie nodded, and Cass opened the door to a red-faced Tank. He glanced back and forth among the three of them and the dog, his gaze finally settling on Cass. "Lose something?"

She frowned but stayed quiet.

Tank glanced back over his shoulder, out into the darkness, and then quietly closed the door behind him, keeping one hand behind his back. *Uh-oh*.

"Where were you three tonight?"

"Uhh . . ." Cass glanced from Stephanie to Bee, but neither of them seemed ready to offer an explanation. "Ummm . . ." She caught her lip between her teeth and settled on saying nothing.

"Well, let me tell you where I was." He took a step toward them, and the three of them backed up together into the living room.

The dog kept pace at Cass's side. When they hit the back of the couch, they stopped.

"I was answering a call at Marge Hawkins's house. Seems the neighbor saw someone over there."

Cass racked her brain to figure who could have seen them.

"Her six-year-old saw two ladies, a dog, and a bear on stilts." Tank eyed Bee up and down, from the top of his bleached blond hair to his platform shoes and back.

Bee answered with a very uncouth and indignant snort. He turned away from Tank, walked into the living room, and flopped back into an armchair to pout.

"I held on to some small shred of hope that it wasn't you three, because of the dog." He frowned at the massive hound at Cass's side. "Should I even ask?"

"Probably not." Cass figured honesty was the best policy here. Besides, there was a chance, however small, he'd let it go at that.

"Would it have anything to do with this?" He pulled the tire iron from behind his back and held it up in front of him.

Cass cringed. *So much for letting it go.* "Possibly?"

Tank lifted an eyebrow and waited, but when Cass opened her mouth to speak, he raised a hand to stop her. "You know what? I don't want to know." He shook his head and turned his attention to Stephanie. "How could you get involved in this?"

Cass intervened. She couldn't let Stephanie take the heat for what she'd done. "It's not what you think."

He gave her his full attention. "It's not breaking and entering?"

Heat crept up her cheeks, and a bead of sweat trickled down the back of her neck. "Okay, it *is* what you think, but with a really good explanation."

Tank leaned back against the wall and crossed his arms over his massive chest.

The dog moved closer to Cass.

"We were looking for Ellie."

"And?"

"We couldn't find her."

"Why were you looking for her?" At least he finally seemed interested.

Cass tried to decide how much to tell him.

"Well?"

She jumped, startled by the volume of his voice. "I gave Ellie a reading yesterday. After she left, I wanted to warn her, but I couldn't get in touch with her."

"Warn her about what?" He tilted his head, his expression telling her this had better be good.

Cass sucked in a deep breath and braced herself to be ridiculed. "A shadow crossed my vision while I was doing the reading."

Tank shifted away from the wall. "So . . . let me get this straight. You had to find Ellie, right after her mother was murdered." He pointed a finger at Cass as he inched forward. "A murder, I might add, you've been suspected of committing." A vein pulsed frantically in his temple. "So you broke into Marge's house."

Cass was pretty sure smoke was coming out of his ears.

"Because a bird or something flew between you and the sun while you were looking into your crystal ball?" He clenched his teeth, seemingly struggling for control. "Do I have this right?"

Cass nodded vigorously.

"Are you crazy?"

She shook her head. "It wasn't like that. The shadow wasn't caused by anything like that."

"All right, I'll probably be sorry I asked, but . . . What was it caused by?"

"I don't know. It's only ever happened to me once before."

"And?"

"The person died."

She held her breath and waited, watching Tank stare at her. He didn't laugh at her or blow up, though, as she'd expected.

"Explain."

"It was before I came home, while I still had my practice in the city." The memory was painful for Cass, even now.

She leaned back against the couch and reached down to pet the dog's head. Before she'd returned to Bay Island, she'd been a psychiatrist. She'd always been intuitive, and the profession had suited her well. "I had someone in for a session, which I can't divulge any details of."

Tank nodded his understanding.

"During the session a shadow crossed my vision. It was the weirdest thing, but I had no idea what to make of it, so I let it go. Something kept nagging at me all day, but I repeatedly ignored it." She paused and struggled to swallow the lump that had formed in her throat. She lowered her gaze to the floor. "My patient was found dead the next day. Suicide."

No one said anything.

Tank's breathing was heavy for an endless minute. "I'll check on Ellie. You three stay far away from her." He pinned Cass with a hard look. "If anyone else had answered that call tonight, you'd be in jail." His tone softened. "I'm serious, Cass. You're in a lot of trouble right now. Promise me you'll stay out of this."

Cass swallowed hard and nodded. "Thanks, Tank."

"You're welcome." He looked at Stephanie. "I'll see you at home." He turned to go.

"Tank?"

He paused and glanced back over his shoulder at Cass.

"How did Marge die?"

He hesitated and scrubbed a hand over his face. Cass was sure he wasn't going to answer.

"She was shot."

6

Cass gripped the steering wheel tightly. "How bad was it?" She didn't even wait for Stephanie to get all the way into the car. Bee leaned forward between the seats, obviously waiting for an answer as well.

Stephanie smiled. "It was fine. He yelled a little, and then we . . . made up, so it's all good." She batted her big brown eyes.

A pent-up breath whooshed out, and Cass shifted into gear and pulled away from the curb. "Tony's?"

"Is it Sunday?" Bee asked.

She peeked in the rearview mirror to see his eyebrow lifted sarcastically.

She laughed. Sunday was the only day Tony made cannoli balls—little fried dough balls, filled with cannoli filling and dipped in sugar. Her mouth started to water at the thought.

"Hey, Cass. What'd you do with Marge's dog?" Stephanie cracked the window and cool, fresh air filled the car.

Cass inhaled deeply, the scent of the sea filling her lungs. "I left him at home."

Traffic was heavy this morning, for Bay Island, anyway. Both churches were letting out, and the people all flocked to one of three places—the deli, the diner, or Tony's Bakery. She settled back and resigned herself to the ten minutes it would take to get to the center of the island.

"You really think that was a good idea?"

She shrugged and stared out the window. It was still warm enough for people to walk, and they swarmed the sidewalks, talking and laughing. Cass recognized a few, but others were strangers to her. Of course, it was still tourist season. By the dead of winter, she'd at least recognize most of the people she came across. "What else would I do with him?" Maybe she'd take the dog for a walk later.

"I don't know, but what are people going to think when they see you with Marge's dog?" Stephanie asked.

Hmmm . . . she hadn't thought of that. Maybe the walk would have to wait.

"Yeah, that's not going to be easy to explain." Bee leaned forward between the seats again, and Cass nudged him back with her elbow.

"Sit back, will you? I can't see through your big head."

Stephanie laughed, and Bee slid over a little. Cass hit the right-turn signal, glanced in the rearview mirror, and joined the line of traffic turning into the small bakery parking lot. Her gaze shot back to the mirror. "Hey, isn't that Jay Callahan?"

Stephanie looked where Cass indicated and turned to

look back over her shoulder. Bee was already turned around, staring out the back window. "Where?"

"Driving that black car."

"Yeah, that's him. Too bad it's not Ellie snuggled up against him." Bee turned back to face Cass as Jay passed them. "Hey, what are you doing?"

"I'm trying to pull back out so I can follow him." Cass hit the left-turn signal and waited patiently for a break in traffic.

"For what?"

"I don't know. I just wonder what he's doing with some-one other than his wife practically sitting in his lap."

Bee snorted. "What do you think he's doing?"

"The same thing he's always doing." Stephanie stared longingly at the bakery.

Cass relented and flipped off the signal. "True, I guess." Her mind stayed on Jay and his—most likely—newest lover. "How does he get all these women?"

"I have no idea. The guy looks like a weasel and has the personality of a wet dish towel."

Cass mulled that over. Bee hated Jay, but she had to admit his assessment wasn't far off.

"Plus, he's nasty, abusive, and makes no attempt to hide it." Stephanie pointed to the left. "There, grab that spot."

Cass waited while a woman strapped a young baby into a car seat. "Did Tank say if he found Ellie?"

Worry filled Stephanie's eyes, and she shook her head.

The urge to follow Jay hit Cass again, but she dismissed it. She'd never be able to find him now anyway. She parked, climbed out, and got in the back of the line that weaved around the side of the bakery, still lost in thoughts of Ellie.

"So, how many people are coming to the reading to-night?" Bee looked hopeful.

"Sorry, Bee. You're not getting out of helping."

He folded his arms across his massive chest, leaned against the brick wall, and sulked.

"That was the deal. I help you with the fashion show, you help me with the group readings."

Stephanie laughed. "She's right, Bee. You're the one who suggested the arrangement."

"Yeah, well, it hardly seems fair. I only have one fashion show a year—Cass has readings every month." He perked up and pushed away from the wall. "Hey. Do you think now that Marge is gone I can keep the original date for the show?"

Cass looked around to see if anyone was listening. "Do you think it would be appropriate to ask . . . considering?" She wondered if the crime scene tape had been removed.

"I don't see why not. It's not like Marge had any day-to-day involvement at the theater. She practiced with her theater group for a few months and ran a performance once a year," Stephanie said, and gestured for her to move up in the line.

"Still . . ." Cass inched forward. "She was the president of the board of directors, and she did die in the theater."

"Oh, for crying out loud. We'll have a moment of silence or something if you have to," Bee said. "It's not like the old crackpot's going to be missed."

Cass sucked in a breath and looked around. Did anyone hear Bee's comment? "Shh . . ."

He rolled his eyes but didn't say anything more on the subject.

Cass crossed through the front door, and the aroma of

freshly baked dough made saliva pool in her mouth. She'd have to run extra hard tomorrow to make up for today's indulgence. Maybe.

"Hey, Cass."

She looked up. Tim Daughtry was blushing adorably.

"Hey, Tim. How are you doing?"

"Good. I just started college, and so far I like it."

"Local?"

"Nah . . . I'm in Philadelphia. I'm majoring in fashion design." He shot Bee a grin. "Thanks to you, I got into the program. I appreciate the reference."

"No problem. If you're ever looking for a summer job, stop in and see me. You're very talented."

"Thank you. I'd like that." Tim's blush deepened. He shook the long blond hair out of his eyes. "I was originally going to major in performing arts, but I liked working with you at the shop a lot better than working with you and Ms. Hawkins at the theater." His eyes shot open as if realizing he'd said something wrong. "I mean, she was a nice lady and all. I don't mean to speak poorly of the dead." The blush ran straight up into his hairline. "She just wasn't as easy to work with as you, Mr. Bee."

"Sure, Tim. She was . . . ah . . ."

Cass glared daggers at him.

"Difficult." He smirked.

Tim turned his attention to Cass. "Is the shop going to be open today, Cass?"

"I have a group reading later, so I'll be there. Why? Do you need something?"

"A friend of mine at school has been going through a really rough time lately, and I wanted to do something special for her. My mom loves all the candles and lotions and bath stuff you have, says it makes her feel better when she's down, so I thought maybe you could put together a basket for me."

"Sure. I just got a new fragrance in. It smells kind of like peaches, and it's supposed to help you relax and center yourself. I'll throw a black tourmaline in with it for protection against negative energy. Tell her to keep it close to her. Your friend will love it." She moved forward with the line.

"That's perfect. Thank you. I'll pick it up Tuesday morning, if that's okay."

"I'll have it ready for you."

"Well, I gotta go." Tim held up the white bakery bag in his hand.

"Sure. I'll see you later."

Cass pulled her gaze from his and moved forward to order.

"Well, what do you think we should do?" Cass lifted the bakery bag a little higher, letting the scent entice her.

"What do you mean? We should go in and take the measurements you didn't get to take yesterday." Bee leaned closer to read the paper sign tacked to the front door.

"It says 'closed until further notice,'" Stephanie said.

"I can read, Steph." Bee spared her an eye-roll before ripping the sign from the door and crumpling it into a ball. "There. Problem solved."

Cass shrugged and dug the keys from her bag.

"What time is everyone supposed to be at the shop?" Bee glanced at his cell phone.

"In about an hour." Unsure exactly what time it was, Cass glanced at Stephanie for confirmation.

She nodded.

Cass lost track of whatever Stephanie was saying as they entered the theater. She paused at the auditorium entrance and took a deep breath before flipping the light switch. Images of Marge Hawkins assailed her, squeezing her lungs and shortening her breath.

A warm hand landed on her shoulder. "Are you all right?"

"I will be." Was that true? She loved working with Bee on the fashion show. Volunteering had provided a distraction when she needed it most. Would the theater forever be tarnished by the images of Marge? She shook her head to try to dispel the thoughts and turned on *all* of the lights, chasing away as many shadows as possible. She reached up and squeezed Bee's hand before starting down the center aisle with Bee and Stephanie on either side of her, lending her strength.

She couldn't keep her gaze from falling on the section of the pit where Marge had been found. Several seats, including the one she'd been propped in, and a large patch of the carpeting, were missing, apparently taken by the police as evidence.

"They're supposed to put the runway in tomorrow. Do you have any sketches for me yet for the stage design?"

She pulled her focus from the pit and smiled at Bee, grateful for his attempt to fill her mind with something other than thoughts of murder. For all his dramatic tendencies, he had a deeply sensitive side as well.

"I think I pretty much know what I want, but I haven't sketched it out yet." The vision of what she wanted to do gripped her, sending waves of excitement rippling through her. Bee was going to love it.

"Just make sure everything I need is there," Bee said.

"Don't worry. It'll be great." Cass climbed onto the stage. She opened the bakery bag. The scent of warm cannoli balls wafted out. "Let's just take the measurements and get out of here before we end up in trouble." She looked up and held the bag out to Bee, shaking it a little so the aroma drifted to him.

"That works." Bee reached into the bag, pulled out a cannoli ball, and popped it into his mouth.

She held the bag toward Stephanie, who took one, bit into it, and moaned.

Cass followed. Her eyes fell shut as she savored the rich flavor. "So, Bee. I didn't realize you worked with Marge at the theater."

Bee dug through his bag and, for a minute, Cass didn't think he'd answer. "It's not that big a deal. I only worked with her for a year. I met her through a friend of a friend. I was looking to settle somewhere new, and she asked if I'd be interested in a position playing piano and making costumes for a small theater group." He shrugged as if it was unimportant. "The pay sucked, but I fell in love with Bay Island and the dream of having a shop on the boardwalk, so I tolerated her for a year until I got the shop opened." He whipped a tape measure out of the bag and grinned. "Then I made sure my fashion show sold out the theater, knowing it burned her gut that her plays couldn't."

Cass propped the bakery bag on a podium at the side of the stage and studied her friend. He fidgeted nervously, pulling the tape measure open a bit, then hitting the button and retracting the tape.

"You never mentioned that before."

"Because it wasn't a big deal, Cass." He held the tape measure out to her, tapping his foot impatiently.

Cass sipped her coffee, then reached for another cannoli ball, giving herself a minute to think about whether or not she should push the issue. He was obviously either lying about something or keeping something secret. Bee's words came back to her, *"The world would be a better place without that woman."* Hadn't he said that when they received the letter from the board? Suspicion niggled at the back of Cass's mind, and she worked hard to dismiss it. She grabbed the tape measure and held it against the edge of the stage while Bee pulled the other end out as he walked to the opposite side.

"What's going on in here?" The booming voice froze Cass mid-bite.

7

Chief Langdon strode down the center aisle toward them. "I asked you, what's going on in here?"

"Uh . . ." Cass grabbed the bag from the podium and held it out to him. "Cannoli ball?"

Bee hissed under his breath but moved closer to Cass.

"Shh . . ." Cass licked sugar from her lips.

Chief Langdon ignored her and climbed the side steps to the stage, his cowboy boots clunking loudly against the hardwood.

Uh . . . oh.

"You shouldn't be on the stage with those boots on. You're going to scratch the wood."

Ugh . . . Bee. Will you shut up?

Chief Langdon stopped when he reached them and stood, hands on his hips, chewing on the inside of his cheek. Anger poured from him.

Cass cringed.

"I asked you a question. What are you three doing in here?"

Cass met his gaze. "We just stopped by to measure the stage so I can draw up the design for the fashion show." She forced her eyes to remain focused on him, not wanting to look suspicious by letting her gaze drop, or even worse, dart around.

"This theater is closed until further notice, as indicated by the sign that *was* posted on the door."

Look at his eyes, look at his eyes . . . "What sign?" She'd kill Bee for taking it down later. For now, she had to get through this conversation with Langdon.

"Let's not play games, Ms. Donovan."

Ms. Donovan? He only called her Ms. Donovan when she was in serious trouble. *Great.* "Look, Chief. I have a reading scheduled in a little while, so all I want to do is take my measurements and go."

"What's the big rush? Did you not receive the notice from the board of directors saying the date for the show would have to be changed?" He rubbed at the back of his neck and glanced around the empty stage.

"You can't do that, Chief." Cass wanted to cower at the look he pinned her with, but she held her ground. "Bee has worked so hard on this. It's not fair to change the date at the last minute. I don't understand what the problem is." Heat crept up the back of Cass's neck as the volume of her voice increased. She bit her tongue. No sense reminding him the reason they no longer needed the date changed was because the director of the conflicting program had been found dead. In the theater. By Cass. *Ah jeez* . . .

The chief put up a hand. "It's not my decision. The board voted, and they decided to honor the change." He shrugged nonchalantly, as if he had no involvement in the decision.

Cass opened her mouth, but Stephanie intervened before she could launch into a temper-fueled tirade. "Chief, the board meeting isn't until next month. Isn't there any way we can go before them sooner and ask them to retract the decision?"

"You all seem to be forgetting one small factor." His eyes narrowed on Cass. "The board no longer has a president."

Cass swallowed hard. Guilt tugged at her. Not because she had anything to do with Marge, but because it felt as if his gaze bored through to her very soul, witnessing everything she had ever done wrong. If Bee hadn't stepped in front of her and interrupted, she might have blurted a confession to every sin she'd ever committed.

"As much as Ms. Hawkins will be missed, I'm sure the board will elect an interim president. The show must go on and all that nonsense." Bee waved a hand dramatically.

Chief Langdon continued to stare as if not sure what to make of the other man. That was a pretty standard reaction to Bee, even when you'd known him for a while.

Stephanie forged on before Langdon could object. "You know, ticket sales from these productions pay the rent on the theater. If we're forced to cancel the fashion show, well . . . that show does bring in a lot of money." She shrugged, then turned to Bee. "You know, Bee, it might be easier to change the venue instead of the date. The hotel probably has a ballroom open."

Bee paled and opened his mouth, but Cass discreetly pinched his arm.

Langdon ran a hand over his thinning hair. "Fine. If you

DEATH AT FIRST SIGHT

can find a board member to initiate a meeting, we'll consider your arguments. In the meantime, get out of here. Now."

"All right. Thank you." Stephanie jumped in front of Bee before he could say anything.

A deep shade of purple crawled up Langdon's cheeks, and a large vein throbbed at his temple. He turned to walk away but glanced back at Bee. "By the way, you might want to put a plan in place for who's going to take Cass's place if the trial date comes before the fashion show."

Cass froze as a chill ran down her spine.

"Don't worry about it, Cass. I told you, he's just trying to scare you." Bee squeezed her shoulder, then brushed past her to greet the guests who'd begun to enter Mystical Musings. He lifted the wind chimes from their hook above the door and set them aside, then shot her a sheepish grin. Listening to them sound thirty or more times would probably be a bit much.

"Everything is pretty much ready." Stephanie handed Cass a cup of tea.

"Thanks." She surveyed the small shop. The table had been pushed to the far corner, and some of the display cases had been moved to the back room, which was actually a small room at the side of the shop, blocked off by a curtain. She hoped to seat as many people as possible, so they'd set up three more tables. "I really appreciate you guys helping out."

"No problem. You know I love this stuff." Stephanie snorted. "Poor Bee, though." She glanced at Bee, then shot

Cass a conspiratorial grin. "You know how he feels about your 'hocus-pocus, mumbo jumbo.'"

The short burst of laughter was just what she needed. Stephanie was right. Bee stayed far away from anything to do with Mystical Musings, psychic powers, contacting the dead . . .

Not that he believed in any of that nonsense, of course.

Bee waved at Stephanie.

"Looks like he needs help." She started toward him but glanced back over her shoulder and giggled. "Or maybe he just got spooked."

Stephanie and Bee pulled folding chairs from the back room, handed out foam cups filled with tea and coffee, and placed a tray of cookies in the center of each table. Their efforts to make everyone comfortable paid off, and a steady stream of relaxed chatter filled the room.

Cass busied herself behind the counter, rearranging perfectly aligned gemstones into small clusters in the glass display case, not quite ready to interact with anyone yet.

She didn't really believe the stones did anything magical, but her customers loved them. Years of psychiatric training had taught her the incredible power of the mind, but she still found it fascinating people could talk themselves into believing a bag of rocks cured their ailments. But they made people happy and, however they worked, they made people feel better, and that was all that mattered to Cass.

A woman entered the shop and approached the counter. Although she looked familiar, Cass couldn't quite place her. One of the guests? "Can I help you?"

"Hi. I'd like to have a reading." The woman fidgeted,

twirling a long strand of blond hair around her finger, obviously nervous.

"I'm sorry. We're closed today for a private group reading, but if you'd like to come in tomorrow, I'd be more than happy to do a reading."

Her hand fluttered to her chest. "Oh, of course. I'm so sorry. Tomorrow would be great."

Cass pulled her appointment book from beneath the counter, opened it, and skimmed through her readings for the day. "Would three o'clock be okay?"

"Perfect."

"I'm sorry, I didn't get your name."

"Carmen."

Cass scribbled her name in the book, then grabbed a business card from the holder on the counter, jotted down the date and time of her appointment, and handed it to the woman.

"Hey, Cass."

She glanced over at Stephanie, who was gesturing wildly for her to join them.

Cass smiled and ushered Carmen toward the door. "I'll see you tomorrow." Regret tugged at her. Maybe she should call her back and do the reading to avoid dealing with her own insecurities a little longer.

Although Cass usually enjoyed interacting with people, her nerves were getting the better of her. Did any of them think she was actually guilty? She kept the groan to herself—the sound would echo through the room if she let it escape—and joined the small crowd.

"How are you holding up, Cass?" A warm hand slid up

and down her arm, and Cass looked into large, brown, sympathetic eyes. Sara Ryan, whose daughter Jess would be wearing the yellow dress in the fashion show, eyed her warily, as if she might crumble under the strain at any moment.

"I'm doing okay, thank you." She returned the woman's wary smile and risked a quick search of the other faces gathered.

Their expressions ranged from sympathy, to wariness, to curiosity, but not a single one held suspicion. A tear formed at the corner of Cass's eye, and she reached up to wipe it away. Sara squeezed her arm in a silent gesture of support and then moved to take an empty seat.

"Well, I for one think it's ridiculous Cass is a suspect." The voice came from the back of the crowd, but a low rumble of agreement quickly surged through the room.

Cass scanned the crowd, relieved the other thirty or so people also offered their support. Emmett Marx leaned against a case toward the back, nodding in agreement. Cass's gaze skimmed over him at first but was pulled back when she noticed he glanced furtively around, his gaze darting rapidly from one person to the next. She might have dismissed his sneaky demeanor if he didn't own the garage where Jay Callahan worked. He wiped a sleeve across his forehead and finally settled on looking at the floor. Now wasn't the time, but she'd definitely seek him out at the first opportunity and see if he knew anything.

Stephanie stood, cutting off any more talk about Cass's predicament.

Cass breathed a sigh of relief and stepped back. While she leaned against the counter, waiting for her turn, she continued to watch Emmett discreetly.

Even though most of the guests had attended group readings before, Stephanie would go through an explanation of how things worked and answer any questions before she introduced Cass.

Bee perched on a stool beside her and leaned close. "What's the deal with Emmett?"

Okay, maybe she wasn't as discreet as she'd thought. "What do you mean?"

"Oh please, honey. You haven't taken your eyes off him. And in case you hadn't noticed, he's sweating like a pig in a slaughterhouse."

She turned to look at Bee. "You noticed that, too? I thought maybe it was just me."

"Nah. Something's weird."

Cass glanced back toward the guests to assure herself no one was listening, and sucked in a breath. Emmett's spot was empty. Where could he possibly have gone that quickly? She started toward the door.

"Cass?"

She glanced back over her shoulder at Stephanie. *Uh-oh.* Had Stephanie already introduced her?

"Go. I'll take care of it." Bee brushed past her and headed for the door.

Cass reluctantly took her place facing the group. "All right." She struggled to bring her mind back to the reading. The group readings she offered one Sunday each month had become very popular with the locals. Whether it was more of a social gathering than an actual psychic event, she had no idea, but every month a few more people attended. Soon she'd have to either limit the number of guests or open a second reading each month.

"As most of you already know, a group reading is different from an individual reading."

Movement at the door pulled her attention. Bee slid back into the room and shook his head. He leaned his back against the wall and folded his arms.

Hmmm . . . weird. Where could Emmett have possibly disappeared to? He'd attended every group since she started and was usually one of the last to leave.

"I can't target any specific person in the group. I simply relay the messages as I receive them."

Bee rolled his eyes, and Cass bit the inside of her cheek to keep from grinning.

She searched the crowed as she spoke, calling on her training and her instincts to guide her.

A young woman toward the back nervously twisted her fingers, worry filling her eyes.

"You're upset," Cass said to the woman.

"I'm sorry. I . . ." She pulled a tissue from her bag and wiped a tear.

"No need to be sorry."

The man seated next to her had already attended several readings, and he stood when Cass approached and offered his seat.

Cass nodded a thank-you and sat facing the woman. She gripped one of her hands.

A sense of loss emanated from her. Not the deep, grief-filled loss of losing someone you love, but still loss. "You've lost something important to you."

She sucked in a breath. "Yes. How did you know?"

Cass ignored the question. Now to figure out what she'd

lost and where she'd lost it. "When was the last time you remember seeing it?"

"Well, I remember wearing it to my sister's wedding."

Okay. What would she have worn and lost? Probably a piece of jewelry. "What else did you wear to the wedding?"

The woman frowned. "I had it pinned to my blue dress." Her free hand fluttered to her chest.

Bingo. "Do you remember seeing the brooch after the wedding?"

She gasped as if Cass had done something incredible. "How did you know? I have to find it. My mother left it to me, and I'll be devastated if I can't find it."

"Don't worry. She'll help you find it. You just have to think back and listen for guidance while you look. Can you remember taking it off after the wedding?"

In her mind, Bee was rolling his eyes again. She resisted the urge to look at him and confirm her suspicion.

"We stayed at my sister's that night, and I was afraid I'd forget it, so I left it pinned to the dress. I remember that." Her eyebrows drew together in concentration.

Cass waited.

"When I went to drop it off at the dry cleaners on my way home the next day, the brooch was still on it. They took it off and handed it to me, and I put it in the zipper compartment of my purse. At least I thought I did. But now it's gone."

Cass closed her eyes, partially for dramatic effect and partially to help her concentrate. She blocked out the small sounds people made even in silence. A cough, a sniff, the rustling of clothing as someone shifted position. Where could the brooch have gone? Cass thought about her own bag, so filled with stuff she could hardly find anything, and yet she always knew what was in there. Unless she cleaned it out or switched bags. Then she tossed things and forgot she'd taken them out. Wouldn't you switch purses for a wedding? Maybe take something smaller that matched your dress? Had she still been using that purse when she went to the cleaners the next day?

Cass opened her eyes.

The woman was staring at her, lower lip caught between her teeth.

"Is that the purse you had when you went to the cleaners?"

"Yes, I've had this purse for—" Her eyes went wide, and she slapped a hand over her mouth. "Oh no." She lowered her hand. "I never went home before I dropped the dress off. I still had my black clutch from the wedding. It's in there." The woman threw her arms around Cass, and a smattering of applause broke out. "How can I ever thank you?"

Heat crept into Cass's cheeks. "I'm just happy I could help." She stood, and the man who'd given up his seat patted her back as he returned to his seat.

She continued through the crowd, seeking out the people who seemed to need her attention the most. An old woman who missed her husband and wanted to say hello. A young woman who wanted to know if she was going to have a boy or a girl. From the way her stomach protruded straight out in front, but the rest of her seemed stick thin, Cass had guessed a boy. A young man who'd blushed adorably while he asked if Cass thought his girlfriend would say yes to his proposal. Who could say no to such a sweet kid?

When the allotted time ended, Cass thanked everyone for

coming and invited them to hang around as long as they'd like. Hopefully, some of them would shop while they chatted.

She moved toward Bee as everyone stood and began collecting their things and mingling.

"Poor thing . . . sorry for Ellie . . ." Bits and pieces of a discussion stopped her.

"Have you seen Ellie?" Cass joined Sara Ryan and another woman she didn't recognize.

"No. As far as I know, no one's seen her since her mother was killed." Sara shook her head and leaned closer to Cass. "Rumor has it, she went a little nuts when she found out, but that's all I've heard."

The other woman jumped in, making no attempt to lower her voice. "And that no-good husband of hers was running around town with some blonde all weekend."

Sara's eyes widened. "Really, where'd you hear that?"

The woman settled back, obviously excited to have gossip to share. "I saw them. I was walking into town the other day, and Jay flew past me, way too fast, mind you, driving a black car with a woman sitting in the front."

"Are you sure it was him?"

Cass thought briefly about confirming the woman's suspicions, but her fondness and concern for Ellie held her tongue. A flicker of memory surfaced of the blonde practically sitting in Jay's lap. Was it the same woman who'd come in a little while ago for a reading? Her concentration faltered. She couldn't be sure.

"I was pretty sure it was Jay, but then I saw them again later getting into the car in the parking lot at the Bay Side Hotel."

"Are you kidding me?" Sara's eyebrows shot up into her hairline.

A smug, knowing look crossed the woman's face. "Nope. I was out at Emmett's picking up my car, and I saw them with my own eyes. The hotel's right across the street. He even helped her into the car like a gentleman, with his hand on her . . ." She cleared her throat and puckered her lips in distaste.

Cass backed away from the women, leaving them to their gossip, and went in search of Bee.

He was in the back of the room talking to a young couple. He looked up as she approached. "Sorry, hon, I couldn't find him."

"Did you look outside?"

"I went as far as the parking lot, but his truck is gone. By the way, great job tonight." He leaned close to hug her and lowered his voice so only she could hear. "You always make that look so real. It's a little spooky." He shivered as he pulled back.

Cass laughed.

He went back to his conversation, and she moved away. *Looks like a trip out to Emmett's Garage is in order.*

8

Cass tucked the fast-food bag beneath her arm, unlocked the front door, and pushed it open. Silence. *Hmm . . . that's weird. Don't dogs usually make some kind of noise when you come home?* She peered into the shadows bathing the front foyer. Empty. She glanced back at Stephanie and Bee, who simply shrugged in return.

She flipped on the light and moved into the living room. Stephanie and Bee followed so closely they ran into her when she stopped short. Cass sucked in a breath. Her heart hammered wildly in her chest. Had someone broken in?

The room was in shambles, cushions torn from the couch and shredded, stuffing floating like fat, puffy snowflakes around the room. The coffee table had been overturned and magazines reduced to confetti and spread across the floor.

Then her gaze fell on *the dog. Oh . . . no.*

He cowered in the far corner behind an armchair, puffs

of white stuffing hanging from his mouth. He peered at her from beneath drooping lids, his wide eyes begging for forgiveness.

A snort pulled her attention, and she glared over her shoulder at Bee.

"Oh . . . dear." The words were muffled by the hand he'd slapped across his mouth, but the smirk he was trying to hide glistened in his eyes.

Stephanie didn't bother to hide her amusement. She laughed out loud, and Bee gave up his struggle and joined her in a full-out belly laugh. Tears poured down his cheeks as he clutched his sides and fell onto the remnants of the couch.

"Did you . . ." Stephanie sucked in a breath and regained some semblance of control. "Did you really leave the puppy free in the house?"

Cass glared at her friend. "Well, what do I know? I've never had a dog before." She lifted the coffee table back into place and dropped the fast-food bag onto it.

The dog sniffed and crept toward her.

"Bad dog." Cass reached out and petted his head when he reached her. "You're not supposed to wreck the house."

The dog whined. She rubbed behind his ears, and his eyes closed as he melted into a puddle at her feet.

"Well, I guess I can forgive you this time."

He rolled onto his back, baring his belly, which she knelt down to rub.

"But don't let it happen again."

Cass stood and surveyed the damage. Stephanie had already started trying to salvage the couch cushions.

Carrying a garbage bag, Bee walked into the room.

"Come on. Let's get this mess cleaned up, then we'll pop the food in the microwave."

"Thanks, guys."

The dog jumped up beside Cass, frantically wagging his whole back end and knocking over a lamp Stephanie had just righted. Cass sighed.

A flashing red light beneath an overturned chair caught her attention, and she bent to retrieve the answering machine.

"Hey, what are you going to do with this thing?" Bee asked.

Cass turned to see what he was talking about.

He flipped the dog a french fry and clapped when he caught it. "Good boy!"

"What thing? The dog?" Cass turned back to the answering machine and placed it on the side table. It was the shop line, so someone must have called after she left. Had someone forgotten something?

Bee laughed at something behind her back. "Yeah, the dog. Are you going to keep it?"

Cass shrugged and hit the play button. "I guess I'll give it to Ellie when we find her."

"Hi. My name is Luke Morgan. I'm new in town, and I'd like to make an appointment for a reading at your earliest convenience." The smooth southern drawl poured from the speaker. "You can reach me at—"

"Mmmm . . . sexy." Bee had come up behind her and nudged her with an elbow.

Heat crept up her cheeks.

Stephanie pushed herself up to sit on the table beside the answering machine. "Nice accent." She waggled her eyebrows playfully.

Cass scooped a ball of fluff from the table and threw it at her.

"So . . ." Bee leaned against the table and crossed his arms over his chest. "Are you going to call him ba—" His gaze darted past her. "Hey, stop that."

Cass turned.

The dog had half a hamburger hanging out of his mouth. He gulped it down when she started toward him.

"Ugh . . ." She weaved her fingers into her hair and squeezed.

"Forget about the dog. Call the sexy stranger back."

Cass ignored Bee and looked into the mostly empty bag. She crumpled it and threw it into the garbage bag, then she glanced at the clock on the cable box. It wasn't really that late yet. The dog made a noise that sounded suspiciously like a burp.

"Would you take him out to the beach while I return the *client's* call?"

"Sure." Bee smiled suggestively. "Come on, Steph. We can take a hint."

Cass rolled her eyes. When they left, she listened to the message again. The smooth, velvet voice filled the room. *Bee is right . . . very sexy.* She smiled as she dialed the number, then cradled the receiver between her ear and her shoulder.

As she listened to the phone ring four times, she couldn't help but wonder if his looks matched his voice. When she was about to hang up, his breathless drawl came through the line.

"Hello?"

"Uh . . . Hi, this is Cass Donovan. I'm returning your call."

"Well, hello, Cass." His accent didn't seem quite as thick

as it had on the machine. Maybe it was because he sounded out of breath, speaking in more of a raspy whisper.

"Did I catch you at a bad time?"

"No, no. Not at all. I just came in from a run on the beach. Can you just give me a second?"

"Sure."

Something banged around for a minute and then he was back.

"Sorry. I heard you're a great psychic, and I'd like a reading."

"Sure. Um . . . When would you like to come in?"

"Would tomorrow be okay?"

She worked to place the accent. Definitely southern, but not as heavy as she originally thought. "I can do tomorrow morning, if that works for you. I get in around ten."

"Perfect. I'll bring coffee. How do you take it?"

Ooohh . . . a gentleman. "Just milk. Thank you."

"No problem. I'll see ya then." His voice held the promise of something special, and a shiver ran up her spine.

She disconnected and set to picking up the mess.

The cushions were ruined, but there wasn't much damage to the couch frame. Once she had all the stuffing and magazine remnants picked up, it really wasn't that bad. The thought of giving the dog to Ellie brought on a wave of panic. *Where can she be?* Tomorrow, after the reading, she was going to find out where the other woman was, once and for all. She was just finishing up with the vacuum when Bee and Stephanie returned with the dog.

"So?" Bee stared at the cushionless couch and sat on the armchair instead. He crossed his legs gracefully and then slid back.

"So what?"

"Did you call him back?"

Bee and Stephanie were always trying to fix her up with someone, no matter how many times she begged them to let it go.

"Yeah, I called him back."

"And?" Stephanie perched on the arm of the chair beside Bee.

"And he's coming in tomorrow morning."

The two of them glanced at each other.

"Will you two knock it off? He's probably ninety years old and shaped like a question mark." She turned her back on them and headed to the kitchen for something to eat, sparing a scathing glance at the dog for eating her dinner. A small trickle of disappointment made her hope she was wrong. A voice as sinful as his deserved the looks to go with it.

Cass walked up the beach toward Mystical Musings. Since the back of the store faced the beach and the front faced the boardwalk, she had signs and display windows on both sides. A large wraparound porch ran all the way around the old two-story building. She'd painted the shingles a deep red and hung flowers from all of the window boxes and along the porch. One of these years, she'd find the time and money to finish the upstairs. Then she'd have the reading room upstairs and the shop down. She used her sleeve to wipe a smudge from the glass door as she entered.

Cass flipped the sign on the door to OPEN and stared out the large picture window. A view of the bay greeted her, the lighthouse standing sentinel at the tip of the island. She paid a little more to rent this building, but the view made it worth every extra penny. During peak tourist season, when crowds flocked to the Bay Pointe Lighthouse next door, her small shop would often be packed. She refused to hire help, though. Mystical Musings was her baby, the cozy shop having brought comfort when she needed it most. She'd placed small seating arrangements sporadically around the shop, with space for refreshments, and if the customers wanted to wait for her, they could. Most often, they did.

A shiver coursed through her, raising goose bumps across the back of her neck, and she rubbed her arms as she turned away from the window. She studied the colorful, flowing robe she typically wore at the shop but decided against it. She usually wore leggings and a tank top beneath the robe, but the air had been too chilly this morning and she'd wanted to walk, so she wore jeans and a heavy cowl-neck sweater instead.

She started straightening knickknacks and trinkets, though there really was no need. She kept the store immaculate, even during the busy season, often staying late into the night to keep things organized. Stephanie and Bee understood and had stayed with her after the reading to make sure everything was back in place. She hadn't always had that need for control and organization, but now . . . she did.

A lighthouse replica clattered against the glass shelf when she went to set it down. Her hands were shaking. "What the heck is wrong with me this morning?" Her voice echoed loudly in the empty store. "Great, now I'm talking to myself." She sighed. *Ellie.*

The wind chimes she'd returned to their hook above the door signaled a customer. She looked up and would have gasped if her breath hadn't caught in her lungs. *Don't even tell me . . .* But, there was no doubt in her mind. "Mr. Morgan?"

His killer smile turned her insides to mush.

"Luke. Nice to meet you." He extended a hand, and she wished she could wipe the sweat from her palm before accepting it. He didn't seem to notice, though, as he shook her hand and placed the cup holder on the large, round table beside him. His eyebrows drew together. "At the risk of sounding cliché, have we met? You look very familiar."

Sure, I'm the woman you were staring at in the deli when Marge had her snit and then again when the sheriff dragged me out of the theater. She'd keep that to herself for now. "Not that I remember." *Liar.*

His cocky grin spread and his incredibly deep blue eyes sparkled. He remembered exactly where he'd seen her.

She cleared her throat. No way would she admit to checking him out or even noticing him. "Come on in and have a seat." She gestured to one of the large, velvet-covered chairs at the table, then took the seat across from him.

He placed her coffee in front of her, and she took a sip, grateful for the warmth, before she set the cup aside. "Thank you."

"No problem. I can't wake up without my coffee." He set his cup aside and folded his hands on the table in front of him, seeming completely at ease.

"Have you ever had a reading before?"

"I have." He didn't elaborate.

"Do you want a general reading, or is there something specific you'd like to talk about?"

"Why don't you start, and we'll see where it leads?" He

smiled, and the dimple in his right cheek caused her heart to trip a little.

An image of Bee fanning himself came to mind, releasing some of the tension.

"Okay." Her voice sounded breathless. She fidgeted in the seat to buy herself a minute to settle down. *This is ridiculous.* She hadn't been this nervous doing a reading since she was seventeen and working at the beach to put money away for college. Of course, back then she'd only been afraid Chief Langdon would catch her and accuse her of harassing the tourists. Now . . . She shivered.

Cass pushed the crystal ball aside and pulled out a small stack of white paper and a basket of colored pencils. "Have you ever had a color reading?"

His eyebrows drew together, and he shook his head, studying her closely while she selected a variety of colors. A calm settled over her as she spread the pencils she'd chosen out beside her, rolled them back and forth a bit, and set the basket aside. She lit a candle.

His deep voice startled her from her preparations. "You're a medium, then?"

A smile tugged at the corners of her mouth, but she didn't allow it to form. "Yes." She straightened her paper once more, even though it was perfectly aligned already. She cleared her throat. "So, are you here on vacation?"

The cocky grin returned. "Why don't you tell me?"

This time she couldn't hold the smile back. "I love a challenge."

He sat back, and she studied him for a moment before lifting a violet pencil. She began to scribble back and forth on the paper. "This purple is an odd choice for me this early in a reading." She frowned, because it actually was.

He leaned forward, his interest obviously piqued. "Really? Why?"

"It indicates a certain level of psychic awareness on your part." She looked at him.

He lifted a brow, and she laughed at his skepticism before returning her attention to the curved shape emerging on the paper.

"Not necessarily something you pay attention to, but an"—she lifted her gaze to meet his dark stare without slowing her drawing—"intuitiveness."

A dark shadow crept over her. Her heart stuttered. *Oh no. Please. No. Not now.* Darkness crept into her peripheral vision, and her hand began to shake.

Luke reached across the table and gripped her hand. "Are you all right?" He frowned, deepening the lines in his forehead.

· A tear tipped over the edge of her lower lashes and rolled down her cheek. She forced the rest back.

"Ms. Donovan?"

Cass struggled for some semblance of a smile. "Cass." She pulled her hand from his and wiped away the tear. "Please, call me Cass."

His gaze held hers, the intensity of his stare not allowing her to pull away. "Are you okay, Cass? You seem awfully pale all of a sudden."

The tinkling of the chimes above the door drew her gaze reluctantly from his. She gasped as she surged to her feet, knocking the heavy chair to the floor behind her with a crash.

9

"Oh my . . ." Cass rushed across the room, careful to avoid running into one of the many freestanding glass display cases. "Are you all right? Where have you been? I've been looking all over for you." She grabbed Ellie by both arms and barely kept from shaking the young woman.

Tears poured down Ellie's face. "Did you hear about my mom?"

Cass paused, unsure what to say. Didn't Ellie know she'd found the body and been questioned about the murder? "Umm . . ." She glanced past her at Luke, who just shrugged and shook his head. What did he know?

"She's dead. Murdered." Ellie sobbed and collapsed into Cass's arms. "Who would want to hurt my mother?" She lifted her head and stared beseechingly at Cass, and Cass bit her tongue hard enough to choke on the coppery taste of blood.

"Come sit down, Ellie. Do you want a cup of tea?"

Ellie nodded and sniffed. Cass led her toward the table, and Luke reached out to help. They settled her in the chair where Cass had been sitting.

Luke grabbed a box of tissues from the counter and handed it to Ellie before pulling another chair up to the table. Okay. Apparently Mr. Southern Drawl planned on hanging around.

Cass dropped a tea bag in a mug and poured hot water over it. She added a bit of honey and brought the mug to Ellie. She glared at Luke, hoping he'd take the hint and leave, but he only stared innocently back at her. A little too innocently.

Fine. She'd ignore him. "Ellie, where have you been?"

"Jay let me go into the city for a few days to show his sister around."

A whole range of emotions shot through Cass, mostly anger, but she suppressed them and struggled to keep her attention on Ellie. "Didn't he call you to tell you about your mother?"

Ellie shook her head. "He says he didn't want to ruin my trip."

Cass rubbed the bridge of her nose between her thumb and forefinger as she searched for patience. "Well, I tried to call. Why didn't you answer your phone?"

"Jay told me to leave it home so no one would bother me while I was away. He really wanted me to have a nice trip."

Creep. He just didn't want his weekend tryst interrupted. Cass clenched her fists and lowered them into her lap so Ellie wouldn't notice. Luke didn't miss the gesture, though. He raised an eyebrow in question, and she discreetly shook her head. Thankfully, he let it drop . . . for now at least. The look he pinned her with told her she'd have some explaining to do later.

"I can't believe this. I don't know what to do." Ellie hiccupped and blew her nose. "Please, Cass. You have to help me."

"Me?" Her jaw would have fallen open if she hadn't gritted her teeth. "I'm sure the police are doing everything they can to find out who did it. I don't know how I could possibly help."

Ellie stared at her with childlike wonder. "You know . . ." She gestured toward the crystal ball sitting on the edge of the table. "You can look and see who killed her."

Heat blazed up Cass's cheeks. She could feel Luke's gaze drilling through her, but she didn't dare turn her head. "Ellie—"

"Please. You have to. I don't know where else to turn. You can't say no." Ellie broke down in a fit of hysterics.

Ah jeez. Cass shoved her hands into her hair and squeezed. A headache had begun to throb at her temples. "Okay, okay. Stop crying, Ellie. I'll try."

"Oh, thank you. I knew you'd help. I know you and Mom had your differences, but deep down I think you really liked each other."

The harsh laughter erupted before Cass could stop it, and she slapped a hand over her mouth and started choking in an effort to cover it up. Ellie scowled but didn't say anything. The woman really was clueless.

Luke handed Cass a glass of water. When she looked up to thank him, she couldn't miss the amusement dancing in his eyes.

Ugh . . . How do I get myself into these messes?

"Excuse me a minute." Cass jumped up and ran for the

back room. She closed the bathroom door behind her and stared at her reflection in the mirror. How could she do this? She took a deep breath and ran the cold water. She scooped some up in her hands and splashed it onto her face. How could she do a reading for Ellie and pretend to look for her mother's killer when she was already suspected of killing the old bat? She couldn't. She'd have to tell her the truth.

But how could she confess to Ellie with tall, dark, and gorgeous sitting there listening? She couldn't. She'd have to get rid of him. With that decided, she opened the door and stifled a scream. Luke stood directly in front of her.

"What are you doing back here?" She pressed a hand to her heart.

He grinned and reached out to tuck her hair behind her ear, smoothing his hand down the wavy strands. "You were gone for a while. I wanted to see if you were all right. You seemed a little shaky before we were interrupted."

Cass had forgotten about the incident before Ellie barged in. Another shadow. Was it meant for Luke? Or was it for Ellie? "I'm fine. Thank you." She started to move forward, but he took up too much space, crowding her when she tried to pass. She pressed her back to the wall instead and waited to see what he really wanted. He moved closer and put a hand on the wall beside her head.

"Are you sure you're all right?"

Could he see her pulse fluttering out of control? She simply nodded.

"Good." When he smiled, something wicked danced in his eyes. But was it evil or just mischief?

She swallowed hard, hoping to dislodge the lump before

she choked on it. "You can't stay while I do Ellie's reading. It's personal."

He shrugged. "Sure, I understand. We can finish what we started another time."

Heat surged through her. She nodded again, and he backed away.

She pushed away from the wall and headed into the main room.

"I'll call you," Luke said as she passed him.

Be still my heart.

He followed her into the room and grabbed his coffee from the table. He put a hand on Ellie's shoulder and leaned over to say something before turning away. He stared at Cass for a moment, his eyes holding the promise of something— she couldn't figure out what—in their stormy depths.

The tinkle of the door chimes as he left pulled her out of her trance, and she tore her gaze away.

She sighed and turned.

Ellie was watching her.

"Ellie." She paused. How could she tell this woman who trusted her so much, and had no one else to go to, that she'd been questioned by the sheriff about her mother's murder? Cass approached the table, but instead of taking her usual seat, she sat beside Ellie in the seat Luke had vacated. She took Ellie's hand.

After a deep breath, Cass tried again. "Look, Ellie. We need to talk. You know I would never hurt you. And I would never lie to you." She made sure to maintain eye contact, willing Ellie to believe her. "I'm the one who found your mother."

Ellie sucked in a breath.

"I unlocked the theater Saturday morning and found her in the pit." Tears spilled down Cass's cheeks. Not for Marge, but for the pain in Ellie's eyes. "I didn't hurt her, Ellie. I promise you I didn't."

Ellie pulled her hand away. "What are you talking about?"

Cass shook her head. The ridiculousness of the whole situation weighed heavily on her. She couldn't raise her voice past a whisper, didn't even want to say the words, never mind out loud. "Chief Langdon thinks I murdered your mother."

"What?" Ellie shook her head. "That's crazy. You'd never hurt my mother."

Well, I wouldn't go that far, but I didn't kill her. She kept that thought to herself.

Ellie twisted her fingers, weaving them together then taking them apart. Cass stayed quiet, allowing Ellie whatever time she needed to digest the information.

After a few minutes of silence, during which Cass prayed fervently Ellie would believe her, Ellie lifted her gaze to Cass. "Will you try to do the reading? Try to see who hurt Mom?"

The plea in Ellie's eyes was impossible to ignore. Besides, she was so grateful Ellie believed her, she'd have done pretty much anything Ellie asked at that moment. "Sure. Come on."

Cass moved to her seat and set the paper and pencils aside. She stared at the violet scribbles for a minute as memories of Luke played through her mind. His intense stare, the knowledge darkening his blue eyes. The certainty he was hiding something slammed through her, and her breath caught in her throat.

With her hands shaking, Cass pulled the crystal ball in

front of her. She closed her eyes, took a deep breath, and worked to clear her mind. She couldn't think about Luke right now. *Okay, concentrate.* She envisioned a clear blue lake, the waves gently lapping against the white sand of the shore. She pictured herself sitting with her feet dug into the warmth of the sand, the sun's rays cocooning her in their heat, Luke lying beside her, stretched out—

Ellie blew her nose, ripping Cass forcefully from the vision.

"Are you ready?" She knew her voice shook, but there was nothing she could do about it for now.

Ellie nodded, and Cass forced her concentration to the reading. She stared into the clear crystal of the ball, trying to focus her energy on reading the other woman. She sensed pain and sadness, the same emotions anyone would pick up just by looking at her. The red eyes, puffy, dark circles beneath them, the strained lines bracketing her mouth. The way she wrung her hands repeatedly played through Cass's thoughts. Ellie's hands turned over and over in Cass's mind, palms turned up, then down, up—

"What happened to your hand?" The words blurted out on their own before she had time to think. She looked up just in time to see Ellie shove her hands into her lap beneath the table, effectively blocking them from Cass's view. Guilt was etched in every line of her face.

Ellie shook her head. "Nothing."

Cass lifted a brow and waited.

"You know what? Maybe this was a bad idea."

"Ellie—"

"No, really . . ." She pushed the chair back and jumped to her feet in one motion. "I don't know why I thought you could see the killer in your crystal ball. That's probably stupid, right?" She stuck her hands in her pants pockets, pants that hung a little too loose. Had Ellie lost weight? She was already so thin it was hard to tell.

Cass shrugged. "It's not likely I would see who killed your mother while doing your reading . . ." An idea struck her. "Unless you know who killed her."

Ellie's face paled. "How would I know who killed her?" She pulled one hand—the uninjured one—from her pocket and grabbed her bag from the back of the chair.

Cass jumped up. She couldn't let Ellie leave in this condition. She was shaking uncontrollably and wore a look of sheer terror. "All right. Calm down, Ellie. I'm not saying you know. I'm just saying it's not likely I'd be able to tell who killed your mother *because* you obviously don't know." *Though I have a sneaking suspicion you suspect someone.*

Who could Ellie be so afraid of? That thought almost knocked her back into the chair. *Duh.*

Cass searched her mind frantically for something to keep the other woman there until she calmed down. "Please, Ellie, sit down a minute." The memory of the shadow she'd felt right before Ellie walked in haunted her. Was Ellie in danger?

"I really have to go," Ellie said. "Thank you for the reading."

Panic gripped Cass. "Uh . . . I have to talk to you about something. It's important."

Ellie paused halfway to the door. She turned a skeptical gaze on Cass.

Okay. Got her. Cass heaved in a cleansing breath. "Please, sit down, Ellie. I have a confession to make."

Ellie's eyes widened, and she returned to the chair.

Cass moved the crystal ball aside and fell into her own chair. "I couldn't find you after I . . . well . . . after. So, I went to your mother's house, hoping you'd be there. When I got there, I heard someone crying. At least I thought it was someone crying." She was rambling and tried to order her thoughts. "I broke the back window and went in thinking it might be you and you might be hurt."

Ellie stared back at her.

Cass waited, but when she got no response, she pressed on. "Anyway, I found a dog. A puppy, I think, but it's huge, and I . . ."

If possible, Ellie's face paled even more. Her eyes grew wide, and she shook her head.

"What?"

"Where's the puppy now?"

Cass's cheeks grew hot, and she knew she was blushing. "It's at my house." The admission didn't come easy.

Ellie visibly relaxed. "Could you take it to the pound for me?"

"The pound? Why?"

"I don't like dogs, and that thing is huge." Ellie trembled and dropped her face into her hands. She shook her head but didn't lift it, and Cass had to strain to make out her muffled words. "I don't know why she had to get such a big dog. I begged her not to, and I haven't been to her house since she brought him home."

Cass frowned, confusion pounding at her already throbbing temples. "Then why did she get it?" Marge never struck her as the maternal type, even with her own daughter. Why would she suddenly have the urge to nurture a puppy? It made no sense.

Ellie finally lifted her head and shrugged. "She said she wanted it for protection."

"Protection from what?"

"I have no idea. I asked her why she suddenly needed a big dog for protection when the alarm had been good enough all these years."

Alarm? What alarm? No alarm had gone off when she'd broken into . . . uh . . . *went* into Marge's house to save the dog.

Ellie shook her head. "She wouldn't answer me, just told me to stop being ridiculous and get over it." She met Cass's gaze.

Perhaps Ellie was over her earlier . . . suspicion. Or perhaps she was just desperate to be rid of the dog.

"Will you get rid of it for me? Drop it at the pound or whatever?"

"Umm . . ."

"I know," Ellie said. "Why don't you keep it?"

Cass tried to be gentle, but Ellie had to accept the truth. "How am I going to explain that I went into Marge's house and took her puppy? Chief Langdon already suspects me of killing her."

Ellie waved her hand, dismissing Cass's concerns. "Don't worry about it. I'll tell him I gave it to you. Besides, no one could really think you hurt Mom."

Relief coursed through Cass at the idea that Ellie trusted her, but then an image of her shredded living room popped up. "I don't know, Ellie."

"Please, Cass. I have all I can deal with right now. I can't have to worry about that, too." A look of outright fear crossed Ellie's face. It only lasted a split second, but Cass caught it.

She sighed. "Sure, Ellie. I'll keep him for now. At least until we figure out what's going on."

Ellie's face brightened. "You mean you're going to help me?"

"Uh . . ." *Oops. That wasn't exactly what I meant.*

Ellie's expression shone with anticipation Cass didn't have the heart to shatter.

She blew her hair up off her forehead, resignation frustrating her. "I'll see what I can do."

{10}

Cass locked the door and flipped the sign from OPEN to CLOSED. She never closed up Mystical Musings during the day, but she didn't want to risk someone walking in. She grabbed her phone and dialed. While she listened to it ring, she began to clean up. She lifted Ellie's full mug, emptied it into the sink, and washed it out. The coffee from her own almost-full cup followed.

Come on, Steph. Pick up.

She grabbed the glass cleaner and paper towels and started to clean the glass display cases that dotted the store, sporadically spaced between seating arrangements.

Stephanie's voice finally came over the line. "Hello . . ."

"Hey, Steph. You'll never believe who—"

"Hah. Gotcha. I'm not here. Leave a message."

A tone sounded, and she hit the off button. Definitely not as satisfying as slamming the receiver down would have been. She blew out a breath. *Okay. Bee's been working on the show at night, which means he's probably sleeping now. Which also means he'll kill me if I call and wake him up.*

She counted four rings before Bee's sleep-filled voice blared in her ear. "This better be good."

"Oh, it's good. Well worth getting up for."

"Who said anything about getting up?" Bee yawned. "Nothing's worth getting up for."

Cass grinned. "Guess who I just found?" The rustling of sheets made Cass laugh.

"How'd you find her?" He didn't sound half as sleepy now.

"I'll tell you what. I'll get coffee and pick you up in forty-five minutes. Then you can take a ride with me, and I'll tell you all about it." Cass grabbed her bag and keys.

Bee groaned, but she knew she had him. Bee loved nothing more than good gossip. "Fine, but I want a donut, too."

"Don't sulk. I'll bring donuts." She placed the phone on the base without waiting for him to complain anymore and ran out the door. She had just enough time to run home and get her car if she walked down the road instead of on the beach.

While she drove, she tried to order her thoughts. Ellie was definitely scared. Could she know who killed Marge? If she did, why wouldn't she tell Chief Langdon? It didn't make sense. And how had Jay gotten away with not telling Ellie her mother had been killed? Surely Chief Langdon would have insisted on speaking to her. And no one in town would believe for one minute that Jay didn't know where his wife was. He kept tight reins on Ellie.

She pulled into Tony's parking lot. If Bee was getting out of bed for her, deli donuts would definitely not do. She ordered half a dozen donuts and went to pour two coffees while she waited.

"Hello there." The smooth southern drawl sent shivers down her spine, and she jerked her hand, sloshing coffee across the counter. Deep, rich laughter followed. "Here, let me help you." Luke grabbed a stack of napkins and mopped up the spill.

"What are you doing here?" Cass pinned him with an angry stare. Was he following her? Suspicion narrowed her eyes.

That laughter raked her nerve endings again. "Nothing sinister, I assure you. I'm just waiting for someone to finish with the coffeepot."

"Oh." Her cheeks burned as she finished pouring the coffees and wiped off the cups. "Sorry."

"No problem." He leaned against the counter and folded his arms across his chest. "I'm in no hurry. How did your reading go this morning?"

"Fine." No way would she discuss Ellie with Luke.

"What's the deal with her husband?"

All right, him she'd discuss. "He's a creep." She stopped, not sure where to go from there without invading Ellie's privacy. Oh well. That about summed it up anyway.

He lifted a brow and waited, but when she didn't continue, he shrugged. "So . . . did you find the killer yet?"

Cass stiffened, but then remembered he'd been sitting there when Ellie asked her to do the reading. She bit her lower lip and lowered her gaze. "Very funny."

His warm laughter teased her.

She lifted her gaze and looked into a grin that stopped her heart.

Luke glanced at his watch, then back at her. "Do you always close up this early?"

"I . . . uh . . . no." *Okay, that was smooth.* "Mondays are kinda slow, and I had errands to run. So . . ." She lifted the cups and shrugged.

"Would you like to reschedule my reading now?" He pushed away from the counter and leaned closer to her.

She inhaled deeply, the fresh, spicy scent of his after-shave invading her senses.

"Or should I call you?"

There. He did it again. The southern accent was suddenly heavier. Sexy. Was he flirting? Fire rushed through her. "Sure." *Whoa. Too breathless.* She cleared her throat. "I mean . . . you can call to reschedule."

"I'll talk to you soon, then." He held her gaze a moment longer, and she finally understood the term *smoldering gaze.* Half the romance novels she read used it, but she'd never seen it in action. Until now. Luke had it mastered.

"Kay." *Holy cow.*

He lifted a brow. "I'm looking forward to it."

Me, too. Since her mouth was too dry to form words, she simply nodded and walked away.

"All set?" Tony's wife, Gina, smiled knowingly.

"Um . . . yup." Cass ignored the implication and placed the coffees on the counter beside the bag of donuts. Great. By the time she reached the car, half of Bay Island would know she was flirting with a tall, dark stranger in the bakery. And not doing a very good job of it. Gina was a sweetheart— the stereotypical older, Italian woman—but the bakery and the deli were pretty much gossip central. If you wanted to know anything that was happening on the island, you simply went into town for coffee. *Hmm . . .* "Hey, Gina. Have you heard anything about Marge?"

Gina looked up from the register, crossed herself, and muttered something Cass didn't catch. "Can you believe it? Murdered?" She handed Cass her change without counting it out, and Cass stuffed it into her bag. Gina folded her arms on the counter and leaned in for a chat.

"I know. No one gets murdered on Bay Island." Cass caught Luke in her peripheral vision, pretending to study the cakes displayed in the glass case. The tension lifting his shoulders belied the casual, disinterested stance. She shifted her weight so her back would be to him and leaned a hip against the counter.

Gina frowned. "Well, old man Tucker was killed last year, but that's because he was messin' around with Crazy Larry's wife."

Cass nodded. "I don't know what he was thinking."

"Me neither." Gina shook her head and tsk-tsked. "Everyone knows how possessive Larry was with his Jenny." Gina circled her finger beside her head. "And how crazy." She looked around Cass toward Luke and lowered her voice. "Don't you worry, dear. No one believes you killed her."

Relief rushed through Cass. She'd been gone from Bay Island a long time and had come back only recently by island standards. Even though people didn't like Marge, she was still a local and deserving of their loyalty.

Gina frowned. "Well, maybe some people believe it, but probably not too many." She paused and stared for a moment. "Except, of course, the chief." She patted Cass's hand as if to offer comfort.

Cass forced a smile for the other woman. "I guess. Anyway, I gotta run. Thanks, Gina." She ran out of the bakery without looking back.

She climbed into her car, tossed the bag on the seat, and put the coffees in the cup holders. She took a minute to rub at the tension headache gathering in her temples. While it was nice to know most of the town probably didn't think she killed Marge, it was a little disconcerting to know she was the new big gossip topic.

She dug through her bag for her keys. Where had she put them? She patted her pockets. Nothing. She leaned over to check if they'd fallen on the floor and found them hanging in the ignition. Had she already put them there, or had she forgotten them on her way into the bakery? Maybe the stress was getting to be too much.

Cass blew out a breath, flipping her hair out of her eyes. She stepped on the brake, put the car into reverse, and looked back over her shoulder. *Well, well, well. What have we here?*

Luke stood beside a black Jeep Wrangler, looking around. He rubbed a hand over his mouth, seeming disturbed. She couldn't quite place her finger on what it was that made him appear agitated, but he did. He pulled out a phone, dialed, and put it to his ear before climbing into the Jeep and taking off.

Hmm . . .

She thought briefly of following him but dismissed the thought just as quickly. She had no reason to distrust him. And what would she do if he caught her? She didn't have to glance in the rearview mirror to know her cheeks had gone beet red.

"**H**ey." Bee opened the car door.

"Watch where you sit."

He glanced in just as Cass lifted the bakery bag from the

seat. "Mmm . . . Is that Tony's coffee I smell?" He slid into the seat, leaned across the center console, and kissed Cass's cheek. "You're a lifesaver." He lifted a coffee. "Of course, if you hadn't woken me, I wouldn't need saving, but that's beside the point." Bee waved his hand in a dismissive gesture and took the lid off the cup.

He blew on the coffee before replacing the lid and turning slightly in the seat to face her. "Well . . . tell me everything. And give me one of those donuts. Please." He flashed her his most charming smile, and she handed him the bag.

"I get the chocolate one." She put the car in gear and pulled out onto the street.

Bee handed her a chocolate donut. "Where are we going? Don't you want to sit and eat first?"

"Nah. I can eat while I drive. I want to get to Emmett's while he's still there." She bit into the donut. *Oooh.* Tony really knew how to make donuts.

"Emmett's. Why? Is something wrong with the car?" Bee broke off a small piece of powdered donut and nibbled at it.

"No. I . . . um . . . sort of promised Ellie I'd look into who killed her mother."

Bee gasped and pressed a hand to his chest. "Are you crazy?"

Oh, great. Here we go. Maybe she should have left Bee home. *And what if Emmett's the killer? Then I'd be alone with him.* No. Better to deal with Bee's dramatics.

"Look, Bee. You didn't see her. She was a nervous wreck, and she had a strange cut down the back of her hand."

Bee spoke around a mouthful of donut, obviously giving up on being dainty. "What do you mean, strange?"

"I don't know." She thought back to the mark on Ellie's

hand. It had gone from her wrist to her knuckles. Not too deep, but more than a scratch. An image of Marge's bloodred nail, sharpened to a dagger, popped into her mind. "Just in a weird spot, I guess." She shrugged it off. "Anyway, Ellie wanted me to do a reading and see if I could name the killer."

She glanced at Bee and caught his eye-roll.

He shrugged. "Sorry, but you know how I feel about that mumbo jumbo."

"I know." She was never quite sure if Bee didn't believe in talking to the dead, or if he was afraid it might be real. A visible tremor ran through him, and she figured it was most likely the latter.

She finished her donut and took a sip of coffee before saying anything else. Bee waited her out while they ate.

"Since the chief seems convinced I killed her and doesn't appear to be looking for anyone else, I figured I may as well see what I can find out." She tried to keep the hurt from her voice, but if the sympathy in Bee's eyes was any indication, she didn't succeed. "I might not be able to look into my crystal ball and see who did it, but I *can* ask some questions. Emmett was acting strange the other night."

"Emmett *is* strange, dear."

"I guess, but he was acting strange, even for him."

Bee held the coffee cup in his hand, rhythmically tapping the lid in time with some imagined tune playing out in his mind. "So, what are you going to do? Walk into the shop and say, *Hi, Emmett, you're acting weird. Did you kill Marge?*"

Cass laughed, some of her earlier tension finally draining away. "No. I thought I'd ask him about building something for the shop. He did some of the renovations last year, and they came out really good. Plus, he didn't kill me on the price."

"This I gotta see," Bee said under his breath as he stared out the window.

Emmett's garage sat at the southwestern tip of the small, oddly shaped island. Not much else was around, except for the Bay Side Hotel and a small family-style restaurant. She'd never paid much attention to how secluded the area was. Until now.

She pulled into the small lot and parked against the chain-link fence that bordered the hotel parking lot. Now for the hard part. "Could you do me a favor, Bee?"

"Sure, hon. What do you need?"

"I want you to wait here."

"What? And miss this?" Bee pouted. "Then what did I get out of bed for?"

"Tony's donuts and coffee. What else?" She grinned.

"Well, there is that, but I'm still coming." He opened the door to get out.

"I'll make you a deal."

He paused and looked back at her. "Oh yeah? What's that?"

Cass shot him her most wicked smile. "If you wait here, I'll tell you who else came into the shop today." She waggled her eyebrows.

"Give me a hint."

Cass thought of Luke. What hint could she tease him with that would keep Bee in his seat in exchange for information? "Fine. His looks match that sexy southern drawl."

She grinned again, blew him a kiss, and got out of the car.

"You witch."

She shut the door and walked away, confident Bee would do as she asked.

{ **11** }

Cass looked around nervously as she crossed the lot to the small garage. She'd hoped at least one of the bay doors would be open, but they were all closed up tight. Maybe Emmett had left? The sign showing through the salt and dirt clinging to the door said OPEN. She pulled open the door and walked into the waiting room. "Emmett?"

Empty. *Hmm* . . . She poked her head into the small office behind the counter. No one.

"Emmett? You here?"

A second door, this one closed, stood beside the open office door. She pushed, and it swung wide. "Emmett. You in here?"

Something loud clattered against the floor. "Aww . . . dang it."

Cass smiled. Yup, that was Emmett.

"Who's there?"

"It's me, Emmett. Cass Donovan. Where are you?" She moved into the garage, the smell of old grease in the closed-in space turning the coffee in her stomach.

"I'm right here." He walked out from behind a car, wiping his hands on a shop towel. "What's up? You having car trouble?"

"No, nothing like that. I came about . . . uh . . . something else." She fidgeted with the strap on her bag while Emmett stood still and stared at her.

She waited, but he made no move to say anything. "Um . . . I noticed you left early last night, before the reading, and I wanted to make sure everything was all right."

His cheeks flamed red. "Yes, everything's fine. I just had something to do."

Okay, not getting anywhere that way. "Um . . . I was also wondering if you'd be willing to do some work in the shop for me again."

A ready smile crossed his face. "Sure, Cass. You know I love helpin' out."

Emmett's wife died when their son, Joey, was a baby, and Emmett had raised him on his own ever since. For all his quirks, Emmett was a wonderful father. Even though he'd played every sport there was in high school, and he was good, he accepted it wasn't his son's thing. Instead of mulling over not having anything in common, Emmett jumped wholeheartedly into the activities Joey enjoyed and stayed very involved with all of the people in Joey's life.

"Great." She gave him her biggest smile. "I was thinking of doing some renovations upstairs. Nothing major, but maybe a storeroom and a small office for now. Then I could open up the back room and use it for more display cases."

Emmett scratched his chin. "Hmm . . . We could probably do that."

"Well . . ." She studied the garage behind him.

Emmett kept the space immaculate. She'd never been in such a clean garage. Even the floor appeared clean. Emmett shifted from one foot to the other. He lifted a large wrench from the nearest counter and polished it with the rag he still held.

She'd always hoped to renovate the upstairs of the shop but hadn't really given it any serious thought. Suddenly, the idea excited her. "Eventually, I'd like to make the shop bigger and put in more display cases and stuff, but for now do you think you can put a stairway in without losing too much space?"

Emmett hung the wrench from a hook above the counter and tossed the rag into a small bucket on the floor. He took off his red baseball cap and smoothed back a wild mane of hair, then, without a word, he walked past her into the waiting room.

Cass took a last glance around the garage, with no clue what she expected to find. Nothing seemed out of place and, as organized as Emmett was, the smallest detail would probably jump out at her. She shrugged and turned to follow him. Bee was right. Emmett always acted strange. He was a sweetheart, but his social skills were . . . a little lacking. Oh well, the way he adored his son made up for it.

He was hunched over the desk, scribbling furiously. She tried to peek over his shoulder but gave up when she couldn't see anything. Instead, she moved to the grimy window and looked out to see if Bee was still waiting in the car. Yup. There he was, head bopping to music she knew would be blasting. Good to know he wouldn't hear a thing if she screamed for help. She glanced nervously over her shoulder, but Emmett was still in the zone.

Her gaze caught on a figure moving through the hotel parking lot across the street. Even with his hat pulled low and a very large bag slung over his shoulder, there was no mistaking Jay Callahan. *What is he doing?* He opened the back of his beat-up SUV and dumped a bag about the size of a body into it before slamming the door shut. With one last furtive look around, he jogged to the driver's door and jumped in.

"I'll be right back, Emmett." Without bothering to look back, she ripped the door open and ran out into the sound of "It's Raining Men" blaring from her car. She waved frantically, but Bee never even looked in her direction. She crossed the lot, jumped into the car, and hit the off switch.

"Hey." Bee's indignation was short-lived.

She slammed the car into gear and tore out of the lot.

"What happened?"

"I just saw Jay Callahan leaving the hotel. I think he put a body in his car."

"What?"

She cringed as Bee's high-pitched screech pierced her brain.

Bee grabbed the dashboard as she took the next corner too quickly.

She reached the front of the hotel. "I think he came out the back door. He was carrying something over his shoulder, wrapped in some kind of plastic or something. It looked like a long bag." She searched the parking lot, cut through to the back exit, and shot out onto the small back road. "Where could he have gone?"

"Are you sure it was him?"

"Positive. He was driving that old truck he uses for work." There were only two exits from the hotel parking lot. He'd been closer to the back one, but maybe he'd gone out the front. She pulled a quick U-turn in the middle of the road.

"Hey. What are you doing?" Bee braced himself against the dashboard.

"He must have gone out the front entrance. I was right behind him." She scanned the only side street she passed but didn't see any sign of Jay or the truck. "There's nowhere to go. I don't understand. How could I have lost him?"

"Lost him? Why on earth are you trying to find him?"

She pulled her gaze from the road for a second to glance at Bee. "Didn't you hear me? I said I think he threw a body in his car."

"So you're looking for him? What if it was a body? Don't you think maybe you should let the police handle it?"

"Yeah, right. All Chief Langdon is interested in is proving me guilty. He's probably poring through every minute of my life trying to pin this on me."

Every side street they passed was a potential escape route for Jay, every parking lot a potential hiding spot. They'd come too far into town to expect to run across him. There was no way she'd find him like this. "Who knows? Maybe Langdon's trying to get all of my friends as accessories."

She'd been kidding, but one look at Bee's face told her he wasn't amused. He'd gone deathly pale, his eyes wide, and didn't say a word.

"What's the matter with you?"

"Nothing."

With no idea where to look for Jay, she turned around with less urgency this time.

"Where are you going?" Bee finally relaxed his death grip on the dashboard and sat back.

"I guess I'll go back to Emmett's." Frustration beat at her, and she drove slowly through the hotel parking lot once more before giving up and returning to the garage. "I don't know where Jay could've gone."

"Maybe he went down one of the dirt roads into the woods."

She shrugged. A maze of small dirt roads used by hunters and dirt bikers zigzagged through the entire area. "I guess, but there's no way I'd be able to find him if he did." She shifted into park and lowered her head to rest against her hands on the steering wheel. "You know we're gonna have to go check on Ellie again, right?"

Emmett must have seen Cass coming, because he opened the door for her. "Is everything all right?"

"Um . . . yeah, sure."

He frowned and scanned the parking lot, then looked back at her but didn't press the issue. "I sketched a few different ideas. You can pick what you want."

What? She'd come back to the garage intent on questioning Emmett about Jay. What was he talking about?

He laid several sketches out across the counter.

Oh right, the renovations.

"Do you want the office at the top of the stairs?"

Cass struggled to concentrate on what would be most convenient. She hadn't given it much thought, since she'd only come up with the idea on the way into the garage. It had been more of a ruse to talk to Emmett than an actual idea for the shop, but the more she thought about it, the more excited she got. "That would be good, but will the stairway take up a lot of room?"

"If I remember the layout correctly, we can put a spiral staircase in the back corner. It'll look nice and fit in great with the design of the shop." He fumbled through the sketches. "Here." He handed her two sketches.

She studied them for a moment. "Oh, this is great." She cringed. "How much do you think it'll cost?"

"It really shouldn't be too much. The biggest expense will probably be the staircase." He shrugged. "Other than that, it's just the wood and stuff. You're not going to add display cases upstairs?"

"No, not yet. Eventually, I'd like to, but right now I just want to make a little more room downstairs. If I don't do something, I'm going to have to start limiting how many people can attend the group readings."

Emmett used his thumb and finger to smooth his goatee. "I'll tell you what. I'll stop by the shop this week and check everything out. Then I'll write you up an estimate."

Cass nodded. "That would be great. Thank you."

"Sounds good. I'll get started on them over the weekend. Joey can help me." Pride filled his voice when he spoke of his son.

"He's a great kid," Cass said.

Emmett beamed. "He sure is."

She racked her brain for a way to question him about Jay but couldn't think of a way to guide the conversation in that direction.

Emmett started cleaning off the counter. "Do you want any of these other sketches?"

Cass shuffled through them quickly. "No. The ones you already gave me are perfect."

He took the papers back, crumpled them, and tossed them in the garbage pail.

"Where's Jay today? Doesn't he usually work on Mondays?" *Okay. That was smooth.*

Emmett didn't seem to think it strange she'd ask. "Yeah. He had stuff to do, so he left early."

"He must be really upset about Marge."

Emmett shrugged. "Seemed okay to me."

Ugh . . . Getting answers out of him is like pulling teeth. "Has he said how Ellie's doing?"

"Nah. She's a nice kid, that one."

"Yes, she is. It's hard to believe her mother's gone."

"Yeah."

Cass gave up. She obviously wasn't going to get any information from Emmett. When it came to talking about something that excited him, like his side business doing renovations or Joey, Emmett could hold a conversation. When it came to making small talk . . . not so much.

"Anyway, thanks for the sketches." Cass tucked them into her purse. "And for working on the shop."

"No problem." Emmett walked to the door with her, keys in hand. "Ya know, it *is* kinda weird her car's not there."

"Whose car?" Cass pulled the door open and waited for Emmett to answer, her mind already racing ahead to what she still had to do. The blonde who had shown up before the group reading should be at the shop soon, and she still had to set up for her reading. She inhaled deeply. She loved the smell of the sea. It never failed to soothe her nerves.

"Ms. Hawkins." Emmett stuck the key into the lock on the door.

Cass's heart started to pound harder. "Her car's not where?"

"By the fence."

"What are you talking about?" She massaged the tension gathering in her temples.

Emmett smoothed a hand over his goatee, and Cass instantly regretted being short with him. He appeared to be lost in thought, though. Maybe he hadn't even noticed. "I always thought it was strange she was hangin' around the hotel." He pursed his lips, and for a minute she thought he was done talking. "Every Monday and Wednesday her car was parked right there beside the fence, but on the hotel side." Emmett pointed toward the spot where Jay's truck had been parked.

"Are you sure it was her car?"

Emmett wasn't the most observant person.

Indignation filled his scowl. "Of course, I'm sure. Knowing cars is my business."

She nodded. She had to concede, if there was one thing Emmett knew, it was cars. "Are you sure she was driving?" An image of Jay sneaking to his truck flashed into her mind. "Could someone have borrowed the car?" Cass thought frantically about what Marge Hawkins could have been doing at the Bay Side Hotel twice a week.

"Nah. I saw her getting in it a coupla times. Never could figure out why she'd be there." He stared at the empty parking spot for another second, then cleared his throat. "Anyway, I gotta make dinner for Joey."

"Oh, sorry. Thanks, Emmett."

He smiled. "Sure. See ya later."

"Yeah. See ya." She never took her eyes from the empty parking spot at the hotel while she ran to the car. She opened the door, tossed her purse over the seat, and hopped in. Then she sat, hands resting on the wheel, and stared at the hotel parking lot. What in the world could Marge have been doing at the hotel twice a week?

"Well?" Bee frowned at her. "Are you going to sit there all day without telling me about the stranger?"

Cass laughed. He'd obviously forgiven her for the mad dash in search of Jay. She shifted the car into gear and backed up. She glanced at the dashboard clock. She still had time to drop Bee off at home before heading back to Mystical Musings for her appointment, but she'd have to visit the hotel later. Or tomorrow. Maybe it would be best to come back on Wednesday and see what was going on that Marge could have been a part of.

"Is the rest of him as sexy as his voice?" Bee sounded like he was losing patience fast.

"Nope."

His grin faltered.

"Sexier." She pulled her gaze from the road for a second to wink at him, and his grin returned full force.

{ 12 }

Cass climbed the steps to the porch of Mystical Musings and walked around the shop to the beach side. She tossed her keys into her bag, dropped the bag onto a scuffed wooden table, and flopped into one of the rocking chairs scattered along the porch. She propped her feet on the railing and rocked slowly back and forth as she stared out at the bay. Small ripples from a boat's wake lapped at the shore.

She leaned her head against the high back of the chair, let her eyes fall closed, and tried to relax. The gentle breeze carried the buzz of the boat's motor, joined with children's laughter, seagulls screeching, and the clinking of the wooden wind chimes dangling from the porch roof. A seagull shrieked. A shadow drifted over her.

Cass shot upright, dropping her feet to the porch. A seagull.

Ugh . . . What is wrong with me? She rubbed her hands over her face and stood. *So much for relaxing.*

She grabbed her bag on her way into the shop that usually brought her such peace. She had to settle her thoughts, keep them from battering her so continuously. Jay, Ellie, Marge . . . Luke. A small smile tugged.

She pulled out the small basket of colored pencils and set it on the table beside a stack of white paper. A color reading would be good today. Maybe it would help relax her. She set a candle in the center of the table.

She tried to remember the blonde who'd been cozied up to Jay. Was it the same woman? No use. She'd glimpsed the woman for only a brief moment through the car window. But she was definitely going to find out. She just had to figure out how. Maybe she could ask the woman if she knew him.

At the tinkling of the chimes, she turned. "Hi, Cayden."

"How are you, Cass?"

She smiled. Cayden and his wife, Sophie, had been customers since Cass opened. "I'm doing well. This is a pleasant surprise."

"We were out for the weekend, and I stayed an extra day to stop in and visit."

Cass laughed. "Sure you did." She pulled a small pouch from a drawer beneath the counter. "Your usual?"

His good-natured smile crinkled the corners of his eyes. "Yup."

She sorted through several bins, choosing the combination of crystals Cayden always carried. "How have you been feeling?"

"Much better since I listened to you." He winked, humor dancing in his blue eyes.

Cayden was an ironworker in the city, almost forced to quit the job he loved because of rheumatoid arthritis. At his wife's urging, and as a last resort, he'd visited Cass. Now he credited Cass's assortment of crystals with healing him.

"By the way, can you give me something for morning sickness?"

Cass lifted a brow. "Something you want to tell me, Cayden?"

He chuckled softly. "Sophie's having a tough month. She told me to see if you had anything that might help."

"Of course." She reached beneath the counter and grabbed a red pouch, then, suddenly quite certain Sophie was having a boy, thought better of it and chose a blue one. She added a few extra gems. "Tell her I hope she feels better."

When she held out the pouch, Cayden gripped her hand. "I will." He frowned, an unusual expression for the typically happy man. "Listen, Cass. I heard you had some trouble . . ."

Ahh . . . The real reason for his visit.

"And . . . well . . . I just wanted to let you know Sophie and I don't believe a word of the gossip. If you need us, just call, and we'll come out."

A surge of warmth shot through Cass. She held back tears as she patted his arm with her free hand. "Thank you, Cayden. I appreciate the support."

His already ruddy cheeks reddened even more. "Yeah, well. I'm gonna stop in at the sheriff's office before we head back and let him know how I feel about him considering you a suspect."

A vision of Cayden's strong hand around Sherriff Langdon's throat made her laugh out loud. "Thanks. I'm sure he'll appreciate that."

She rang up his crystals, giving him a discount because he was such a sweetheart. "Tell Sophie I hope she feels well enough to stop in next time you're out."

"You bet. Take care of yourself."

She smiled as he strode out the door, almost feeling sorry for Langdon. Almost.

She glanced at the clock and was surprised it was well after three. A chill ran through her, raising the hairs along the back of her neck.

Cass returned the bins of crystals to their proper places. She strolled through the shop, rearranging knickknacks, adjusting the stock to make sure the shelves all looked full, without being cluttered. Some of the things she carried were simply souvenirs—small statues, lighthouse replicas, wine-glasses, and other paraphernalia sporting the Bay Island logo.

But most of her stock held some meaning. The stones, which helped people heal and feel good. Creams, lotions, and candles designed to help people relax and reduce stress. A small assortment of various good luck charms and potions lined the shelves along one wall.

She polished the driftwood counter, set aside the paper and pencils, and gave up. The blonde hadn't left a phone number, so there was no way to contact her. She hoped the woman wasn't Jay's mysterious girlfriend, because if she was, she would be the second of Jay's women to disappear. She thought of the body-shaped bag slung over Jay's shoulder, and a chill coursed through her.

She glanced up at the tinkling of the chimes, relieved the woman had finally made it, but ready to tell her she no longer had time for the reading. Luke's grin stopped her short.

"I brought a gift." He lifted a cup holder with two cups from Tony's.

Cass laughed. "We have to stop meeting like this. People are going to talk."

His languid chuckle seeped through her. "So, what are you doing now?"

"Now? Getting ready to close up and go to rehearsal."

He handed her a cup. "Do you have a little time?"

She glanced at the clock. Surely Luke Morgan was a Bee-worthy excuse for being late. "Sure. What do you need?"

"I thought maybe you could finish my reading?"

"Oh." She sipped her coffee and studied the colored pencils and paper she'd put aside. She didn't have the right sense of peace to work with them with Luke in such close proximity. "Sure. Have a seat." She sat across the table from him and pulled the crystal ball toward her.

Luke lifted a brow but didn't question her. He leaned forward, elbows resting on the table, hands clasped.

Cass sipped her coffee again and reluctantly set the cup aside. She stared into the glass and brought an image of Luke to the front of her mind. It wasn't hard. She let her eyes fall closed.

His dark good looks, the intensity of his gaze. She thought back to the bakery, where he had leaned against the counter with his arms folded across his chest. Defensive. A barrier . . . designed to hold people at a distance. And yet . . .

An image of him leaning close to her, invading her space, lifting a hand to tuck her hair behind her ear. She longed to lean her cheek into that cupped hand and feel the warmth and strength of it against . . .

Cass gasped.

Her eyes shot open.

He was staring at her, his expression amused. "Did you see something scary in there?"

If she said yes, she wouldn't be lying. Any level of intimacy scared her. She shook off the thought of Luke touching her and tried to concentrate. "You tend to hold people at a distance. Only letting them in on your terms, when you want to invite them in."

He frowned a little and sat back. "I guess that's fairly accurate." He crossed his arms.

A small smile played at the corners of her mouth. Following the movement of his arms, her gaze traveled to his chest. Toned, muscular, but not big. She jerked her eyes back up to meet his. She blew out a breath and caught her lower lip between her teeth. *What in the world is wrong with me?*

She forced herself to concentrate on his eyes. The eyes held so much information about a person if you knew what to look for. And Cass did.

Luke's eyes were guarded. His expression hard. Disciplined.

"You have secrets you keep well guarded. Important secrets that play a big role in your life . . ."

His jaw clenched, but he didn't respond or acknowledge her statement. His expression brought a memory into focus. She pictured the look on his face when he'd been talking on the phone outside of the bakery. Jaw clenched, eyes on fire. The words blurted out. "You're passionate."

His posture changed completely and relaxed. He leaned farther back. The hot, sexy grin returned, and his eyes held the promise of . . .

Cass jumped from her seat. Flames raced up her neck, and her cheeks burned. "You know what?"

He continued to watch her, his gaze holding hers in an iron grip. He stood and let his hands drop to his sides. "No . . . what?"

Cass held her ground as he skirted the table and walked toward her, her gaze never faltering from his. She tipped her head back to maintain eye contact as he moved closer.

When only an inch or so separated them, he stopped.

She took a deep breath in and held it, clinging to his scent.

"I have an idea." He ran a finger along her cheek.

A chill raced through her body. Heat followed in its path.

"Why don't I tell you *your* future?"

That smooth, southern drawl made her heart skip a beat. She nodded and checked the urge to reach up and make sure she wasn't drooling.

He held his finger beneath her chin, forcing her to continue looking at him. "You are going to meet a tall . . ." He leaned closer. "Dark . . ."

The warmth of his breath tickled her in places she didn't want to think about.

"Handsome . . ."

Her insides melted.

"Stranger." His laughter was as sexy as the rest of him. He lowered his lips toward her. His voice dropped to a husky whisper against her ear. "Here's where you're supposed to say: *I already did.*"

The door chimes tinkled, and she jumped back like a cat hitting water. She nodded to a young couple, who started to browse.

Luke laughed, all the smoldering heat gone in an instant. "Saved by the bell?" He lifted a brow, obviously amused at her reaction.

Ding! It's a defense mechanism. The thought slammed through her with absolute certainty. The increased southern accent, the sexy, smoldering gaze, the featherlight caresses. She shivered. It might be a defense mechanism, but it was certainly effective.

Luke had secrets he no doubt wanted to keep hidden.

He lifted his leather jacket from the back of the chair. "I'll catch you later."

"Sure." She had no doubt he'd show up somewhere throughout the day.

Now that she understood the whole sexy act, would she be immune to it? She watched him walk toward the door and groaned. *Probably not.*

She couldn't help but admire the way the tight jeans accentuated the muscles of his thighs. Her gaze traveled upward to where his pants hugged . . .

Fear clutched her throat, its grip so tight it threatened to strangle her. Clearly defined beneath the form fitting T-shirt, tucked into his waistband, was the shape of a gun.

"Excuse me? Miss?"

She jumped, startled by the man at her side, his expression caught somewhere between *Is this woman all right?* and *Is this chick crazy?*

"I'm sorry. Can I help you?" She glanced toward the doorway again, but Luke had already disappeared through it.

13

Later that evening, Cass pulled into Stephanie's driveway and parked. She grabbed the box of Chinese food from the backseat. "Can you get the sodas, Bee?"

"I already did, dear."

They carried everything to the back door and knocked before they walked in. "Stephanie?" Cass dropped the box on the kitchen table. She poked her head into the living room. "Hello? Stephanie, you here?"

"Be right there." Stephanie's footsteps sounded on the stairs, and Cass grabbed a small stack of napkins from the holder on the counter.

Bee already had the table mostly set, but he took glasses and ice out while Cass set out the food.

"Hey." Stephanie pulled out a chair. "Mmm . . . smells good. How long do we have?"

"We're good. We still have a little over an hour before we have to be at the theater."

Stephanie blew on a spoonful of wonton soup. "Are you allowed to run rehearsal? Did Langdon release the theater?"

Bee loaded his plate with fried rice. "He released it and removed the crime scene tape today, so we're allowed back in."

Stephanie reached for an egg roll. "Did you get in touch with any of the board members? Is anyone willing to initiate an emergency meeting?"

Cass cringed. "No. I'm sorry. I know I said I'd call them, but I didn't get a chance today."

"Can you do it tomorrow?" Stephanie grinned. "You know we try not to let Bee interact with the board members if we don't have to."

Bee snorted. "One little snit with a board member, and suddenly I'm not allowed to talk to them anymore."

"It was more than a snit, Bee." Stephanie laughed. "You threatened bodily harm if he walked on the stage with his cowboy boots on again."

Bee shrugged and laughed with her. "Yeah, but he didn't walk on it again, did he?"

Stephanie just shook her head.

"Hey, in my defense, the stage had just been refinished. Besides, Cass got into a fight with Marge, and she's still allowed to talk to them."

Cass looked over at Bee, fully expecting to find him pouting, but a flash of humor lit his eyes.

"No. Marge told Cass off. Cass was smart enough to keep her mouth shut." Stephanie filled her glass. "So, *anyway* . . ."

She glared at Bee before turning her attention to Cass. "Why didn't you get to call today? The shop's not usually that busy on Mondays."

Cass's mind flashed to Luke. Heat flared, but she kept his visit to herself. Cass told Stephanie about the trip to Emmett's, Marge's twice-weekly visits to the Bay Side Hotel, and the large bag she'd seen Jay toss into his truck. She skipped over the fact that she'd followed him, knowing it would only earn her a lecture. When Bee opened his mouth to rat her out, she pinned him with a death stare.

"Do you really think it was a body in the bag?" Stephanie sat back and studied Cass.

Cass shook her head. "I don't know what to think. It was long, and he had it slung over his shoulder. It's not like there were feet hanging out the bottom or anything, but it seemed like the right shape and size."

The rumble of a car on the gravel driveway interrupted them.

"Is that Tank?" Bee frowned and looked over his shoulder toward the back door.

"I don't know. He was supposed to work tonight, and I told him you guys were bringing dinner." Stephanie glanced pointedly at Bee.

Bee and Tank tended to avoid each other whenever possible.

Cass shrugged. "Maybe he's hungry."

"I guess."

Tank walked in and wiped his feet on the mat. Then he pinned Cass with a look that had her halting her fork halfway to her mouth. "What?"

"We need to talk." He pulled a plate from the cabinet and sat at the table with them, but he didn't reach for any food. Instead, he clasped his hands together and rested them on the table.

"About what?" She lowered the forkful of chicken chow mein to her plate, suddenly not as hungry as she'd been. "Is something wrong?"

"Look, Cass. I'm really not supposed to tell you anything about the investigation." He sat back and rubbed a hand over his closely buzzed hair.

"Well, then, why bring it up?" Bee lifted a brow, the challenge evident in his tone.

"I'll get to you later, Bryan."

Bee snorted and rolled his eyes.

Tank stared hard at Bee. "*Maxwell*, is it?"

Bee's eyes halted mid-roll, and all the sarcasm quickly fled his expression. His face paled. He sat back, crossed his arms over his chest, and held Tank's gaze. But he didn't say another word, and his eyes lit with fear.

Tank turned back to Cass. "This conversation has to stay between us, but I *would* like to ask you some questions."

She nodded, never taking her gaze from his.

"Chief Langdon seems to be really stuck on fresh coffee stains on the front stoop of the theater."

Cass frowned.

"Can you explain how they got there?"

"Hey, shouldn't she have a lawyer or something?" Bee shoved his chair back and stood.

Tank stood as well, the two of them facing off, chests puffed. Bee's cocked hip sort of ruined the tough guy look he seemed to be aiming for.

"That's enough." Stephanie jumped to her feet. "Both of you."

Bee pouted, and Tank's eyebrows rose almost to his hairline, shock widening his eyes.

"I can't take you two fighting anymore. I don't understand what the problem is between you two, but get over it. I'm sick of listening to you bicker. Cass might be in real trouble here. We're going to have to work together to help her."

Bee shrugged and spoke quietly. "I don't really have a problem with Tank." He glanced at the other man, then quickly looked away. "I just always got the impression he doesn't like me. Sorry, Steph."

Both women stared at Tank. Waited.

"I'll reserve judgment until after I find out how Butch Hawkins became Bryan Maxwell."

Cass sucked in a breath. *Hawkins? As in* Marge *Hawkins?*

Bee's eyes widened, then he flopped back onto the chair and sulked.

"Is that true, Bee?" Stephanie asked.

Bee clamped his mouth closed defiantly.

"Don't worry, we'll get to that soon enough." Tank sat, pushed his empty dish aside, and resumed his interrogation pose. He focused his attention on Cass. "Do you know how the coffee got spilled on the stoop?"

Cass shrugged. Her mouth went dry.

"This isn't an official interview or anything. I'm just trying to figure out what happened so I can try to help you. I suggested to Chief Langdon that he ask you, but he seems more interested in building a case against you than actually trying to find out what happened." Tank's eyebrows drew together. "Is there a history between you two I don't know about or something?"

Cass worked to pull herself together. This was Tank. They were friends. There was no way he'd do anything to hurt her. "I don't know what his problem is. He and my dad were friends. He was always a bit stern, but I don't remember him being like this." She *had* been gone a long time, though. Had something happened between Chief Langdon and her father?

Tank shook his head. "Anyway, tell me what happened the day you found Marge."

She blew out a breath, flipping her hair out of her face, and sat back. "I spilled coffee on the way into the theater. It was no big deal. My hands were full and I dropped the cup when I tried to unlock the door."

Tank rubbed his hands over his face and sat back. He crossed his arms over his chest and seemed to relax a little. "Did you have any sort of altercation with Marge?"

"No . . . Well, not that day, anyway. I had a run-in with her the day before at the deli over doing a reading for Ellie. But it wasn't anything that hadn't happened before." She weaved her hands into her hair and squeezed. "I don't understand what the big deal is."

"Do you have any idea why she might have had a Mystical Musings business card in her hand when she died?"

Fear clutched Cass's throat. She shook her head.

Tank didn't say a word.

Cass began to wonder if he was going to say anything else when he sighed and sat forward.

"Langdon has it in his head that you and Marge struggled on the front steps of the theater. Marge has a bruise on her right cheekbone. He thinks you put it there. Obviously you dropped your coffee when the fight started. I have no idea what he thinks she was doing with your card—maybe sending a postmortem message that you killed her?" He caught her gaze and held it. "The fact that your fingerprints were found all over Marge's house didn't help matters any."

Uh-oh . . .

Tank clenched his teeth, then worked to relax his jaw. "Can you explain that?"

Cass winced. "Sort of?"

"Make sure you can do better than that."

She nodded. Ellie had already said she'd tell everyone she gave the dog to Cass. *Oh no . . . the dog.* She'd forgotten all about it. One glance at Tank's rock-hard expression told her she was not going anywhere. A glimpse at the clock told her she wouldn't have time anyway.

"We really have to get going, Tank, or we're going to be late for rehearsal." Stephanie stood and started clearing the dishes. "Do you want me to leave the food out?"

"Yeah. I'll put it away after I eat something." Tank turned his attention to Bee, and Cass jumped up to help Stephanie, relieved to be off the hook. For the moment, anyway.

"Look, Bee." Tank paused and studied the other man, distrust lining his face. "No one else knows about this but me, and I only found out right before I came home. I'll wait until after rehearsal, but I want an explanation tonight. If I don't get one, I'll take you to the station and get it there. I'm giving you the benefit of the doubt because you're friends with Stephanie, but that only goes so far. Understood?"

Bee swallowed hard, his Adam's apple bobbing as he nodded.

* * *

"See, Bee, I told you everything would come together. The models looked much better tonight." Cass pushed the front door of Mystical Musings open and flipped on the light.

He shrugged. "Yeah, but what does it matter if I can't have the show as scheduled?"

Bee had been unusually quiet since leaving Stephanie's house. Any attempts by Cass or Stephanie to find out what Tank was talking about had been met with moody silence. His heart had definitely not been in the rehearsal.

Could Tank be right? Could he really be related to Marge Hawkins?

"We could do away with Marge. The world would be a better place without that woman, anyway." Bee's words after he read the letter from the board haunted Cass's thoughts, allowing doubt to creep into her certainty that Bee was innocent. Could he have really meant it?

"Cass?"

She shook off her unease. "Sorry, Bee. What did you say?"

"Would it be too much trouble to pay attention here?" Bee stood with one hand on his hip, anger etched into every line of his face.

She opened her mouth, intent on a witty retort, but snapped it shut just as quickly. His face might be lined with anger, but his eyes were drowning in worry. "Sorry."

He turned away and headed for the door. "I'll be at Dreamweaver if you need me."

Dang. Now his feelings are hurt. Could someone that sensitive really be a killer? In her experience, Bee tended to sulk when he was upset. Had Marge hurt his feelings enough to make him snap? *Well, if anyone could push someone that far, Marge could.*

Cass sighed. "Don't go, Bee. I'm sorry. I'm just a little preoccupied. I have to put these orders together for tomorrow." She pulled out three baskets and started sorting through a variety of scented candles and stones. "Would you grab the order slips from behind the register, please, and tell me what else I need?" She separated the stones she needed into small piles, started on the basket for Tim, then glanced toward Bee.

He stood behind the register with the forms spread out in front of him, his hands resting on the counter. His concentration was fully focused on the pages . . . or on some demon in his mind.

She rolled the black tourmaline around in her hand, the warmth and movement bringing comfort, then moved to stand next to him and nudged him with her elbow.

"Yeah?" He didn't even bother to look up.

She studied his profile. He was a good-looking guy, with a strong jaw, high, almost feminine, cheekbones, but otherwise masculine features. "You okay?"

He huffed out a breath and squeezed the bridge of his nose between his thumb and forefinger. He stayed that way for a minute.

"What's going on with you?"

He shook his head. "Let's just get these orders together, drop off the dresses at Dreamweaver, and we'll talk after." He waited a beat, his eyes pleading with her to drop it. "Okay?"

Cass studied him another moment. Was he guilty of something? Well . . . something was obviously on his mind. But, having a secret didn't necessarily make you guilty. "Sure."

The smile didn't reach his eyes. "Thanks."

"Give me your hand."

She couldn't help laughing at his warily lifted brow. "What's the matter—don't you trust me?"

He blew out a breath and held out his hand, palm down.

She gently turned his hand over and placed the black tourmaline in the center of his palm, then closed his fingers over the stone and held his hand in both of hers. "I know you don't really believe in any of my hocus-pocus." She shrugged. "Who knows? Maybe some of it's true and maybe not, but people really seem to think these help. This stone is supposed to help protect you against negative energy."

His gaze remained on their joined hands.

"Keep it with you." She grinned. "It can't hurt."

He lifted his gaze to hers, and tears shimmered in his brown eyes. He cleared his throat. "Thank you."

"Whatever's going on with you, Bee, I'm your friend. If you need help or need someone to talk to, I'm here." She patted his hand, then returned to her orders, leaving him to ponder whatever was tormenting him.

Chimes sounded. "Hey, guys. Sorry I'm late. I stopped for caffeine." Stephanie grinned and held up a cup holder with three large sodas. She placed them on the table beside Cass and nodded toward Bee. "Is he all right?"

"I honestly don't know."

"Do you think his name really is Butch Hawkins?" Stephanie studied him from the corner of her eye as she whispered.

Cass stared openly. Why would he change his name? Had he changed it? Was Bryan Maxwell an alias?

Bee walked over, moved a few things aside, and slid onto

the counter to sit behind them. "Psst." He tapped Stephanie's shoulder and stage-whispered, "He's fine."

Stephanie feigned shock, pressing a hand to her chest and batting her eyelashes.

"Don't you bat those lashes at me, toots." He leaned over and kissed her cheek, then Cass's. "Thank you for worrying about me. I really am okay." He smiled and lifted his gaze to the door as the chimes sounded. "Mmm . . . Looks like this night is finally looking up." Bee grinned, leaned back on his hands, and crossed one leg over the other.

Cass turned around to see what he was drooling over.

Her heart stuttered to a stop.

What's he doing here? Cass stared, mouth hanging open.

Luke Morgan walked toward them, his cocky grin firmly in place. "Don't stop on my account."

"Not at all, dear. We were just hanging around while Cass puts an order together." Bee gestured dismissively toward Cass, hopped down from the counter, and moved forward to greet Luke. He extended a hand, and Luke gripped it and shook. "I'm Bee Maxwell."

"Good to meet you, Bee. Luke Morgan. I was actually looking for you. I stopped by the theater, but you'd already left." Luke stepped back and glanced past Bee at Cass. "I'm taking Ms. Harper's place on the board, and I thought I'd stop by, introduce myself, and say hello."

Bee harrumphed and leaned toward Cass. "Unless there's another sexy, southern stranger in town, I gather you two have already met."

Cass glanced at him only briefly before returning her full attention to Luke. "You didn't tell me you were on the board of directors."

"I didn't tell you a lot of things." Luke waggled his eyebrows. "You were going to do a reading and tell me. Remember?"

Cass clasped her hands together to keep from fanning herself. She wished she could say the same for Bee.

Luke's grin widened. At least he seemed to take it all in stride.

Stephanie intervened. "The board must be disorganized with Marge gone."

Luke shrugged. "It does seem a bit . . . chaotic. I thought maybe y'all could tell me a little about what's goin' on." He increased the laid-back, southern drawl, turned to lean against the counter, and crossed his arms over his broad chest.

Smooth and sweet as melted chocolate. What is he up to? "What do you mean, going on?" Cass asked.

Luke pushed himself up to sit on the counter. "One of the other board members, Marti Symms, said there's a problem with the date for the fashion show. She said there was a conflict because the play was scheduled for the same day."

Stephanie gestured from just out of his line of sight.

Huh? Oh, right. "Umm . . . Since you brought it up, I was wondering if you could do me a favor?" Cass peered at him from beneath her lashes and caught Bee's eye-roll in her peripheral vision.

"Really. And what's that?" Luke looked thoroughly amused, and she gave up on flirting. She simply wasn't good at it.

Bee opened his mouth to say something, but she stopped him with a glare.

She dug through her bag, pulled out the letter Bee had given her, and handed it to Luke. "Chief Langdon said the board would consider rescheduling the play instead if we could get a member to call an emergency board meeting." *Well . . . maybe that's not exactly what he said, but it was something along those lines. Sort of.*

Luke studied the paper for another minute, raked a hand through his hair, and smiled. "Why not?" He shrugged a broad shoulder and handed her the letter.

"You mean you'll do it?" Excitement coursed through Cass, in addition to the thrill Luke caused when he brushed her hand with his.

"Sure." Luke glanced at his watch. "I better get going if I'm going to reach all of the board members tonight, though. I'll let you know what happens."

"Thank you so much. That's great."

Luke leaned close enough for Cass to inhale the woodsy scent of his aftershave deep into her lungs. He tucked a loose strand of hair behind her ear. "But you're going to owe me one."

Her heart fluttered and her stomach flipped. The man had a way of making everything sound like an innuendo. She looked into his eyes. *Maybe he really is dangerous.*

14

"Do you want to stop at the diner?" Bee stared into the rearview mirror at Cass, his eyes filled with hope.

"Tank wanted to talk to you as soon as we were done."

His face fell, and he flopped against the back of the seat and pouted.

Cass ignored him and turned to Stephanie. "Can you call him and ask him to come to my house?"

Stephanie shrugged. "I guess. Why?"

Cass could only free one hand while driving, so she massaged her right temple first then switched hands and did the left. Neither helped. "I kinda forgot about the dog."

"What do you mean, forgot about?" Stephanie sounded wary. Not that Cass could blame her.

"I fed him and took him out this morning before I left, but then I was running around all day."

"Cass, it's ten o'clock at night. The dog hasn't been out since this morning?"

"Weeell. I was busy." The excuse sounded lame even to her own ears, and Bee's mocking laughter filled the car.

"Look. I'm not used to having a pet. I never had a pet as a kid. What do you want from me?"

"Did you at least confine him this time?"

"Yes." *Sort of.*

"You better do something with that dog before he eats your whole house."

"Ellie's just going to have—oh no—Ellie." With everything going on, Cass hadn't even thought about her all night. She looked at the dashboard clock. No good. It was too late to call. Maybe she should ride past and see if everything seemed all right. The memory of her living room in shambles ended that thought. "I have to get in touch with her tomorrow anyway. I'll see if she's changed her mind about taking the dog."

Splatters of rain started to hit the windshield. She turned on the wipers. *Great.* Now she'd have to walk the dog in the rain. The swish, swish of the wipers kept time with the pounding in her head. All she wanted to do was go to bed. "Did you get ahold of Tank?"

Stephanie frowned. "No. He didn't answer. That's weird, because he was very insistent about talking to Bee as soon as we were done."

"Does that mean you want to go to the diner?"

"No!" Cass and Stephanie answered in unison.

Cass pulled into the driveway, shifted into park, and turned off the car. She was out and running toward the front door before she heard either of the other car doors close. She fumbled the key in the lock but managed to get the door open without dropping the key. She stopped dead in her tracks. *Holy* . . . She slapped a hand over her mouth and nose and backed out onto the porch, slamming into Bee.

"Ah, jeez, what is that smell?" He pushed her toward the door.

"Are you crazy? I'm not going in there." She twisted out of his grasp.

"Well, someone has to, and it's not going to be me."

Stephanie kept her distance, leaning against the porch railing in the far corner, shaking her head.

A cold breeze blew in off the bay. If she held her breath and ran in and opened some windows, the smell should dissipate. She hoped. She inhaled deeply, filling her lungs with the fresh scent of the sea, and ran. She flung the front window open, then ran through to the kitchen. She froze in the doorway, and the breath shot from her lungs.

She'd left the dog in the laundry room with the lower half of the Dutch door closed. He had gotten out.

Thankfully, from what she could see, the damage was confined to one chair he'd apparently spent all day chewing apart. *That* she could live with. The mess in the corner by the door, she couldn't. She gagged and covered her mouth with her hand. Tears formed in her eyes, but she refused to let them fall. *Ugh . . . I'm not cut out to be a dog owner.*

She opened the window over the sink and bent to get the rubber gloves from the cabinet underneath. She pulled out a roll of paper towels, bleach, and a garbage bag.

Once she had the mess cleaned up and outside in the trash, she sprayed the entire downstairs with Lysol and opened all of the windows. At least the smell was starting to lessen. Of course, she'd have to mop up all the rain soaking the floors, but better a few wet floors than that smell. She lit a few candles.

She fed the dog and took him for a walk on the beach. It was empty this time of night, even though the rain had stopped, and she was grateful for the peace. The soothing lap of the small ripples against the shore worked to calm her nerves. The reflection of the moon danced along the surface of the water. She imagined Luke walking beside her, his strong hand enveloping her smaller one. *Okay, enough of that.*

When she dismissed the images of Luke, a vision of Ellie took his place. Cass wrapped her arms tightly across her chest and whistled for the dog. She needed sleep. She needed to warn Ellie to be careful. After she found her, of course. And she needed to be done with all of this stress. She'd come back to Bay Island to eliminate the stress she'd been under. She didn't need this.

With that decision made, and the disaster at the house behind her, she breathed a sigh of relief, allowing the nip of the cool, salty night air to cleanse her mind. The dog followed her back to the house. "What am I going to do with you?"

He tilted his head and perked up his ears.

She reached out and petted his head. "I know. It wasn't your fault. It was mine. I'm sorry I forgot about you . . ." *Hmmm . . .* Even if he was only going to be with her a little longer—she offered up a quick prayer—he was going to need a name. She opened the door. "Come on, fella. Time for bed. We'll worry about everything else tomorrow."

Cass walked into the living room. Bee and Stephanie were waiting for her. She flopped onto the cushionless couch, propped her feet on the coffee table, and dropped her head back. "That's it. I'm done. I don't want to hear another word about murder, or Marge Hawkins, or Ellie, or this dang dog, or anything else." She rubbed her eyes. It didn't help. They burned with exhaustion. "Let the police handle the whole thing. I don't care anymore. They can't prove I did something I didn't do, so I'm not going to worry about it anymore."

Bee and Stephanie didn't argue. Heck, they were probably relieved she was going to stay out of the investigation. Stephanie's cell phone rang.

Cass stood. "I'm going to bed. Lock up on your way out."

Stephanie checked the caller ID and answered.

"Bee, you can sleep in the guest room if you don't want Tank and Stephanie to drop you off." Cass pushed to her feet and started toward the bedroom.

"Oh no. Are you serious?" Stephanie's voice sounded almost shrill.

Cass stopped. She didn't want to know.

"Who?"

Keep walking. She turned around.

"When?" Stephanie had a finger pressed against one ear and the phone pressed in a white-knuckled grip to the other.

Cass stared at the look of horror on Stephanie's face. *Great. What now?*

"No. Don't worry about it. I'm sure Cass will drive me home. Yes. I'll tell him." Stephanie said good-bye and hung up. She looked straight at Cass. "That was Tank. They just found a body on the beach by the Bay Side Hotel."

* * *

The room spun. Cass's legs gave out. She sat down hard on the coffee table, dropped her head between her knees, and crossed her arms over her head.

"Are you all right?" Bee stood over her, rubbing circles on her back.

Ellie. She shook her head but didn't lift it. "Who is it?"

"They don't know. Or at least that's what Tank said. An unidentified woman's body was found on the beach by the Bay Side Hotel."

Unidentified. Surely someone would have recognized Ellie if it was her. Cass took a deep breath and struggled to control her erratic heartbeat.

"We're going to have to go to Chief Langdon and tell him what we saw." Bee's voice shook.

Cass finally looked up. Bee, Stephanie, and the dog stared warily at her.

"I'm fine, guys." Cass stood and started to pace. All three backpedaled to get out of her way. Back and forth, back and forth she paced across the small living room, hands pressed to her temples.

She stopped to face Bee. "Look, Bee, I don't know what's going on with you, but you didn't actually see anything this afternoon. I did." She sighed. "I'll go into the sheriff's office tomorrow and report what I saw. There's no sense going tonight. I'm sure they're all out at the scene, anyway."

Relief visibly relaxed Bee's stance, and he didn't argue. They stood staring at each other for another minute before Cass turned away. Bee obviously had his secrets, but he'd been a good friend to her this past year, and she trusted him. Mostly. And even if he did kill Marge, she'd probably given him good reason.

"Come on. I'll drive you guys home." She grabbed her purse and keys and started for the door, then turned back. She stared at the dog for a split second before deciding she couldn't deal with another mess tonight.

The dog tilted his head and his tongue dropped out the side of his mouth.

"Yeah, come on. You can come."

He barked once and ran after her.

Bee stopped when they reached the car. Cass climbed into the driver's seat and Stephanie opened the passenger door.

"Hey. What do you think you're doing?" Bee said.

Cass looked around. What was the problem now?

"I am not sitting in back with this monster." Bee folded his arms across his chest.

Stephanie held the door open but didn't get in. "You always sit in back."

"I know, but there's no room back there for both of us. That dog is huge."

Cass studied the little silver Volkswagen Jetta. Bee was right. It would be a tight squeeze. "Well, what do you want me to do with him?" Frustration shortened her temper. "I can't leave him here, and I'm not driving one of you home and coming back for the other. I'm backing out of this driveway in one minute. I don't care who's sitting where when I go, but whoever's not in the car is spending the night." She pulled the door shut, turned on the car, dropped her head on the wheel, and waited.

A minute later the back driver's side door opened and the dog hopped in, followed by a moody Bee.

Stephanie slid in next to Cass. No one said a word.

Cass shifted into reverse and turned to back out of the driveway . . . and found herself staring at two big heads. Laughter born from exhaustion erupted from her throat.

Bee scowled.

Cass laughed harder. Tears poured down her face and a cramp bit into her side. "Owww."

Bee ignored her and spoke to Stephanie. "I think she's finally lost it."

Her laughter must have been contagious, because Bee and Stephanie soon joined her. The dog barked once. The tension that had gripped them for most of the evening finally started to ease.

Cass sucked in a deep breath and tamped down the hysterics. "Will one of you two please get your big head out of the way so I can see to back out?"

"Lie down, boy." Bee put a hand on the dog's massive head and lowered it onto his lap.

Cass started to back up. "Do you think we oughta give that thing a name? I mean, I'm going to find Ellie tomorrow and tell her she has to take it, since I'm obviously not cut out to be a dog owner."

Bee snorted.

Cass ignored him. "But I'm getting tired of calling him *the dog*."

Bee looked at the dog and petted his head. "Why don't we call him Tank? He's certainly built like one."

Stephanie bristled.

"What? Just a thought."

Stephanie turned to glare at him, and Bee looked innocently back at her. "Okay, fine. What do *you* want to call him?"

Stephanie studied the giant animal. "How about Warrior?"

Cass shook her head. "I'm not chasing this thing around yelling *Warrior.*"

Bee laughed. "I like Monster."

They tossed names around for a few more minutes—Bruiser, Giant, Chief Langdon—laughing as they got sillier.

"I know." Bee sat up straighter. "It should be something from a musical. Hmm . . . What about Beast?"

"Yeah, Beast." Stephanie looked over at Cass.

"Beast, huh? I like it. Beast it is."

Beast barked once.

"I guess he likes it, too."

The three of them settled into silence, and Cass watched the scenery go by, enjoying the peace and quiet of the late hour. It wasn't often the island was this deserted.

"It's not that big a deal, you know."

"What's not?" Cass hit the turn signal, even though there was no one around for miles, and turned onto Bee's street. She glanced over her shoulder at him.

He slid lower in the seat and rested his head back. "Changing my name."

Light, dark, light, dark. The hypnotic effect gripped her as she passed beneath streetlight after streetlight, waiting silently for him to say more. She hit the turn signal again, turned into Bee's driveway, shifted into park, and sat quietly, waiting.

Bee made no move to get out of the car. "Do you have any idea what it was like growing up *Butch Hawkins* when you're . . . like me?"

So he *was* related to Marge. Cass turned to face him. "You mean gay?"

He studied her face. "Flamboyantly gay . . ." A self-deprecating smile touched his lips. "Feminine, sensitive. The Hawkins men are a tough breed." Bee swiped at a tear tracking down his cheek. "Hell, so are the women."

An image of Marge, spine rigid as she argued, flashed into Cass's mind.

He focused his attention on Stephanie. "Tell Tank he can stop by tomorrow, and I'll answer his questions." He lifted the dog's head from his lap and slid out. He crossed the small lawn, shoulders hunched, without ever looking back.

❦ 15 ❧

Cass contemplated the situation as she drove home. She and Stephanie hadn't spoken about Bee once they'd dropped him off. Instead, Cass had remained quiet, lost in her own thoughts until she'd dropped Stephanie at her house. How had everything gotten so messed up? She was a suspect in a murder case—a chill ran through her. Bee was being accused, and was possibly guilty, of something, but she had no idea what.

Beast snored loudly from the backseat. She looked into the rearview mirror to find red and blue lights pulsing through the night. Annoyed, she hit the turn signal and pulled to the side of the road to allow him to pass, even though he had plenty of room to go around her on the deserted road.

The police cruiser pulled off behind her. *Uh . . . oh.* Had she been speeding? She watched in the side mirror as Chief

Langdon climbed out, her eyes drawn to the holster hanging from his left side as he pulled up his belt.

When he turned and started walking toward her, she sucked in a breath and looked around. The stretch of road was far from deserted—small houses lined each street of the small residential neighborhood—but at this time of night, it might as well have been. *Don't be ridiculous. What's he going to do . . . shoot me?* She rubbed her eyes, too exhausted to even think straight.

Chief Langdon knocked on her window and she rolled it down. "Hey, Chief. What's up?" She smiled, hoping to let him know she held no hard feelings toward him for suspecting her of murder. *Yeah, right.*

He didn't smile back. "What are you doing out driving around at this time of night?"

"I just dropped Stephanie and Bee off." Her hands shook a little, so she put them beneath her legs, hoping he wouldn't notice how nervous she was.

"Keep your hands where I can see them, please." One hand hovered over the gun at his side, the other held the flashlight trained steadily on her.

Is he serious? Her heart rate accelerated as she whipped her hands out from beneath her legs and placed them on the steering wheel.

"What were you three doing out so late?"

"We . . . uh . . ." She didn't want to mention she knew about the body, or Tank wanting to question Bee. "We were going over some stuff for Bee's show."

"When are you going to give up and realize you are not—"

"Ruff!" Beast chose that moment to stick his head between the seats.

Langdon jumped back, the look of shock that crossed his face almost comical as he moved the light to land on Beast.

Cass bit back a smirk.

"Step out of the car, please."

What! "But I—"

"I said get out of the car. Now." He stepped back as he opened the door a crack. "And don't let the dog out."

She moved slowly, her mind racing as she climbed out and slammed the door shut, careful to keep Beast in. "Look—"

"Turn and face the car." He guided her gently to the front of the car and turned her toward it. "Hands on the hood."

Anger surged through her. "Are you kidding me?"

He didn't answer.

Adrenaline pumped wildly as he patted her down. When he finally turned her to face him, she swallowed the tirade she'd been about to let loose.

His face burned purple with rage. "Where did you get that dog?"

"Uhhh . . ."

"Answer me."

"Ummm . . ."

"That dog belonged to Marge Hawkins. How did it end up in your car in the middle of the night?"

She swallowed the lump she couldn't seem to get any words past, and still all she could manage was a whisper. "Ellie gave it to me."

"Really." It was obvious from the sarcastic inflection he didn't believe her.

She nodded.

"I have *another* dead body on the beach down the road.

It's the middle of the night. And you're out driving around with a dog belonging to the last woman you were suspected of killing."

Even Cass had to admit it didn't look good. She prayed fervently the dead woman hadn't been mauled by a dog. Sweat trickled down her back, cooled by the sea breeze, and she shivered. She clamped her teeth together to keep them from chattering.

"I don't know what's going on with you, but I intend to find out." Langdon pointed a beefy finger an inch from her face. "And when I do, you're finished. Do you understand me? You'll be rotting in jail for a long time, missy."

Missy? Who says that? Indignation crept in to replace some of the fear. How dare he try to pin all of this on her?

He propelled her toward his car, shoved her into the back-seat, and slammed the door. Then he pulled out a cell phone and moved a little ways away. She couldn't hear a word he said, but he didn't look happy.

Panic raged through her. He couldn't arrest her. She couldn't abandon her car here in the middle of the night. Who would take care of the dog? He'd probably eat the whole car before she could get back.

When Langdon returned a few minutes later, he didn't say a word. He simply opened the car door and let her out. Cass forced herself to hold his gaze. No way would she allow him to intimidate her. Her insides turned to mush.

"You're lucky Ellie admitted to giving you that dog, or you'd be on your way back to the station right now." He walked her back to her car and closed the door behind her when she got in. He leaned into the window.

A thought popped into her head and, unfortunately, out

of her mouth before she could stop it. "How did you know it was Ms. Hawkins's dog?"

He frowned. "I saw it when she called me to her house about your run-in at the deli. She wanted me to keep you away from her daughter since you're obviously a bad influence."

Cass bit back any response.

"License and registration, please."

What?! She handed him the information without saying another word.

He pulled out a pad and pen, paused for a minute, then started writing. He ripped off the top page and handed it to her.

"What's this?" She stared uncomprehendingly at the ticket.

"Speeding. You did thirty through the school zone." He tucked the pen back into his shirt pocket and flipped the ticket book closed.

"Are you kidding me? It's the middle of the night."

"The sign says twenty when the yellow lights are flashing." He smirked. "The lights are flashing."

He strutted back toward the cruiser, and she thought briefly about telling him she saw Jay carrying something that looked like a body out of the hotel this afternoon but quickly dismissed the idea. *Maybe now's not the best time.*

A new sense of determination filled Cass as she walked down the beach the next morning with Beast on a leash at her side. No way was she going to let Chief Langdon get away with pinning not one, but two murders on her. She was going to have to find out what was going on. She sighed. *So much for giving up the murder investigation and eliminating stress.*

She tried to order her thoughts as she and Beast walked toward Mystical Musings. She closed early yesterday, so she had to go in today. At least for a while. Rehearsal for the show started at six tonight, so she'd have a few hours if she closed up at three. But what could she do?

A trip out to the Bay Side Hotel topped her list. Followed by what? A visit to Ellie? Cass knew she was all right, as of last night anyway, because Chief Langdon had talked to her. That made seeing her less of a priority. Unless, of course, she wanted to get rid of Beast. She glanced at the big dog trotting happily beside her. Nah . . . maybe that wasn't such a priority, either. He was starting to grow on her. Maybe he just needed some attention.

She would have to call Luke Morgan and see if he was able to get in touch with the board members to call a meeting. She'd do that as soon as she opened the shop and returned any business calls. If he hadn't had any luck, she'd have to call and beg each of them.

She also had to make time for a trip to the mainland with Bee and Stephanie. They had to go to the local vineyards and pick up the wine for the show. Bee always used local products for his shows. He liked to keep businesses in the area thriving. She sighed as she turned toward Mystical Musings. So much to do—how would she ever get it all done? She probably should have driven today, but the sun had been shining so brightly, she couldn't resist the temptation to walk along the mostly empty beach. It wouldn't be long before winter—or prison—made early morning walks impossible.

She climbed the two steps to the front deck of Mystical Musings. "You have to behave yourself here, Beast."

He looked at her and licked his lips.

Uh-oh. She laughed and unlocked the door. "Come on, boy." She'd have to make time for a quick stop at the pet store to buy some toys for him to chew on or something. She settled him in the back room with a piece of driftwood she'd picked up on the beach. "This'll have to do for now, boy. Later we'll go get you some toys. Now, stay. And be good."

He looked at her, cocked his head, and snorted.

The tinkle of wind chimes had her returning to the shop. "Good morning."

An older woman with a kind smile returned her greeting. "I was wondering if you could help me."

"Sure. What do you need?"

"Well . . ." She blushed, looked around the empty store, and lowered her voice. "I was hoping you had a love potion."

Cass bit back the urge to laugh at her stealth and walked around the counter to help her. "I don't have a love potion, but I do have some crystals that might help."

"Really?" The woman's excitement brought a smile to Cass's face.

"Sure." She pulled a small pouch, suspended on a leather cord, from beneath a glass display case. "Do you know who you'd like to attract?"

"Yes. He's been a friend for a long time, but I invited him for dinner tonight, and . . . well . . . I'm hoping he'll be interested in something more."

Cass pulled a selection of crystals from the case—a beautiful rose quartz for love, a bright, sunny citrine for confidence, positive energy, and success, a pink and white swirled rhodochrosite for love and balance, and a green aventurine for luck—and filled the pouch. "Turn around."

The woman obeyed, and Cass held on to both ends of the cord and dropped the pouch over the woman's head. "Hold it against your heart." While she did as instructed, Cass tied the cord to a length that would allow the small pouch to sit directly over the woman's heart. "There."

The woman turned back to face her. "Do you really think it'll help?"

"Sure." *It can't hurt.* "Just tuck it under your shirt and wear it during the day, and then tuck it under your pillow at night." If nothing else, it would give the woman confidence.

"Oh, thank you."

Cass rung up the purchase. "Good luck."

The woman waved happily on her way out the door, and Cass smiled after her. The smile was short-lived, though. Why was the dog so quiet? She ran to the back. He lay belly up, spread-eagle on the floor. *Hmmm . . . I guess the walk tired him out.* He didn't even stir at the sound of the chimes.

She smiled as she headed back toward the showroom. "Did you forget somethi—"

The words froze on her lips. She'd expected to see the woman who'd just left. Instead, she stood face-to-face with an irate Jay Callahan. The breath whooshed out of her lungs. *Oh crap.*

Jay stood, hands on hips, just inside the doorway. "Where is she?"

Cass's heart stopped. She sucked in a breath but couldn't get it back out again.

"Did you hear me?"

She nodded frantically as true fear prickled every nerve ending.

"Where is Ellie?" His eyes narrowed, and he moved toward her.

She took a step back and hit the wall. *Ah jeez* . . . "I don't know w-w-what you're talking about, Jay. I haven't seen Ellie." She shouldn't show she was afraid of him, but she couldn't help it. Once the words started to flow, she couldn't turn them off. "I haven't seen Ellie since . . ." *Oh crap . . . when was the last time I saw Ellie?* Her mind was a total blank.

Jay moved forward slowly—a man who was obviously used to intimidating women and knew how to make the most of each second of fear he inflicted—until he stood about a foot in front of her. "The sheriff woke me up in the middle of the night asking questions about you. He talked to Ellie, and she told him she gave you her mother's mutt." A vein in the side of his forehead throbbed wildly. "When was that?" Jay lifted his fisted left hand, and Cass recoiled.

"Uh—"

A vicious growl at her side saved her. Beast poked his head through the curtain separating the store from the back room. Teeth bared, hair on the back of his neck sticking straight up like a lion's mane, Beast crept toward Jay.

Jay stumbled back, with the usually good-natured, kinda goofy dog keeping pace, stalking him.

A tremor ran through her. Should she try to call the dog off? She didn't really want Jay ripped to shreds in her store. At the same time, she did want him to leave.

"This isn't over. I want to know where Ellie is, and I'll be back if I don't hear from her." He lifted a hand and Beast barked. Jay backed quickly through the doorway, pulling the door shut behind him, effectively barricading the dog in the store . . . with Cass.

Beast continued to growl at the closed door, and Cass didn't know whether to be grateful or terrified. So, she settled on both. With the threat apparently gone, Beast turned to Cass. She held her breath. He padded over to her and licked her hand.

With her back pressed to the wall, she slid down to sit on the floor, pulled her knees to her chest, and wrapped her arms around them. She lowered her forehead to rest on her knees and tried to control the tremors that shook her body. Beast lay at her side, nuzzling his head against her.

She pressed her hand into his warm fur and took comfort from the sheer size of him.

16

The chimes sounded, and Cass jumped. How long had she been sitting there, lost in a haze of fear and self-pity? She sniffed and wiped the tears from her cheeks.

Beast lifted his head but didn't growl or bark. He didn't even stand, just stayed at Cass's side, alert.

"Are you all right?"

She looked up and sobbed. She couldn't help it. The sob tore free before she could control it.

"What happened?" Luke was at her side in an instant. He knelt in front of Cass and petted the dog's head. "Good boy." He showed no fear of the animal, and Beast dropped his tongue out and drooled.

Laughter mixed with the tears, and Cass swiped at her face again.

"Are you hurt?" Luke put an arm around her and helped her to her feet. He led her to a chair and pulled it out for her to sit.

Her heart rate kicked up, but this time it had nothing to do with fear and everything to do with Luke's close proximity.

Instead of moving away, he squatted down in front of her and took her hands in his. "Your hands are like ice. Do you want a cup of tea?"

She did want a nice warm cup of tea, but she wanted him to keep holding her hands more. "No, thank you."

"Can you tell me what happened?"

She glanced toward Beast, who lay alertly on the floor beside her.

Luke followed her gaze and eyed the dog warily. "Did the dog do something?"

"No." She shook her head. "Well, not exactly." She took a deep breath. "Remember Ellie, the woman who came in when you were here yesterday?"

"Yes. Did she come back?" He frowned, obviously confused.

"No. Her husband came in looking for her."

Luke stood. "Did he do something to you?" His jaw clenched.

A small thrill tickled her at the thought of her knight in shining armor rushing to defend her honor. *Okay, enough of that.*

It was a little easier to think rationally now that Jay wasn't standing in front of her. "No. Well, not really . . . I guess. He just wanted to know if I'd seen Ellie." It didn't make any sense. Where was Ellie that Jay couldn't find her? "I think I'll make that cup of tea now." Now that Luke had stood and let go of her hands, she wanted to hold something warm. "Would you like something?"

"No. Thank you." He took a seat, and Beast plopped his head in Luke's lap. "He's a beautiful animal. Where'd you get him?"

She hesitated. Would it matter if she told him the truth? Probably not. The sheriff already knew, so what difference did it make? "He belonged to Marge Hawkins."

"The woman who was murdered?"

"Yes." She poured the water over a tea bag and brought it to the table to sit beside him.

"Mind if I ask how you ended up with her dog?"

"You can ask . . ."

That gorgeous grin returned, dimpling his cheek. "But you're not going to tell me?"

"I'll give you the short version. Ellie gave him to me. Of course that was after I already had him, but that's okay." She smiled at the confused expression that stole over his face.

"Maybe one day you'll trust me enough to give me the long version."

Her smile faltered for an instant. "Sure. Maybe." Though highly unlikely. Trust didn't come easily for Cass. She'd been hurt too badly to ever have complete faith in someone again.

"So what did the dog do?"

"What do you mean?"

"When I asked you if he did something, you said 'not really.' Which means he did *something*."

She laughed. "He pretty much chased Jay out of the store."

Luke pushed his hands through Beast's fur. "Really? He doesn't exactly seem vicious."

"I know. That's what was so weird. I've only had him a few days." She swallowed hard. "I was never afraid of him before. Even when I first found him . . . uh . . . I mean . . . uh . . . when I first *got* him, he was friendly." Luke's eyes held a question, but she ignored it. "But when Jay came in here and yelled at me, Beast went ballistic. He growled at him and backed him out of the store." She glanced at Beast. "He can be really scary."

Luke's eyes filled with genuine admiration as he looked at the dog and laughed. "Nah. He won't hurt you. He's just doing his job. He's supposed to protect his owner. These dogs are extremely loyal, but they're friendly, for the most part, as long as you train them well."

"Wait a minute. You mean you know what kind of dog he is?" Cass studied Beast's reddish-brown fur tipped with black, and the thicker fur that had bristled into a mane and surrounded his massive head when he'd been defending her.

"Sure. He's a Leonberger. A gorgeous one, too, aren't you, boy?"

Beast tipped his head to the side and snapped his mouth closed. He looked almost proud. Regal.

"Do you know if he's full grown?"

Mischief gleamed in Luke's eyes. "Nope. He's more like . . . a teenager."

"Ugh . . ." The thought of this dog growing any bigger was more than she could deal with at the moment. "What are you doing here anyway?" She didn't want to be rude, but why was he all of a sudden popping up every time she turned around? It seemed strange she'd never seen him before that day in the deli, and now he was everywhere, his dark, dangerous good looks making her crazy.

"I actually came to tell you I was able to reach all of the board members about scheduling an emergency meeting."

Cass held her breath as hope soared through her. "And?"

"They all agreed, except one."

Her sense of anticipation fled. "Let me guess. Chief Langdon."

"Yup."

"So, does that mean we don't get to go in front of the board?" The kids would be crushed. They'd worked so hard for this.

"Nope. It means I . . . persuaded him. The meeting's at ten tonight at the theater."

Excitement sent butterflies dancing in her stomach. "Oh my . . . How can I ever thank you?"

Luke stared at her, his dark eyes intense, his expression serious. "Have dinner with me."

Cass's hand fluttered to her chest. It had been a long time since she'd gone out on a date. She loved to socialize and go out with friends, in groups, but she hadn't gone on a date since she'd broken up with her ex. Was she ready? She enjoyed flirting with Luke, and he definitely elicited an interesting response every time he touched her. She smiled and had no doubt her cheeks flamed red. "Sure."

Cass turned off the car and sat staring at the hotel. She glanced at her cell phone. Four o'clock. She'd hoped to make it to the hotel sooner, but she'd gotten caught up with a last-minute reading. She scanned the parking lot. No familiar cars. "Stay." She pinned Beast with a glare before opening the windows a bit, slamming the door shut, and hitting the lock button. He licked his chops. Hopefully, the car would be in one piece when she got back.

She studied the three-story building as she walked across the lot. What could Marge Hawkins have been doing there twice a week? Why was Jay Callahan parked in the back lot? And what did either of them have to do with the body that was found on the beach?

She entered the lobby and looked around. The concierge desk was empty. A lone clerk sat behind the counter, eyes cast downward, and didn't even look up when Cass approached. She cleared her throat, and the young girl looked up sheepishly and closed the cover of her Kindle. "Sorry." She smiled. "I just got to a good part. May I help you?"

"Umm . . ." Now that she was there, she couldn't think of a thing to ask. She couldn't very well ask what Marge was up to twice a week or why Jay was skulking around the parking lot. *Hmm* . . . "Uh . . ."

The girl frowned and eyed the Kindle longingly.

"I was just wondering if Marge Hawkins worked here?" Okay. A little lame, but it was all she had.

The girl's eyes widened. "Didn't you hear about Ms. Hawkins?"

"Well, yeah, but I . . . um—"

"Cass?"

Cass turned at the sound of her name, grateful for the reprieve. "Hi, Elaina."

Elaina Stevens smiled warmly. "I haven't seen you in a while. What are you doing here?"

Cass glanced over her shoulder at the clerk, but she'd already returned her attention to her novel, lower lip caught between her teeth, eyes wide. Cass almost called to her and asked what she was reading but shook off the urge and returned her attention to Elaina. "I was actually looking for some information." She took Elaina's arm and guided her across the sea-themed lobby to a small, discreet seating area. "Do you have a minute?"

"Sure. I just got off." She sat on the couch beside Cass and propped her purse in her lap.

Cass had forgotten Elaina worked as a maid at the hotel. She also worked as a waitress at the diner, so Cass would have to be careful what she said to her. "I'm trying to find some information."

"What kind of information?"

"Well, I'm trying to find out why Marge Hawkins was hanging around the hotel twice a week."

Elaina stood abruptly, knocking her bag to the floor. Her gaze darted around the room. "Sorry. I can't help you." She bent to pick up the bag and gather its contents, and Cass leaned over to help.

She lowered her voice. "Can't?"

Elaina whispered back frantically. "I'll get in trouble if anyone hears me talking about her."

Cass stood and handed Elaina a brush and compact. "Here you go. Sorry. Would you like a ride home? I'm headed that way anyway." She wasn't really, but she desperately wanted to get Elaina alone. It was obvious the young girl knew something.

"Umm . . . Sure. Thanks."

Cass bent to retrieve a lipstick that had rolled beneath a corner of the couch and out the other side. She lifted her head at the sound of footsteps crossing the tile floor. *Surprise, surprise. He just keeps turning up.*

She studied Luke's waistband when he turned toward the elevators, but his jacket covered any telltale sign of a weapon. *What is he doing here?* She paused, torn between the urge to follow him and the need to hear what Elaina had to say. If she let Elaina go now, she might not be so willing to talk next time she ran into her . . . hunted her down . . . whatever.

Dang! She turned back to Elaina, who was grinning from ear to ear. Elaina waggled her eyebrows, but Cass ignored her. "Ready?"

"Yup. Let's go."

They crossed the parking lot in silence, Elaina looking nervously over her shoulder. When they reached the car, she stopped and frowned. She pointed in the back window. "What the heck is that thing? A horse?"

Cass laughed and unlocked the car. "Nope. He's just a really big dog."

Beast stood on the backseat, wagging his tail furiously, rocking the whole car.

"Lay down, boy." She flipped on the air-conditioning. Even though the fall air was cool, the interior of the car was sweltering, thanks to Beast's panting.

Elaina climbed in beside her and patted Beast's head. "You sure are a handsome fella, aren't you?"

Beast yipped.

"Are you going home?" Cass spotted Luke's parked Jeep as she pulled out of the lot.

"Nah. You can drop me at the diner."

That would actually work better for Cass since the diner wasn't far from the theater. Maybe she'd be on time for once, sparing her a lecture from Bee. "So, what's the deal with Ms. Hawkins?"

Elaina blew out a breath. "She already got me in trouble once. And I didn't even do anything."

"Well, if it's any consolation, she can't get you in trouble now."

"I wouldn't be so sure about that." Elaina shrugged. "Anyway, Ms. Hawkins had a twice-weekly, standing reservation. She always took a different room, checked in around noon, stayed for a few hours, and left."

"That's weird."

"Not really. I cleaned her room a number of times. It was always a mess and always the same. Wineglasses, wet towels tossed carelessly around the room, bed rumpled."

"What would she be doing in bed in the middle of the afternoon?" Cass glanced toward Elaina.

Elaina lifted a perfectly sculpted eyebrow, pursed her lips, and waited.

When the image came, it wasn't a pretty picture. "Oh . . . eeeww . . ."

Elaina laughed. "Yeah, well, think how I felt."

Cass struggled to rid herself of the mental image searing her brain. "So, how'd she get you in trouble?"

Elaina waved it off. "Oh, it was really no big deal. Once, when I was cleaning up, I found a pen in the bed. I picked it up and clipped it to my uniform pocket while I stripped the rest of the sheets. It wasn't like I was going to keep it or anything." She looked over at Cass. "Marge came back to the room while I was putting the sheets in the cart. She stopped to ask something, I assume if I saw the pen, but then she spotted it sticking out of my pocket."

Elaina shook her head at the memory. "She grabbed it and accused me of stealing it. Then she went to Uncle Henry and told him I stole her pen." She grinned at Cass. "That's one upside of having an uncle who owns the hotel. He knew darn well I didn't steal anything. He told her he'd look into it, but he just told me to be more careful next time."

"What was the big deal? Was there something special about the pen?"

"Nope. Just a plain gold pen with black script on it. She was just being her usual, argumentative self."

Cass's mind raced. "Do you know who she was . . . meeting there?"

"Nope. I'm not even sure it was always the same person. Although, I can't imagine more than one person would want to be Marge Hawkins's . . . whatever."

They both laughed. No. Cass couldn't imagine it, either. But who on earth could it have been?

17

Cass ran into the theater only ten minutes late and considered it a small victory. Bee stalked toward her, his *You're late* scowl firmly in place, as soon as she entered the auditorium.

"I know, I know." Cass waved a hand dismissively. "Consider me properly reprimanded, and let's get on with rehearsal."

Bee's expression turned to one of shocked indignation. He froze in his tracks, propped a hand on his hip, and stared at her. When she was almost face-to-face with him, he pointed a finger at her and opened his mouth.

She grabbed his finger, leaned close to his ear, and whispered, "I've got dirt that would make it worth having a sleepover in the haunted, old Madison Estate."

He sucked in a breath. "Give me a hint."

She released his finger, waggled her eyebrows, and headed toward the stage to line up the models.

Bee followed, grabbed her arms from behind, and leaned close. "You've gotta give me something. Anything. How about a little tidbit?"

Cass laughed and turned to face him. "Okay. Clue number one. It involves two people and a room at the Bay Side Hotel."

He pressed a hand to his chest. "Pretty please, tell me Mr. Tall, Dark, and Dangerously Southern is one of the two. And then I want all of the sordid details."

"No. He's definitely not one. Besides, that wouldn't be gossip. That would be . . ." Cass sighed.

"Yeah." Bee fanned himself.

"Sorry to ruin your fantasy, but guess again."

Bee frowned. "Is either of the people dead?"

Cass smacked his arm playfully. "No. No one's dead. Oh. Well. Wait. One of them actually is dead now. Or both may be, I guess. But, at the time the gossip-worthy action was happening, all parties were alive and kicking . . . among other things." She grinned, turned away from him, and hoisted herself onto the front of the stage.

They'd run through only half of the show when the board members started to trickle in.

Stephanie came up behind Cass and put a hand on her shoulder. "Bee doesn't want to talk to them."

Cass wasn't surprised. Even though they joked he wasn't allowed to talk to the board, truth was, authority figures intimidated him. Bee was actually quite timid. "I didn't figure he would."

"So, what do you want to do? Do you want to do it, or do you want to flip a coin?"

"Me?" Cass huffed out a breath. "Why don't you do it?

You're the business manager. Do my titles have manager in them? Model? Nope. Stage designer? Nope. Neither one."

"Come on, Cass." Stephanie nudged her. "Let's be honest. My background is in business. You have experience in dance and theater. You're a lot more knowledgeable about what's involved in producing a show than I am."

Cass shrugged. Just because Stephanie was right didn't mean Cass had to like it. "Ugh . . . Fine. I'll do it. But you're taking me for ice cream later."

Stephanie grinned and shot Bee a thumbs-up.

Traitors.

By nine thirty almost all of the board members were seated in the auditorium, watching the show. All except one. Chief Langdon was noticeably absent.

The models finished walking through their routines, in shorts and T-shirts rather than the outfits they'd be wearing, to a smattering of applause and nods of approval. They packed up their things and emptied the room quickly. Maybe they'd felt the pressure as well.

Cass dillydallied as long as she could. The air buzzed with tension. She glanced at the clock. Chief Langdon was obviously not coming. *Okay. Time to start the meeting.* She heaved in a deep breath. *I can do this.*

She approached the small group. Conversation dwindled to silence as they greeted her with cold suspicion. With Marge and Chief Langdon missing, the group consisted of only six members. Luke would vote to let them do the show. Marti Symms stared openly at Cass, her expression seeming to hold curiosity more than anything else. Maybe Luke had already won her over.

That left Jana Sorenson, Debby Watson, Katie Bell, and Kyle Benedict for her to convince.

Cass smiled. Sweat trickled down her back in the air-conditioned auditorium. "Hi."

Luke greeted her with a smile, the women simply nodded and looked at one another, and Kyle glared at her with open hostility.

O-kay. "Thank you all for coming on such short notice."

More nodding. This was getting downright frustrating. Cass bristled. Who did these people think they were?

"We called you here to discuss the notice we received asking us to change the date of the fashion show." *Asking* was being kind, since there was no question involved, but diplomacy was probably a better tactic than confrontation.

Debby's cheeks reddened, and she lowered her gaze. Her hands twisted together nervously in her lap.

"I'd like to ask you to consider rescheduling the play instead of the fashion show."

Jana twirled a lock of her hair, elbow resting on the back of her seat, seemingly disinterested in Cass's argument.

What is going on here? Cass frowned.

Kyle, a nervous little man with horn-rimmed glasses, looked to the others before he finally cleared his throat. "Why can't you just choose a different weekend? What's the big deal?"

Anger rushed through her. She tamped it down. "What's the big deal? Seriously?" *Okay, so much for diplomacy.* She scanned each of their faces, trying to hold eye contact with every one of them. "Do any of you have any idea what's involved in putting on a show of this magnitude?"

They all shook their heads.

What were these people doing on the board of directors of the theater if they had no clue how a production worked? "First of all, Bee has worked really hard to coordinate a time when buyers are available. That's not easy. If he changes the date, he may not get the buyers to attend. Not only will he lose money then, but the entire town will. A lot of the people attending this year's show are coming because of who else will be there."

Cass's cheeks heated as she got angrier.

"Not for nothing, but this show brings a lot of revenue in to the local businesses on Long Island as well as Bay Island. The restaurants, the hotel, the tourist shops. Not to mention, the theater. Bee's show has sold out. The play will be lucky to seat a hundred people." *Besides, Marge isn't even here to run the play. Has anyone even taken her place?* She bit the inside of her cheek, figuring it might not be the best time to ask.

Katie held her hand timidly in the air. "It's not that we're trying to be difficult, it's just we want to honor Marge's wishes. She really wanted to do a fall-themed play this year. She was tired of holiday themes."

Yeah, right.

"We'd hate to go against her after . . . well . . . what happened." Katie blushed crimson.

Cass weaved her hands into her hair and squeezed, desperate to relieve her building stress headache. Her patience had worn thin. She thought of Bee and stopped the angry words from coming out. Unfortunately, they churned in her gut. Bee and Stephanie were going to owe her a whole lot more than ice cream for taking this on. "Look, Ms. Bell. This isn't about Marge Hawkins, or me. I'm telling all of you right now, I had nothing to do with Marge's death. Don't punish Bee for something that doesn't even involve him. Please."

That was it. She was done. Her stomach flip-flopped. Whatever was going to happen would happen. "Thank you all. I appreciate you taking the time to come down here. If you have any questions, Bee or Stephanie will be happy to answer them." She mentally stuck her tongue out at both of them as she turned around, walked back to the stage, picked up her bag, and walked out.

Tears pricked the back of her eyelids. She refused to shed them until she was far away from the theater.

"Hey. Wait up."

Ugh . . . This is the last thing I need right now. She paused but didn't turn around.

Bee ran to catch up with her. He walked around to face her and threw his arms around her in a bear hug. "I'm so proud of you." He released her, stepped back, and pressed his fingers to his mouth. "You did a wonderful job. Thank you."

Cass looked down and shook her head. "Do you think they'll change their minds?"

"Oh, honey, I have no idea. But if they don't, we'll reschedule the show to later in the season. It's not the end of the world. My career maybe, but not the world."

Cass smiled. "Thanks, Bee. You're a good friend, despite the fact you threw me to the wolves in there."

He smiled and tucked a loose strand of hair behind her ear. "Anytime, dear, anytime."

Stephanie caught up. "You did great, Cass. I was eavesdropping while I closed down the auditorium, and it seems as if some of the members are going to give in. I think Debby will, and maybe Katie. Luke Morgan is a definite, and he's still in the lobby trying to convince the others."

"Come on. I know just what you need." Bee hooked his arm through Cass's and started walking toward the car.

"Don't say donuts, unless you want to stop by the shop and let out the dresses I'm wearing for the fashion show when we're done."

Bee laughed. "No way am I altering those dresses, honey. You can have carrot sticks." He grinned. "I'll have donuts."

"Cass. Wait up."

Cass looked back over her shoulder. Luke strolled across the parking lot toward her.

"Could you give me a minute, guys? Please."

"You bet, sweetie. We'll wait in the car."

She handed Bee the keys. If they were all piling in her car, they were obviously going out. She hoped there'd be something to celebrate.

"Hey." Luke's dark eyes didn't give anything away.

"Hey." Cass held her breath and waited to see what the decision would be. Had they even decided yet?

"You're very convincing, you know."

Hope flared.

Luke tucked her hair behind her ear. The gesture, which was so comforting and friendly when Bee did it, brought a completely different response when Luke did it. Cass shivered.

"Kyle Benedict left here looking like he was about to stroke out, and he voted against allowing the show to go on, even gave a heated argument about why the board shouldn't allow Marge's murderer to have her way. In the end, the women and I outvoted him and Chief Langdon's absentee ballot. They're going to let you keep the date."

She sucked in a breath. "Are you kidding me?"

He shook his head. "Nope."

She threw her arms around his neck. "Oh, thank you."

Luke wrapped his arms around her and pulled her against him. "You're welcome." The words were a mere whisper against her ear.

Oh boy.

She pulled back and looked into his eyes.

He grinned. "Looks like I'm not the only one who's passionate."

Her stomach clenched, but the memory of the gun-shaped bulge in his waistband had her pulling away. "Thank you again."

"No problem. Now, how about going to dinner with me tomorrow?"

She briefly considered putting her arms back around him and frisking him but thought better of the idea. She smiled instead. "What time?"

Cass pushed open the front door and sniffed tentatively. *So far, so good.* Only the aroma of tacos and nachos coming from the bag she was holding.

"Is the coast clear?" Bee poked his head in from behind her.

Cass shrugged. "Seems like it. I don't smell anything, at least."

"Good." Bee pushed past her. "Let's eat. If he tore anything apart, we'll clean it up later."

They tromped toward the kitchen, bags in hand. Bee had wanted to go sit somewhere and celebrate, but Cass was too worried about what Beast might get into, so they'd compromised. Taco Bell drive-through.

When she opened the door to the kitchen, Beast greeted her with his tail wagging. She took a cautious look around. "Good boy. You didn't chew anything or make a mess."

They dumped the bags on the table, dropped their jackets over the chair backs, and finally sat.

Exhaustion beat at her. "I need some sleep."

"Sleep is overrated." Bee unwrapped a taco.

"You wouldn't be saying that if it was seven in the morning."

Bee frowned. "There's a seven in the morning, too?"

Stephanie threw a balled-up taco wrapper at him.

Cass stretched. "I hope I can sleep better tonight, now I know the show will go on as planned."

"All right. I've waited long enough." Bee pinned her with a glare. "Spill it." He popped a nacho into his mouth.

Cass grinned. "Marge had a lover."

Bee choked.

Cass got up and ran around the table. She pounded on his back.

Stephanie handed him his Diet Pepsi.

He sucked in one breath, then another.

Cass returned to her seat. "She was meeting him at the Bay Side Hotel twice a week."

Bee heaved in a breath and took a sip of his soda. Tears still pooled in his eyes. "Who was it?" he wheezed.

Cass shook her head. "I don't know. No one seems to know." She took another bite of her taco.

"Do you think it was Jay?"

Hmmm . . . She hadn't thought of him. "No way."

Stephanie shrugged. "Why not? It could have been."

"Sure," Bee added. "He's doing everyone else in town."

Cass had to concede the point. But she couldn't believe Marge was sleeping with her daughter's husband. Or could she?

She pushed her food aside, rested her elbows on the table, and pressed her hands to her head. *Think, think, think.* Something niggled at the back of her brain. She shook her head. No use. She couldn't grab hold of it. Maybe it would come to her.

She turned her attention to what Bee was saying, something about Jay's newest love interest.

Cass interrupted. "Jay came into the shop this morning."

"For what?"

"He said he was looking for Ellie. When I told him I didn't know where she was, he got violent."

"He hurt you?" Bee paused, taco halfway to his mouth.

Cass waved him off. "Nah. He lifted his hand like he was going to hit me, but then Beast chased him out of the shop."

"Good boy, Beast," Bee offered around a mouthful of taco.

Cass started to smile but it froze only partly formed. "I just realized something. When Jay picked up his fist like he was going to hit me, it was his left hand. And when I saw Marge's . . . Marge . . . in the theater, she had a mark on her right cheek." Cass balled up the rest of her food and got up to throw it in the garbage.

Stephanie waved her off. "That doesn't mean they were lovers. Maybe they had an argument that got out of hand before he killed her."

"Possibly, but she had another mark on her neck."

"What kind of mark, a bruise? Like someone was choking her?" Bee held his hands up as if they were around someone's neck.

Cass shook her head. "I didn't think of it at the time, but it looked more like a hickey."

"A hickey? You can't be serious."

She nodded, more and more certain with each passing second. She closed her eyes and brought up a mental image of Marge. The darkening bruise below her right eye, the reddish, fairly new-looking mark—hickey?—marring her neck. "I really think it was a hickey."

They all sat silently for a while, probably contemplating the implications of that.

Stephanie broke the silence. "You know, I was thinking. Do you think Marge was actually killed at the theater?"

"What do you mean?" Cass studied her intently. Was this something that had just popped into her mind or had Tank told her something?

"Well, maybe Jay killed her somewhere else, like a lover's spat or something. You saw him putting what might have been a body in the back of his truck, and a body turned up on the beach the next day. Maybe he killed Marge at the hotel or something and then staged her body at the theater to pin it on you."

Cass opened her mouth to argue but then thought better of the idea. Stephanie could be right.

"Was there a lot of blood at the theater?" Bee crossed his arms and leaned forward on the table. He was obviously considering the possibility.

Cass tried to remember. She clearly recalled every detail of the body, but not much else. She shook her head, frustrated. "I can't remember. I don't think I noticed anything past Marge."

"Surely you would have noticed a large blood spatter if she was shot at the theater."

He was right. Maybe. "You'd think."

"And another thing. Why would Marge be sitting in a seat? If she was arguing with someone, you'd think she would have been standing. What are the chances she'd have fallen back to sit in one of the seats?"

Hmm . . . Cass was going to have to think more about this. She tried to envision Marge's posture. Did it look like she'd fallen back into the seat after she'd been shot? *Not really.* She was slumped, but, at first glance, Cass had thought someone was sitting there waiting. Which meant either Marge was caught off guard and killed quickly and without warning, or she was killed somewhere else and moved. "You might be right. It makes more sense that she was killed somewhere else and propped up in the seat."

The doorbell rang, and Bee stiffened.

Stephanie got up to open the door.

"Are you okay?" Cass placed a hand over Bee's arm.

"Sure." He gave her a halfhearted smile.

"Just answer his questions, and it'll be over before you know it."

"Yeah, well, he better be quick. I want to work on some of the dresses for a few hours tonight."

18

Bee's posture went rigid as Stephanie's and Tank's voices preceded them into the hallway. Tank didn't sound happy. They entered the kitchen and his eyes immediately sought Cass's. "Are you all right?"

She cringed. Apparently Stephanie couldn't wait to tell him about the run-in with Jay. "I'm fine."

"We'll talk about all that after I finish with Bee." Tank pulled out a chair directly across from Bee, sat, and folded his hands on the table. "Talk."

Bee snorted. "You don't have to be rude." He stalled for another moment. He sat back, crossed his legs at the knee, and folded his hands primly on his thigh.

Cass lowered her head to hide the smirk she couldn't keep from forming. Bee was messing with him. Bee was openly gay and quite flamboyant, but that pose was over the top, even for him.

Tank rubbed his hands over his face, his frustration obvious. "Are you ready now?"

"Yes, dear. You may proceed with your questions." He waved his hand dramatically, like some kind of old, washed-up diva.

Tank stared at him for a moment. "Would you rather just tell me what the deal is?"

Dee smiled and batted his eyelashes. "I wouldn't want to divulge any deep, dark secrets unnecessarily."

Tank blew out a breath. "Fine. What is your history with Marge Hawkins?"

"My mother's name was Melody Hawkins. She was Marge's half sister."

Cass frowned. Marge had lived on Bay Island her whole life, as far as Cass knew. She knew Marge had brothers, all of whom had left the island, but didn't remember anything about her having a sister.

Tank closed his eyes, and Cass counted to ten while she waited for him to open them again and speak. "Would you care to elaborate?"

Bee gave up the prima donna act and slid his chair forward. He folded his arms and rested them on the table. "Look. My mother and Marge had the same father, different mothers. My mom was the result of an extramarital affair. She and Marge hated each other. My mother was everything Marge wasn't— sweet, kind, maternal. She was a single mother and raised me on her own. Marge didn't agree with my upbringing, not that it was any of her business." Bee looked at the table. "I never understood why my mother insisted on having contact with those people, but it seemed important to her that I have extended family, since my father wasn't in the picture."

He pressed his fingers to his eyes. "One day, Marge and my mother had a terrible fight. I never did find out what it was about—it was probably me. It usually was." He lowered his hands to the table and sighed. "Anyway, my mother was beside herself for two days. On the third day, I came home from work and found her dead."

Cass sucked in a breath. Her gaze shot to Tank, but his expression remained neutral.

Bee swallowed and wiped at the tears tracking down his cheeks.

Cass handed him a Taco Bell napkin.

"Thank you, dear." He wiped his nose. "My mother had had a heart attack. To this day, I blame it on the stress of whatever went on between her and Marge that day."

Tank frowned. "How did you wind up here on the island with Marge?"

"The small house where I live now was left to my mother by her father. I never even knew about it." His shoulders slumped. "When they read my mother's will . . . Well, I inherited the house. I was having some problems at the time, so I moved here." He stared at Tank. "See? Nothing sinister."

Tank rubbed a hand over his mouth. "Why change your name?"

"I was doing a show in Las Vegas before I moved. Bee Maxwell was my stage name." He stopped talking, seeming to contemplate what to say. "Look, Tank. I know you don't like me, but I have to ask you to keep this information to yourself." He looked beseechingly at Tank. "Please."

Tank nodded.

"I was in some trouble in Vegas. I got involved with drugs

and gambling and owed quite a bit of money. The inheritance was enough to make good on everything I owed, but I wanted a fresh start. I also didn't want to be associated with Marge once I was here. My mother struggled her whole life to support us, when she had a house free and clear on Bay Island. I can only assume there was a reason for that."

"It must have been hard for you to deal with Marge all the time while blaming her for your mother's death." Tank asked the question, but the passion he'd started out with was gone. It seemed more like he was wrapping up loose ends at this point.

Bee nodded. "It wasn't easy."

"You hated her."

"Yes. The world is better off with that woman gone."

"Did you kill her, Bee?"

Cass didn't dare breathe.

Tank stared at Bee but didn't push for an answer, simply waited him out.

Bee sat back and folded his arms across his chest. "No."

Tank nodded. "All right. Thank you. I appreciate you being honest with me. It saved me a lot of time following false leads."

Cass finally exhaled. Apparently Tank was fairly convinced of Bee's innocence.

"No problem." Bee stood. "I'll catch you guys tomorrow. I gotta run."

"Sure, Bee," Cass said. "See ya later."

He shrugged into his jacket, grabbed his soda from the table, and headed for the front door.

Stephanie had remained silent through the interview, but

she looked at Tank as soon as the front door slammed shut. "Do you believe him?"

Tank pushed his hands through his almost-shaved hair and clasped them behind his neck. "Yeah. I think he's probably telling the truth. Unless anything new comes to light, I won't even write any of it up. No sense having everyone in the sheriff's office knowing about the skeletons in his closet."

Stephanie smiled. "Thanks, Tank. You're the best." She got up and kissed him on the head.

"Yeah, yeah, just remember that when you're mad at me for something." He turned a tired gaze on Cass. "And you"—he pointed a finger at her—"you stay away from Jay Callahan."

"He came into *my* business, not the other way around."

"Yeah, well, just stay away from him. The guy's bad news."

"Did you hear anything more about the body they found on the beach?"

"Nah. Not really. She hasn't been identified yet, but there's a hotel guest unaccounted for. They're trying to track her down now." He closed his eyes and rubbed at them.

Stephanie sucked in a breath to say something, but Cass stopped her with a look. She clasped her hands together in a silent plea and mouthed the word *tomorrow*.

Stephanie frowned but nodded her agreement.

She was so tired tonight. If they got into what she'd seen at the hotel, first she'd have to listen to the lecture, then she'd spend however long answering questions. Besides, after the run-in with Chief Langdon, she didn't want to chance having to go into the police station to file a report or anything. She'd deal with it tomorrow, after a decent night's sleep.

* * *

A ringing woke Cass up from a deep sleep, and she fumbled blindly for the phone. She grabbed it just before the machine would have picked up. "Hello?"

Silence.

She slitted her eyes open just enough to see the clock. Three o'clock? In the morning? Who could possibly be calling at 3:00 A.M.? Exhaustion shortened her temper, and the next *hello* wasn't as nice.

"Cass?" The male whisper sounded like . . .

No way. She struggled to free herself from the tangled bed covers and sit up against the headboard. "Who is this?"

"Cass, listen. Please don't hang up."

Her heart strained against the confines of her ribs, pounding so wildly she could barely hear the tense whisper coming over the line. "I said, who is this?"

"It's me, Jay Callahan. I need to talk to you. It's important."

Indignation masked the fear for a second or two. "Are you crazy? Do you know what time it is?"

"Yes. I'm sorry. I—"

A familiar noise in the background cut him off. She tried to make out what it was but couldn't quite catch it.

"I'm worried about Ellie. Not just a little worried, but really scared. I can't go to the police. I don't know what to do. I need help."

She moved the phone away from her ear and stared at it. *Is this for real?* "So, why are you calling *me*?"

"Ellie trusted you." It was a simple statement but tinged with desperation.

Cass's heart was melting a little, and she slammed her guard up. "Fine. I'm listening. What do you want to talk to me about?"

"I can't talk to you over the phone. I shouldn't have even stayed on this long."

"Look, Jay, either tell me what you want, or I'm hanging up." She started counting in her head. If she got to ten before he told her what the problem was, she'd disconnect and then . . . and then what?

"I know who killed Marge."

The breath caught in her throat. She didn't make it past three.

"What?" She worked to bring the high-pitched squeal down a notch. "What are you talking about? Who?" She held her breath while she waited to see if he'd answer.

"I'm not saying anything else on the phone. I'm out by the lighthouse."

Ahh . . . that was the sound she'd heard. A foghorn. But who was out at this time of night? If someone was at the marina, it'd probably be safe to meet him. She caught herself ready to give in. "No way. I'm not meeting you in the middle of the night." Chances were good he'd killed Marge and possibly Ellie as well. How else would he know who the murderer was? She shivered. "I'll meet you at a public place in the morning. That's the best I can do."

"I can't go out in public. Langdon's going to arrest me if he sees me."

I knew it. "Arrest you? Why?"

"I can't get into all of this on the phone. You have to meet me." Anger started to invade the whining tone he'd had up until then.

Fear prickled the back of her neck.

"I'm serious, Cass. Ellie is either in a lot of trouble, or severe danger. I have to talk to you. I'll wait one hour at the lighthouse."

An image of Jay, an inch from her face, fist raised, popped into her head. *No way.* A bead of sweat trickled down the side of her face. She'd have to be totally insane to drive out to a deserted lighthouse in the dead of night to meet with someone who was most likely a killer. "Which lighthouse?"

He let out a breath he must have been holding with a loud exhalation. "Bay Pointe."

She hit off and tossed the phone on the bed. She berated herself the entire three minutes it took her to throw on clothes and step into her boots. What if Jay was the killer and she had to make a run for it? She toed off the boots and put on a pair of sneakers.

Beast followed her from the bedroom to the kitchen, where she grabbed the keys from a basket on the counter. She contemplated the big dog. Should she take him with her? He'd already protected her from Jay once. But even a dog this size couldn't stop a bullet. "Come on, boy. Want to take a ride?" She'd compromise. She'd take Beast with her but leave him in the car. He should be safe there, and she could always open the door if need be.

She stopped halfway to the car. She should let someone know where she was going. She thought of Luke but, for all she knew, he was the killer. Heck, she wasn't even 100 percent sure Bee wasn't the killer. But somehow Bee seemed different now. Less dangerous. She could call Stephanie, but Tank would be all over her before she got anywhere near the lighthouse. She could send a text to Stephanie's cell. But

Stephanie used the phone for an alarm, so she slept with it beside the bed.

Bee. Bee turned his phone off at night while he was working, so chances were good he wouldn't get the text until morning. She typed out a quick text to Bee. *Went to Bay Pointe lighthouse to meet Jay.* That oughta do it. Now, at least sometime tomorrow someone would know where to start looking for her body. She shoved the phone in her pocket and ran to the car before she could change her mind.

Once she had Beast settled in the backseat, she sat and stared at nothing. Was she crazy? Running off to a deserted area of the island at three in the morning? Heck, every area of the island was deserted at three in the morning. Even during the height of tourist season the beach bars closed up by two.

She dropped her head onto the wheel. How had she gotten involved in all of this mess? All she wanted to do was be left alone. What would Jay do if she didn't show up for their meeting? Come and find her? A chill blasted through her.

She shifted into reverse and turned to Beast's questioning gaze.

"It'll be okay, boy." She patted his head, and he lay down on the seat.

She drove slowly, allowing herself time to change her mind. There were too many questions that needed to be answered. Where was Ellie? She didn't just disappear into thin air. Ellie never missed being home to put Jay's dinner on the table. And why would Jay be arrested? Surely Chief Langdon wouldn't arrest him if he didn't do anything wrong.

Of course, he'd brought her in for questioning, and she hadn't done a single thing. She stepped on the gas.

19

The Bay Pointe Lighthouse sat atop a hill on a narrow strip of land that jutted out into Gardiners Bay. Cass drove slowly past Mystical Musings and up the dark, winding road that would bring her onto the small peninsula. She pulled into the deserted lot, gravel and seashells crunching loudly beneath the tires.

Beast popped his head up at the noise.

"It's okay, boy. Lie down." She backed into a spot against the low, sagging split-rail fence—in case she needed to make a quick getaway—and scanned the empty lot. Nothing. No sign of Jay or anyone else. She shifted into park, but left the car running, and climbed out.

Where could he be? She eased the door shut quietly, pulled the cell phone from her pocket, and glanced at the time. It had taken only half an hour to get there, even with the extra time she'd spent driving slowly and beating herself up over whether or not to go. She should have taken Jay's number from the caller ID at the house, but she hadn't thought of it. Now she couldn't even call him back . . . unless she went home first. She blew out a breath.

The small lot was lit by only two streetlights. The big light atop the lighthouse farther up the peninsula scanned the bay, illuminating sections of the darkness briefly before moving on, but it didn't cast any light down toward her. Fear gripped her chest. She looked up the hill toward the lighthouse. Nothing. No sense of movement anywhere. *That's it. I'm outta here.*

She turned toward the car, but her hand froze partway to the door handle. She looked up the hill again. He'd said the lighthouse, not the parking lot. *Dang.*

Crunch! Crunch! Crunch! She winced with every step she took across the lot. Nothing like announcing your position. She held her breath, trying to listen for any sound other than the crunching of her footsteps. The rustling of leaves as the light wind blew through the trees, the lapping of the choppy waves against the shore, and crickets chirping. The usual sounds of night on the island. Nothing sinister.

She blew out a sigh of relief when she finally stepped onto the concrete walkway. A headache beat at her temples, but she didn't dare rub it, too scared of blocking her peripheral vision. She hurried up the walkway to the lighthouse, then followed the path around the back. She'd go around once and then head back to the car. If Jay wanted to talk to her after that, well . . . he was out of luck.

She crept through the darkness, careful to stay on the walkway. As she rounded the side of the lighthouse, wind tore through her hair, whipping it across her face.

"Psst."

She shoved her hair back, holding it with her hand, and searched the darkness. A row of bushes bordered the walkway. Past that was the small cliff that dropped toward the giant rocks bordering the beach below. She squinted into the darkness.

"Psst."

She kept her voice a hushed whisper. "Jay?"

"Yeah. Come around through the opening in the bushes."

The image of her body plummeting over the cliff and landing broken on the rocks kept her from obeying his order. "No way, Jay. I'm here. Now start talking or I'm leaving."

"Come through the opening. We can sit against this side of the bushes."

She crept forward. This was crazy. *This is the kind of stupid everyone talks about when the woman in the horror movie creeps up the stairs in the dark house, where ten people have already been killed, by herself.*

She rounded the edge and sat with her back pressed against the bushes, right next to the opening. She pulled her knees to her chest and wrapped her arms around them. "That's it, Jay. I'm not taking another step. Now, spit it out, or I'm outta here."

"Thank you for coming, Cass." Jay crawled out from beneath the bushes a little farther down the path.

Wow. He really was paranoid.

He moved closer to her and sat, knees to his chest. "I need help, and I don't know who else to turn to."

Cass shivered. The wind whipping over the top of the hill off the bay felt much colder, and she pulled her jacket tighter around her. "What happened?"

Now that she was there, sitting next to Jay, some of the fear began to release its hold. He seemed broken, afraid . . . not the same man who'd barreled through the door of her shop intent on intimidating her.

"I didn't kill anyone, Cass. You have to believe me." His voice held a pleading quality that bordered on whining.

"Why should I believe you?"

"Did you kill anyone?"

"Of course not."

"Chief Langdon sure thinks you did."

Touché. She waited silently for him to continue.

"I know you've been asking questions, investigating Marge's murder on your own. I figure you're trying to clear your name, and I thought maybe you could help me."

"All right. Why don't you start at the beginning? I don't even understand what the problem is."

Jay took a deep breath. He moved closer to her, and his rumpled clothes and wild hair came into view. Jay was a mess.

"I didn't kill anyone . . . but I can see where people might think I did."

Anxiety tightened her chest.

"It's no secret Marge Hawkins and I pretty much hated each other. And, well . . ."

He leaned closer, and she gagged on the combination of body odor and alcohol. Was this the same man who always strutted around town with a woman on his arm and no regard for his wife?

"I have a confession to make." Jay shoved a hand through his tangled mess of hair. "I'm not proud of this, but . . . the woman who was killed at the hotel was . . . a *friend* . . ."

Cass's stomach roiled. Bile crept up the back of her throat.

"My sister took Ellie to the city for a few days, and I spent the weekend with my friend." Jay dropped his head onto his knees and clasped his hands over the back of his neck. "I know it wasn't right. Ellie deserves so much better than me. I'm so sorry. All I want to do is make it up to her, but I can't find her. He sobbed, but something about the sob sounded off. Phony. Contrived.

"So, what do you want from me?" Cass shifted to get upwind of Jay.

"Don't you see? You have to tell me where Ellie is." Jay shifted onto his knees, grabbed both of her upper arms, and shook her. "If Ellie doesn't show up soon, they're going to think I killed her, too."

Sheer terror seized Cass. Her head exploded with pain. A giant vise squeezed her chest. No words could move past the lump in her throat. *Too?* What was he saying?

Jay's mouth dropped open and his eyes went wide. "I didn't . . . I mean . . ." He released her arms, sat back on his feet, shoved both hands into his hair, and lowered his head.

Cass fell back onto her butt when he let go. She worked desperately to force air into her lungs. *In, out, in, out . . .* She choked the lump back down her throat. She crab-walked toward the opening in the bushes, her gaze glued on Jay.

When he lifted his head, she froze. He held his hands up, palms toward her. "I didn't mean I killed Marge and that other woman. I meant they'd think Ellie was dead, too. And they'd think I killed her."

Cass opened her mouth to speak but couldn't force words through the dryness. Between the absolute fear and the sand being whipped into her open mouth by the wind, she couldn't get the words out. She sat, frozen in terror, and stared at him, choking on the sand. Finally, she managed to snap her mouth shut.

"I love my wife, Cass, and I'm worried about her."

He loves himself, and he's worried about going to jail.

"I have to find her and make sure she's all right."

He has to find her to cover his ass.

"Will you help me?"

Not a chance, buddy. She nodded mutely.

Jay smiled, his teeth glowing a sickly white in the darkness. "Great. Where is she?"

"I-I-I don't know." Her throat hurt with the effort to speak.

"You don't know, or you won't tell me?" Jay's jaw clenched.

She shook her head frantically. "I really don't know. I haven't heard from her."

Jay balled his fists and pressed them to his eyes. "All right. Where do we go from here?"

We? Keeping her eyes firmly on Jay, Cass pushed to her feet.

He stood as well.

She had to get out of there. Once she was away from him, she could think more clearly. Maybe she'd just call the police and let them handle it. Not Chief Langdon, but she could tell Tank. "I'm not sure. I need time to think."

With her eyes more adjusted to the darkness and fear magnifying all of her senses, she had no trouble making out Jay's frown.

"I don't have time."

"You woke me up in the middle of the night, dragged me

out of bed, and dumped all of this on me, and now you don't even want to give me time to think about what to do?"

"How do I know you won't go to the cops?"

How could she give him an honest answer when she had every intention of doing just that? "I'm not exactly Chief Langdon's favorite person right now." That was true enough.

"I guess." Jay studied her. "You think I did it, don't you?"

Now that she was standing a few feet away from him, centered in the opening between the bushes, her confidence began to return. "I honestly don't know what to think."

"I'm guilty of a lot of things, Cass, but murder isn't one of them."

She didn't say anything.

"All right. How can I convince you I didn't kill anyone?"

The memory of Jay carrying a . . . something out of the hotel came to her. "What were you carrying out of the hotel the other day?" She clapped a hand over her mouth. What was she, crazy?

"What day?" He actually sounded sincerely confused.

Could she have been mistaken? She lowered her hand slowly. "I s-saw you leaving the hotel the other day with a . . . large bag or something over your shoulder. You threw it into the back of your truck and disappeared." She swallowed hard and backed up one step, then another, ready to run if need be. "The same day the body turned up on the beach." Her teeth chattered, from the cold or nerves, she had no idea which. At the rate she was going, she was probably on the verge of a nervous breakdown. She held her ground. Waited.

Jay laughed. It started as a chuckle but built into something almost maniacal. She turned and ran for the car.

"Hey, Cass. Wait." Jay's footsteps pounded behind her.

She ran faster. The wind tore through her hair, whipping it into her face, blocking her view. Her jacket billowed around her, slowing her down. She leaned forward and tried to propel herself faster. The wind rushing through her ears wasn't loud enough to drown out the steady rhythm of Jay's footsteps, the heavy panting of his breath—coming closer.

Cass hit the gravel parking lot, and her foot slid out behind her. Her forward momentum wouldn't allow her to stop. She went down hard. She caught herself with her hands before she face-planted into the gravel, but she still managed to scrape her chin. A weight on her back crushed her for an instant before Jay rolled over and off her.

She rested her cheek against the ground, unable to do anything but suck air and sand into her straining lungs. She lay in the gravel, seashells poking into her hands and cheek, listening to Jay heaving in air beside her and Beast's frantic barking.

Jay recovered first. "I'm sorry. I didn't mean to scare you." He struggled to his feet. "Are you all right?" He bent over and reached for her.

Cass rolled over twice and stopped on her back, looking up at him.

He held up his hands.

Cass scooted backward until she was sitting, then climbed slowly to her feet.

"Please. Come with me to m—"

"There's no way I'm going anywhere with you, Jay."

Frantic barking pulled her attention, and she looked over at the car. Beast was barking nonstop, alternating between pressing his head against the window and pacing back and forth across the seat. She ran for the car. She cracked the door and reached a hand in to pet him, not wanting to risk him escaping and tearing Jay to shreds. "It's all right, boy. Everything's all right." She eyed Jay warily.

"I understand you won't come with me, but if you could just wait here, I'll go get my truck and prove I wasn't carrying a body out of the hotel."

Cass sighed, too exhausted and emotionally drained to argue. "I'll be here for five minutes. That's it."

"Thank you." Jay backed to the edge of the parking lot without taking his eyes off her, then he turned and ran into the woods.

"Come here, boy." She opened the door all the way, and Beast jumped out. Cass dropped onto the driver's seat. The big dog whined and lowered his head into her lap. Twisting her hands through his long fur brought her as much comfort as it seemed to bring him. "It's all right. You're a good boy." She sat sideways, feet on the ground, and rested her cheek against the seat. "Ouch." She pulled down the sun visor and looked at her face in the mirror. *Great.*

A large scrape marred her chin. A variety of small scratches crisscrossed her left cheek. And a large bruise darkened the skin over her left eye. *How did I get that?*

The sound of a motor reached her before headlights stabbed through the darkness. She stood and put Beast back in the car as Jay's truck rounded the last curve and came into view. No way was she moving away from her car again. She stood still and waited for him to back the truck up beside her.

Jay jumped out, ran around the back, and lifted the back of the SUV open. "See?"

She leaned forward, trying to keep one eye on him and one on whatever he was showing her in the back of the truck.

Even in the dim light cast by the overhead light in the middle of the SUV, Cass could make out a shape similar to what she'd seen him carrying over his shoulder.

Despite her fear and the throbbing of . . . well, pretty much her whole body, her interest was piqued. "What is it?"

Jay grinned and, for just an instant, beneath the glow of the streetlight, the charm that attracted so many women shone through. "It's a carpet."

Her mouth fell open.

"They were remodeling one of the rooms at the hotel." He gestured toward the bundle in the back of the truck. "This was going in the garbage, so I grabbed it for Emmett."

"Emmett?"

"Yeah. When I got to work on Saturday, the carpet in the waiting room had been ripped up. The concrete floor makes the whole room cold, so I figured he could use it."

She frowned as she tried to bring Emmett's waiting room into focus. She could clearly remember the floor in the garage, the cleanliness standing out in her mind. But no matter how hard she tried, she couldn't recall if there was a carpet in the waiting room when she was last there. Of course, she *had* been kind of preoccupied. "What happened to Emmett's carpet?"

Jay shrugged. "I have no idea. You know Emmett."

She did know Emmett. He did things on a whim whenever the mood struck, even if it didn't appear to make any sense. Another question crept in, interrupting her confusion about Emmett. "What were you doing at the hotel, anyway?"

Jay looked at his feet. "Visiting a friend."

"The friend who turned up dead?"

He nodded. Apparently the dead woman wasn't too good a friend, because Jay didn't seem the slightest bit upset about her body being found. He might not be guilty of murder—though Cass wasn't completely convinced of his innocence—but he was guilty of being the creep Cass always knew he was.

Thoughts whirled around in her head. If Jay didn't kill Marge and the other woman, then who did? She clearly remembered the words Jay had spoken earlier, the words that had pushed her out the door in the dead of night on what could easily have been a suicide mission. *I know who killed Marge.*

"Do you really know who killed them?"

Jay nodded. He looked her directly in the eye. "Ellie did."

20

*B*ang! Bang! Bang!

Cass groaned. *What now?* She rolled over and pulled the pillow over her head. There wasn't a single part of her body that wasn't sore.

Bang! Bang! Bang!

Go away.

The front door slammed, and she jerked upright in the bed, pulling the blanket to her chest. Footsteps strode quickly down the hallway. *Ah jeez . . .*

Her bedroom door swung open, and Cass pulled the blanket over her head.

"That ain't gonna save you, sweetie."

The cover was torn from her head to reveal six feet of irate Bee.

She held her hands up as if to ward him off. "I can explain."

"You have exactly thirty seconds. Make them count."

A tear tracked down his cheek, and Cass sighed. "I'm sorry, Bee."

"Sorry? You're sorry?" He swiped the tear away and flopped onto the bed next to her. "Do you have any idea how worried I was when I saw that text message?"

If the rumpled condition of his clothes and the wild hair were any indication, he'd been downright terrified. Guilt stuck in her throat.

He looked over at her for the first time and sucked in a breath. "What happened to your face? Did he hurt you?"

She quickly shook her head. "No. I fell."

Bee eyed her suspiciously. "You fell?"

"No. I really did fall. I was running and slid in the gravel."

"Well, you just about gave me a heart attack." His hand fluttered dramatically to his chest.

Cass bit the inside of her cheek. "You're absolutely right. I'm so sorry. I wasn't thinking."

"You're darn right you weren't thinking. How could you run out in the middle of the night, to probably the most deserted area of the island, to meet someone you think might be a killer—or at least a body dumper? Someone who already threatened you once?"

"I know, Bee. I'm sorry. I didn't mean to scare you. I just wanted to make sure someone knew where I was in case . . . well . . . in case." Cass rolled over and hugged him. "I really am sorry."

Bee pulled her into his arm and hugged her back. The tightness of his grip told her how worried he'd really been.

Footsteps sounded in the hallway. *Now what?*

Before she had a chance to move, Stephanie stood in the

doorway. She lifted an eyebrow. "Well, well, well. Isn't this cozy? Something I oughta know?"

Cass sat up, and Bee scooted back to rest against the headboard.

"Come on in. May as well join us."

Stephanie laughed. "I'm not sure Tank would take that too well." She crossed the room, sat down on the bed, and tucked her legs beneath her. "So . . . to what do I owe the pleasure of Bee's frantic phone call at ten in the morning? And should I even ask what happened to your face?" She squinted at Cass.

Cass scrubbed her hands over her face. *Ugh . . . ouch.* "I got a phone call at three this morning."

"Okay. I'll bite. From whom?"

"Jay Callahan."

The amusement in Stephanie's eyes turned instantly to worry. "And?"

"He wanted me to meet him at Bay Pointe."

"I'd love to think you said no, but from the urgency of Bee's phone call and the condition of your face, I'm guessing that's not the case."

Cass shook her head. "I did find out a few things, though."

Bee snorted. "Nothing worth risking your life for."

Cass reached over and squeezed his hand. "The *body* I saw Jay dump in his car? Turns out it was only a carpet."

"You saw it?"

Hmmm . . . "Well." She frowned. "Not exactly. I saw the package, though. I just didn't see what was inside it."

"So what makes you think it was a carpet?" Bee's voice was starting to rise. Never a good sign.

Cass fidgeted with the edge of the blanket. This had made so much more sense in a dark parking lot, in the early hours of the morning, with adrenaline coursing through her system. "He told me it was."

Bee surged to his feet. "Oh well, then. It must be true, because everyone knows killers don't lie."

Cass glanced at Stephanie for help, but she only shook her head.

Bee paced back and forth across the bedroom. "And what else did he have to say?"

"Remember the blonde he was running around with all weekend?"

Bee paused.

"He was fooling around with her."

After a huge eye-roll, Bee resumed his pacing.

"She was also the body that turned up on the beach."

"Are you kidding me?" Bee's stare went from one of complete aggravation with her, to total astonishment.

"Could I make this stuff up?"

He shrugged. "Probably, but why would you?"

Stephanie chimed in. "Maybe to keep you from having another hissy fit."

Bee grabbed a pillow and threw it at her, then waved her off. "What else?"

Cass swallowed hard. All signs of good humor fled in an instant, and her tone turned serious. "He also said Ellie killed them."

"What?" Bee hit a perfect high note.

"That's ridiculous." Stephanie waved a hand dismissively. "There's no way that timid little mouse killed anyone."

Bee jumped in. "Jay probably killed them, and now he's trying to pin it on poor Ellie."

"Why would she kill her own mother?" Stephanie asked.

Cass pressed her hands to the sides of her head and tried to sort through Bee's and Stephanie's questions as well as her own. "Jay said Ellie lost it when she found out Marge knew he was having an affair. They had a big blowout over it when Marge went to the house to reprimand Ellie for seeing me. Marge screamed at her that she didn't need a psychic to tell her Jay was running around. If she couldn't open her eyes and see it, anyone in town could tell her about it."

"So how would Marge have ended up in the theater?"

"Jay wasn't sure. He thinks Ellie went to the theater early Saturday morning looking for me to confirm what Marge told her. He said the exchange on Friday night was really heated, and he thinks it exploded on Saturday. So Ellie shot her."

"Did Ellie ever strike you as being that unstable?" Stephanie's question didn't seem argumentative, just curious.

Cass looked at Bee, who flung his hands up in a *How would I know?* gesture.

"Ellie was childlike." Cass shook her head. She tried to set aside her friendship with Ellie and view it from the perspective of the psychiatrist she was trained to be. "She was emotionally abused for years, first by her mother, then by her husband. The husband whom she viewed as her savior for getting her out of her mother's house and basically keeping Marge from having *complete* control over her life. The husband she looked up to and admired and trusted." She shook her head. "I don't know. I can't say I think it's out of the question. But . . . I just don't know."

* * *

Cass stood under the spray and moaned as the hot water worked to loosen her stiff muscles. She winced each time it ran over the cuts on her face and hands. She hadn't even realized how scraped up her hands were until the hot water hit them. She blanked her mind and allowed herself a few moments of peace.

It wasn't long before chaos interrupted her peace and quiet. Her mind betrayed her, jumping frantically from one thought to the next. She had to get organized, had to sort through the details she knew and try to make sense of what was going on. Stephanie was pushing her to tell Tank about the carpet in Jay's truck, saying he could have rolled a body in the carpet to dispose of it. Since Cass hadn't seen the carpet opened, she couldn't really argue. For all she knew it was soaked through with blood.

She sighed and turned off the faucet. No sense wasting time. She obviously wasn't going to relax. She climbed out of the tub, dried herself off, and grabbed her robe from the hook. Once she'd put it on and tied the belt, she opened the door to release some of the steam and wiped off the mirror with a towel. She studied her reflection with a critical eye. *Great.*

Since most tourists flocked to the island on the weekends, she always opened the shop on Saturdays and Sundays. Because of that, Mystical Musings was closed on Wednesdays, so that wasn't an issue, but she still had to make it to rehearsal. Her heart sank at the thought of going out to dinner with Luke afterward, her face crisscrossed with cuts and scratches. *Oh well. Nothing else I can do.*

She pulled a tray of makeup from a drawer. She placed it on the counter, opened the big lid, and set it aside. If she used only a little, it should work to cover the bruise, but not leave her looking like a clown.

She leaned closer to the mirror and dabbed a small amount of concealer on each of the small scratches along her cheek and a little heavier amount on the bruise above her eye. She then covered her face and neck with foundation. A little strategically placed eye shadow should draw any attention from whatever bruising still showed through.

There wasn't much she could do with the large scrape on her chin, but at least she no longer looked like she'd gone ten rounds with a heavyweight champion. She applied the rest of her makeup, taking extra care to be gentle on the tender spots. Finally, she glossed her lips and stood back. *There. Not too bad, if I do say so myself.*

She tossed the makeup back into the tray and placed it back in the drawer. With that done, she went to feed Beast. She opened the back door and let him out to run in the fenced yard. She leaned against the doorjamb, arms wrapped around her for warmth. Dark clouds rumbled with the threat of rain. She'd let Beast run off some of his energy for a few minutes before it started.

She pushed away from the jamb and moved to the counter, keeping an eye on Beast through the window over the sink. She eyed the Keurig carousel but passed it up in favor of herbal tea. *Hmm . . . peach, I think.* She didn't want caffeine. She needed something soothing. She filled the kettle and set it on the stove to boil. Another rumble of thunder rattled the windows. She went to the back door and called for Beast.

He bolted through the door as the first fat drops of rain hit the deck. She stood watching the brewing storm and inhaled deeply. There was nothing like a thunderstorm on the island. It was, in a strange way, comforting and befitting her somber mood. If she sat on the front porch, she could watch the churning waters of the bay. The whistle of the teakettle pulled her from her reverie. She shut the door and went to the cupboard, dropped two tea bags in an oversized mug, and poured hot water over it. She set the mug on the table, went to the office, grabbed a stack of printer paper and a box of colored pencils, and returned to the table. Beast settled beside her with a bone. *Hmm . . . I could maybe get used to this.* When she reached to pet him, he snuggled his big head against her hand. "Yup. I could definitely get used to having you around."

Okay, now. May as well put the quiet time to use. She'd promised Bee she'd draw some designs for the stage and runway decorations. Flowers. She started to sketch. Hesitantly at first, not really sure how she wanted to put it together. Flowers were the key, but they had to complement Bee's dress designs.

Random thoughts drifted in and out of her mind while she sketched, erased, adjusted . . .

Where was Ellie? Had she killed her mother and Jay's lover and then taken off? It didn't seem to be a likely scenario, but she supposed stranger things had happened.

She erased three potted plants and drew them farther apart, centering the podium between two of them.

It seemed more likely Jay killed Marge, his lover, and Ellie. Would Ellie's body be the next to turn up?

{21}

Cass pushed the sketches to the side and set a blank piece of paper in front of her. She drew a red circle in the center and wrote *Marge* in black. She studied the name for a few minutes before adding a straight line out toward the top. She drew another circle attached to the top of the line and wrote *Ellie*. On the line between the two circles, she wrote *abusive relationship*. She added another spoke partway around Marge's name with another circle at the end with *Jay* written in black. On the line she put *competition for control of Ellie*. She thought about it for a minute and added *lover?* She drew a line connecting Ellie's and Jay's circles.

She moved the pencil a little farther around Marge's name and added a spoke with the word *argument* on it and attached a circle that said *lover*. It wasn't a thought she really wanted to contemplate, but if she were to be thorough . . . she drew a line between the circles marked *Jay* and *lover*.

She added *one and the same?* She now had two small triangles. One with Jay, Marge, and Ellie at the points, the other with Jay, Marge, and lover at the points.

She studied the diagram. She also had a big triangle with Ellie, Jay, and lover at the points and Marge along the center of the bottom line. How did they all connect?

For the sake of fairness, she added two more spokes and two more circles. She reluctantly added Bee's name to one with *family history* on the line, and Luke's name to the other. *Hmm* . . . What to put on Luke's line? As far as she could tell, he had no connection to Marge. But, he *was* on the board. She added the words *stranger*, *gun*, and *board of directors* to Luke's line.

She studied the diagram again. *Okay. Now. Who can I eliminate?*

No one.

She tried to think. There had to be a way to eliminate someone from the diagram. She studied the names. Maybe she needed to think about the whole thing in a different way. Alibis. Why hadn't she thought of that sooner? Whose whereabouts could she confirm for Friday night and Saturday morning?

Did Bee have an alibi for Friday night? That would eliminate him completely . . . or at least make it highly unlikely he could have committed the crime. She held the red pencil over his name, ready to put an *X* through it. He'd been at rehearsal until eleven. Her heart sank. He'd dropped her off and gone home to work on some of the dresses. Alone.

She glanced at the other names briefly, but she had no way to know where they were during the time in question. Her heart soared a little, though. At least now she had a direction to follow. Maybe she could even clear Bee completely.

The back door opened.

Cass quickly piled the scenery sketches on top of the diagram.

"Boy, you really want to earn the wrath of Bee, huh?" Stephanie wiped her feet dry and shook some of the rain from her jacket.

"What are you talking about?" Cass glanced at the clock, her mind still racing through murder suspects. It took a minute to register. "Oh no!"

"Hurry up. He's going to kill you if we're late again."

"Me? You're late, too."

"Yeah, but I'm only late because you weren't ready." She smirked and leaned a hip against the counter.

"Well, I was sketching the scenery, so at least I was working on the show." Cass dumped the forgotten tea in a to-go cup and popped it in the microwave. She grabbed the stack of sketches and dumped them in her bag with a handful of colored pencils. She ran to the front closet for a jacket and ran back to the kitchen just as the timer on the microwave dinged.

Beast jumped to his feet.

"Sorry, boy. Not this time. If you're a good boy and don't eat any of the furniture, we'll go for a run on the beach tomorrow." She scanned the room quickly to make sure nothing too important was lying around. "Okay. Let's go." She grabbed the tea, slapped a top on it, threw her bag over her shoulder, and ran out the door.

She was soaked by the time she reached the car. *Ugh* . . .

Stephanie didn't waste any time shifting into reverse and backing down the driveway. "Do you want to close the gate?"

"Nah. Don't worry about it. I'll get it later." The last thing Cass wanted to do was get back out in the rain. "Besides, we were supposed to be at Dreamweaver for alterations five minutes ago. If we're any later, Bee's going to have a tantrum." She glanced over at Stephanie. "Have you talked to Tank?"

"Not since this morning. Why?"

Cass sipped her tea. "Did he say anything new about the investigation?"

Stephanie didn't take her eyes off the road, the heavy downpour limiting visibility. "He said the same caliber gun was used to kill Marge and the woman on the beach."

Did that help point to the killer in any way? *Not really.* "Did they think someone else killed her?"

"Not really." Stephanie turned up the windshield wipers.

Cass took another sip of the warm tea, then rested her head back against the seat. "Did he say if they have any suspects?"

"You mean other than you?"

Cass lifted her head and shot her a look, but when Stephanie glanced over at Cass her eyes were filled with humor. *She's only teasing. When did I get so sensitive? Jeez, I'm no better than Bee.* Cass laughed.

Stephanie frowned but kept her attention on the road. "Are you all right?"

Cass sighed. "I have no idea."

O ne of the models stood on a small platform surrounded on three sides by mirrors, and Bee was already making adjustments to the gown she wore. Cass slid in quietly and headed toward the rack of dresses. If she could grab her dress and get to the dressing room, maybe he wouldn't even notice she was late. She dropped her bag on a chair and grabbed the red dress from the rack.

"Ahem."

Uh-oh.

"Nice of you to join us." Bee's voice held a note of frustration but seemed half-amused as well.

"Sorry, I . . . uh . . ."

"Hey. Don't pick on Cass. She was working on the scenery for the show and lost track of time."

Oh, thank you, Stephanie.

"Oh, really?" Bee lifted a brow. "Give me a minute, guys. If I've already done your alterations, you can change into your next outfit."

Most of the models headed toward the back of the store to a row of curtained dressing rooms. A few sat chatting and waited for their turn. Cass started back toward Bee. If she groveled appropriately, he should forgive her.

Movement at the front door caught her attention, and Luke strolled into Dreamweaver Designs. A shiver worked its way up her spine. She started forward to greet him.

"Cass?"

She turned. "Hey, Jess. What's up?"

"Would you mind helping me?"

She glanced at Luke, who'd stopped to talk to Stephanie and Bee. "Sure. What do you need?"

Jess held up a box of bobby pins. The young girl laughed. "Bee will have a fit if I don't put my hair up for him to work on these straps." She glanced over her shoulder at the elaborate pattern of straps. "Gorgeous, aren't they?"

"Absolutely stunning."

DEATH AT FIRST SIGHT

Jess slid her fingers beneath the straps over her shoulders. "They're a little loose, though. Bee's going to have to adjust them a bit."

Movement in her peripheral vision caught Cass's attention. Stephanie bent over and dug through Cass's bag.

Jess pulled the dress up, knelt on a small block in front of the mirror, and pulled her mass of curls into a ponytail. "How many dresses are you modeling this year?" She wrapped her thick hair into a bun and held it in place for Cass to pin it.

"I was only supposed to do the red one, but then I saw the black one in the window and begged Bee to let me model it. So, two." Cass glanced toward Stephanie, Bee, and Luke.

"You're so lucky. I begged him to let me wear that one, but he said you were doing it."

Cass stuck the first pin through the bun and it popped back out.

Jess laughed. "Now you see why I need help." She sobered quickly. "Cass?"

"Hmmm . . ." Cass worked to push another bobby pin through the thick bun.

"Can I ask you something?"

The serious tone in Jess's voice pulled Cass's attention from Bee. "Sure. Is something wrong?" She studied the young girl's reflection in the mirror.

Jess shrugged, and a shoulder strap slid off. "I think maybe Lucas is going to break up with me." A blush stole up her cheeks, and she lowered her gaze to the floor. "I was just wondering if . . . well . . . Can you tell?"

"Aww . . . hon." She smoothed a stray piece of hair back into Jess's bun. The pain etched in Jess's features told Cass she was probably right, and she already knew the answer, but just didn't want to accept it. "I'll tell you what. Stop by tomorrow and I'll do a reading. Just keep in mind, sometimes things happen for a reason. If he does break up with you, it might be there's someone else you're supposed to meet."

Jess lifted her gaze to the mirror and grinned. "If there is, can you tell if he's hot?"

Cass laughed. Jess would be fine. Lucas was a nice boy, but a bit too immature for a serious relationship.

Stephanie handed Bee a stack of papers.

Oh. Oh no!

"You know what? I have the same problem when I try to put my hair in a bun, but I have bigger pins in my bag. Sit for a minute, and I'll get them." Cass didn't wait for a response, just took off toward Bee and Stephanie. "Hey, guys. What are you doing?"

"I'm just showing Bee the sketches, so he believes you were working."

Bee slapped Stephanie's arm playfully with the back of his hand. "Oh, stop. I believe you." He looked at Cass. "I'm just nosy and impatient, and I want to see the sketches."

He slipped another page from the top of the pile to the bottom and studied the next scene. "These are great. I love the whole thing." He pointed to the flowers draped from the front of the runway. "Do you think it would make more sense for these to be over here?" He pointed toward the spot she'd originally had them.

A bead of sweat dripped down her back. "That's the way I originally drew it, but I moved them because it left this front section of the runway too empty." She pointed toward a section of the drawing depicting the empty area of the stage. "So, I figured by putting them here, we have a little something in the front, too. Otherwise, all of the flowers are in the back." She tried to take the stack of papers from Bee.

"Hey. I'm not done yet." He pulled them back.

"I just want to show you something, then I'll give them back." She reached for the drawings again, but Bee held them over his head.

"Tsk, tsk, tsk."

"Quit fooling around, Bee. I just want to see them for a minute. Please?" Her palms had started to sweat, and she wiped them on her jeans.

"When I'm done, dear." He threw her a haughty look and flipped another page over, then brought it in front of his eyes to look. It took only an instant for the line of his mouth to firm. He shot his gaze to her.

Ah . . . jeez . . .

Bee's face fell. Hurt filled his eyes.

Cass lowered her head and put a hand over her eyes. She closed them and searched for a reasonable explanation. "Bee. Please. It's not what you think." She lifted her head to meet his gaze, pleading with her eyes for him to understand . . . to forgive her.

"Oh no?" He stared straight at her, unshed tears ready to tip over his lashes. "What is it, then?"

"Uhh . . . Okay. Actually, it probably is what you think, but let me explain. Please."

He held the stack of papers out to Cass, but she made no move to take them. "You don't owe me an explanation for anything. If that's how you feel . . ." He shrugged.

Stephanie and Luke had watched the exchange up to that

point without saying anything. They both wore looks of confusion, but neither interfered.

"Did you know about this?" Bee focused his full attention on Stephanie.

"Know about what?" It was obvious from her tone she had no clue what he was talking about.

"This." He held the papers out to her.

She looked at the diagram Bee held out. Her mouth fell open, and her gaze shot to Cass. "Seriously?"

"No. Not really. I was just playing around and wanted to be fair and include everyone."

Bee harrumphed. "Well, Stephanie, don't you feel left out?"

"Ugh . . ." Cass shoved her hands into her hair and squeezed. She thought she might cry, and she squeezed her eyes tightly shut to keep the tears from falling.

"Don't worry, Luke. She was fair to you, too."

Oh no. Her eyes popped open.

Luke stood holding the stack of papers, staring at the diagram of suspects. He looked up.

Cass held her breath.

His smooth, rich laughter slid through her, touching her heart.

Bee snorted and tossed the end of his scarf over his shoulder. "Well, I'm glad you think it's funny."

Luke reined in the laughter, but amusement still danced in his eyes. "Stranger, Cass? Really?" He held a hand to his chest. "I'm crushed."

"What are you talking about?" Bee took the papers back from Luke.

"See." He pointed to the line between his name and Marge's, where Cass had scrawled the word *stranger*.

"Hmm . . . Well, that hardly seems like much of a motive." A tentative smile touched Bee's lips. "And she is going out with you tonight. Hardly seems like she'd go out with someone she suspects of murder." He frowned. "Although, she might run out and meet you at a deserted lighthouse in the middle of the night . . . alone." He stared pointedly at Cass before turning back to Luke.

Luke laughed again. "I wouldn't take it too seriously, Bee."

"Well . . ." Bee glanced at Cass. Some of the pain she'd seen in his eyes seemed to have disappeared, but he still eyed her warily.

"I'm so sorry, Bee. I didn't mean anything by it. I was just trying to figure out all of the angles and see how everyone connected. Please believe me." She lowered her voice. "I know you didn't do it. I really, really do."

Bee shrugged but lowered his gaze. "Whatever."

"No. Don't blow it off. I hurt you, and I couldn't be sorrier. You've been nothing but a friend to me since I came here. And I wasn't in good shape. I really needed a friend, and you were there for me. Bee, I don't want this to interfere with our friendship . . ." A tear fell over and tracked down her cheek. "It means too much to me. You mean too much to me."

Bee reached out and caught the tear with a finger. "Oh, quit your blubbering. We're fine. Now stop. You're making a scene." He laughed and pulled her into a bear hug.

When she pulled back and looked into his eyes, she found only honesty.

Oh, thank you. She offered up a silent prayer. Until that moment, she hadn't realized just how important Bee had become to her.

She heaved in a deep breath and let it out slowly. "We're okay, then?"

"Of course we're okay." Bee's expression turned serious. "You're one of my best friends, Cass. I have no family to speak of. You and Stephanie *are* my family. Now, come on. The models are getting antsy, and you know what happens when we let them lose their focus. We'll never get it back."

He was right about that. Bee held out the sketches again, and Cass took them and shoved them into her bag. When Bee turned back to his work, she mouthed a silent *thank you* to Luke.

He lifted a brow and nodded once in acknowledgment.

As she walked toward the dress rack behind Bee, she realized Luke had only poked fun at the *stranger* comment. He hadn't said anything about the word *gun*.

22

Bee leaned over and spoke softly to Cass. "Are you sure this is okay? You don't really think he's the killer, right?" He eyed Luke warily.

Cass smiled. "Nah. I don't think so." *Not too much anyway.* "I'll be fine. Thanks for worrying, though." She reached out to squeeze his hand.

"Yeah, well . . . try to refrain from any late night . . . escapades." He waggled his eyebrows. "Of the meeting-with-killers variety anyway."

Cass laughed. "I'll see what I can do."

"I'm serious. No more running off in the middle of the night by yourself. Promise?"

"I promise. No more meeting with killers or suspected killers. Cross my heart." She made an *X* over her chest with her finger and held her hand palm up toward him in an *I swear* gesture.

"All right, then. Have fun." He ran for his car.

Rain pelted the jacket Cass held over her head as she ran down the walkway. Luke opened the door of the Jeep and, with a hand on the small of her back, guided her into the seat, then closed the door, ran around to his side, and jumped in beside her.

"Sorry. I didn't think to bring an umbrella." He turned the key and started the defogger and the windshield wipers, but he made no move to pull out of the spot.

"No problem. I occasionally think to buy one, but I just end up leaving it somewhere anyway, so what's the point?"

He shifted until he sat facing her. He skimmed a feather-light caress beneath her chin. "Mind if I ask what happened?"

She forced herself not to turn away. "I fell."

He studied her eyes a moment too long. "Fell?"

She smiled, but her heart rate kicked up a bit. "I was running, and I slid on the gravel and fell."

He seemed to accept her explanation and turned to shift into drive. He still didn't move the car, though. "So . . . I'm a murder suspect?"

Hmmm . . . Since he brought it up, should she question him about the gun? "Well . . . I couldn't help but notice the gun-shaped bulge under your waistband."

He looked over at her, his dark eyes more intense than usual, and grinned. "And where were you looking that you noticed my bulge?"

Heat erupted through her face—well, pretty much everywhere, actually—and she quickly averted her gaze to look out the windshield.

He pulled out of the lot. "So, where do you want to go?"

Apparently he wasn't going to answer her question. *Okay,*

then. "The only places open this late are the diner or Atlantis, a small place by the marina."

"Is Atlantis any good?"

She thought of the romantic atmosphere, dim lighting, and large stone fireplace. "Very. They have seafood, but they also have the best steaks around, if you like that better."

"Sounds good."

She directed him toward the marina. They rode in silence for a while, Cass contemplating the chances Luke was a killer, Luke contemplating something she couldn't even guess at. If the scowl was any indication, it was probably something serious. *Hopefully not where to dump my body.* She swallowed hard. "So, you're here on vacation?"

Luke shrugged. "Sort of, I guess. At least that's how it started out. Then, I got a call from my boss asking me to work while I'm here. I guess you could call it a working holiday."

"You can work from the hotel?"

He glanced over at her, but shadows darkened his face, and she couldn't read his expression. If he was surprised she knew where he was staying, he didn't let on. "I can work from pretty much anywhere as long as I have my laptop and Internet service."

Streaks of windblown rain inched along the side windows. Cass gestured toward Atlantis, and Luke hit the turn signal and pulled into the lot. It wasn't packed, but it was definitely crowded for a Wednesday night. Most of the cars in the lot probably belonged to bar patrons.

Luke pulled to the front deck and stopped. "Why don't you get out here? I'll park and meet you in a minute. That way you won't get any more soaked."

She glanced out at the rain pounding against the hood of

the car, the windshield wipers barely able to keep up. Lightning briefly lit the sky. "Sure. Thank you." She hopped out and ran up the stairs onto the deck. Once she was under the awning, she shook the rain off her jacket and caught sight of her reflection in the glass door. *Yikes.* She used the glass as a makeshift mirror to try to fluff her hair.

Cass straightened when the door opened, and grinned at Jim and Tami Mills. They weren't close friends, but she'd known Tami since they were kids. "Hi."

Jim nodded. Tami only eyed her suspiciously and puckered her lips as if she'd sucked on a lemon.

"Uh . . . rough weather, huh?" Cass squirmed. She'd forgotten Jim and Tami lived next door to Marge Hawkins.

Jim nodded again, then turned to his wife. "Do you want to wait here and I'll run and get the car?"

Her gaze lingered on Cass and, for a minute, Cass thought she might rather run through the thunderstorm than stand next to her on the deck.

"Sure. Go ahead."

He left without sparing Cass another glance.

Good sense told Cass she should probably either step inside the door or stand there quietly and ignore Tami until Luke arrived. Of course, good sense wasn't one of her strong points. It probably fell somewhere after arriving on time for rehearsals. "So . . . how have you been?"

Tami rolled her eyes and faced Cass head-on. "Why don't you let it go, Cass? I'm not interested in small talk."

Anger rose. *Sigh* . . . One of these days she'd probably learn to keep her mouth shut. Unfortunately, today wasn't that day. "Do you have a problem with me?" *Duh . . . as if it's not obvious from the attitude.*

She snorted primly. "I don't associate with killers."

Cass's mouth fell open. Was she serious? "I beg your pardon?"

"You heard me."

"I didn't kill anyone, Tami. You've known me since I was a kid. How could you even think I'd do something like that?"

"Wrong, Cass. I knew you *when* you were a kid. Then you disappeared for years and years. When you showed up back here, rumor has it you were . . . troubled, talking to dead people and whatnot."

What?!

"Besides, the sheriff seems pretty convinced of your guilt." She turned away.

"What are you talking about?" Cass balled her hands into fists. This was getting way out of hand.

Tami pinned her with a glare. "When the sheriff came to question us about Marge, we asked him about the killer. Naturally, we were concerned for our safety with a killer on the loose."

Naturally. Witch.

"He told us we were perfectly safe, since they already had the killer under surveillance."

Jim pulled to the curb, and Tami held her head high and her spine stiff as she walked down the stairs to the car.

Cass stood staring after her, mouth open in shocked silence. Was that what Sheriff Langdon was telling people? *It might just be time to pay Otis a visit.*

Luke ran up the steps to the deck. "Sorry for taking so long. I got caught up with a phone call from my boss." He frowned after the BMW as it sped out of the lot. "Everything all right?"

"Yeah. Fine." Cass waved off the incident, but she couldn't completely dismiss the hurt. She turned toward the restaurant and simply stood, staring at the door.

Luke placed a hand on her lower back, the warmth giving her strength. He leaned close to whisper in her ear. "Are you sure you're okay?"

She looked into his concerned eyes and smiled. "I'm sure. Come on. Let's eat." As he held the door open for her to enter, she couldn't help but feel like she was walking into the lion's den.

Luke held the chair out for Cass to sit. They were close enough to the fireplace for the heat to chase away the chill from her wet clothes . . . and the few indiscreet stares that had followed her into the room. Their server greeted them, thankfully with no suspicious glares, and left menus while he went to get their drinks.

Cass opened the menu, more for something to do with her hands than anything else. She already knew what she wanted, the same thing she always had when she came to Atlantis. Steak. Medium well with loaded mashed potatoes and . . . she peered over the menu at Luke . . . well, maybe she'd skip the garlic string beans.

She studied his face in the flickering glow of the candle-light and fireplace flames. He had strong, handsome features, the kind of rugged good looks you expected to see on cowboys or—

He looked up and caught her watching him. "Are the steaks tender?"

"Huh? Oh yeah. You can cut them with a butter knife."

"Sounds good." He closed the menu and set it aside. He clasped his hands and rested them on the table. "You said earlier that Bee's been a friend since you came to the island. How long have you been here?"

"I grew up here, then left for college. I didn't come back after that until last year, when my parents passed away." She took a moment to collect herself, to ease the sense of loss back into that small compartment where she was able to control it somewhat, while the waiter placed their drinks on the table. By the time he'd finished taking their orders with a promise to return shortly with their appetizers, she was once again composed.

He studied her intently. "I'm sorry to hear about your parents."

She nodded her acknowledgment. "I came back here to see to the services, and I never left."

"You mentioned you were in bad shape when you returned. Because of their deaths?"

Cass stirred her diet soda with the straw, clinking the ice against the sides of the glass. She smiled, the sort of smile that came when things were so bad there was nothing else to do but smile or lose your mind. "That was a rough year for me. I'm sure you don't want to hear all the boring details."

"Actually"—he clasped her hands across the table—"I'd love to know everything about you."

He seemed sincere, held her gaze, and rubbed warmth into her cold hands. She shrugged. She may as well give him all of—well, most of—the sordid details of her past. It was nothing he couldn't find out by asking around town. There were no secrets in a community the size of Bay Island. She thought of Marge and her secret lover.

Someone had to know. The idea hit her like a ton of bricks. Her first assessment was right. There really were very few secrets here. People knew what other people were doing. *Someone* knew who Marge's lover was. Now, if she could only find out who.

Luke squeezed her hands, bringing her back to the present. "Are you okay?"

She shook off thoughts of Marge . . . for now, anyway. "Sorry. My mind tends to wander."

The appetizers arrived, and she reluctantly let go of Luke's hands and sat back to give the waiter room. "Can I get you anything else?"

"No, thank you. We're good." Luke returned his undivided attention to her.

"I'm actually a psychiatrist. I used to have my own practice in the city."

"The city?"

She laughed. "Sorry, I forgot you're not from around here. New York. Manhattan."

He nodded.

"Anyway. One of my patients committed suicide right after leaving my office." She lowered her gaze and shook her head, the memory still swirling with regret. Regret she hadn't listened to her instincts, regret she hadn't realized something was that wrong, regret she hadn't looked for him sooner. She blew out a breath. "When I found out, I was devastated. I went home to tell my husband what happened, hoping to find some comfort."

Luke's eyebrows shot up. Apparently he hadn't known she was married. He didn't question her though, simply waited for her to continue.

"When I got there, he was busy *comforting* my best friend."

Luke winced.

"A week later I received word of my parents' deaths." She took a deep breath and reached for a plate. "So, there you have it, my whole sordid past."

Luke shook his head. "You weren't kidding. That really was a bad year."

Cass shrugged. "I got through it, with the help of Stephanie, who's been my best friend since childhood, and Boo, who became one after I came back."

"How did you end up involved in this whole mess with Ms. Hawkins?"

"I have no idea. Enough about me, though. Tell me about you." She took a baked clam and placed it on her plate, ready to be finished with the somber conversation and needing a break from any talk about murder.

"My story's not quite as . . . tragic . . . as yours. I was born on Long Island but moved to Florida with my parents, my brother, and my three sisters when I was young."

"Ahh . . . so that explains the sometimes southern accent."

He laughed. "You caught me."

Cass really liked his easy laughter, the small affectionate touches and gestures, his sense of humor. It surprised her a little to realize she enjoyed his company. But she didn't trust him, and that *didn't* surprise her.

"I always missed Long Island, especially in the fall. When I was a kid, we always used to drive out east on the North Fork, Mattituck, Cutchogue, all the way out to Orient Point. We'd stop at farm stands along the way, stuff ourselves with roasted corn on the cob and hot apple cider, pick pumpkins to carve, and fill the car with bales of hay, scarecrows, and mums to decorate the yard. It was always my favorite time of year, a happy time. When the opportunity presented itself, I moved back up here."

Cass smiled fondly. She loved Long Island in the fall for many of the same reasons. "Have you driven out yet this season?"

Luke laughed. "Actually, no. I haven't had time. I'd love to if you're up for it one of these days."

They talked about all kinds of things through dinner—movies, books, sports, though Cass couldn't contribute much to that conversation. Eventually, they ended up discussing theater. "So how did you come to be on the board of directors at our theater?"

The question had seemed innocent enough. Yet Luke's guard slammed up immediately. His eyes darkened and his lips firmed. He shrugged as if it was unimportant, no big deal, really. He was lying.

"I've always been involved with theater in one way or another. When I was in high school I played the lead in *Bye Bye Birdie*."

Cass couldn't help herself. Laughter bubbled up and out before she could contain it. "I'm sorry." She held up a hand and tried to stem the fit of giggles. "The image of you gyrating around the stage is just too funny."

"Hey. I'll have you know I was a great Conrad Birdie. The girls used to swoon." He laughed with her, obviously comfortable with his role.

He hadn't answered her question, again, but she was getting used to his avoidance tactics. Not that she liked it, but she was beginning to realize Luke was very skilled at keeping his secrets well guarded.

23

It had finally stopped raining, and Cass and Luke took their time strolling leisurely, hand in hand, to the Jeep.

"Can I ask you something?"

Cass glanced toward him. He sounded so serious, and her experience with him so far told her he seldom was. "Sure."

"What were you doing with that suspect list?"

Cass breathed in a deep lungful of the crisp night air. "I was trying to figure out who killed Marge."

He smiled and yanked her hand. "I figured that much. I was wondering why."

Her laughter faded quickly. "The sheriff seems hell-bent on pinning the murder on me. As far as I can tell, I'm his one and only suspect." Anger started to chase away the peace she'd managed to attain with Luke. "He's even telling people I killed Marge." Tears threatened. "I figure the only way I'll get out of this is if I can prove I didn't do it."

She stopped walking to look him directly in the eye. "I was home alone from the time I dropped Bee off Friday night until the time I found Marge on Saturday morning. I don't have an alibi. No one's going to come forward and say they were with me or saw me anywhere." She looked at the wet parking lot and shook her head. "There's no way to prove I didn't do it without finding out who did."

He sighed and pulled her into his arms, a friendly embrace, with no heat, no innuendos, only the offer of comfort. She rested her cheek against his chest and wrapped her arms around his waist.

"Just be careful, all right, Cass? If you need help, you can call me." He released her, placed a finger beneath her chin, careful to avoid her scrape, and lifted her head until she looked into his eyes. "I mean it. If you think you know who killed her, *do not* confront them. Call me or the police. Promise?"

She nodded, and they continued on their way to the Jeep. He held the door for her before rounding the front of the Jeep and climbing in. When he pulled out, he turned on the radio, a soft rock station that suited her mood well.

In the companionable silence between them, Cass laid her head back, letting the music soothe her. The thought of unloading everything on Luke begged for her attention. She tilted her head to study him in the glow from the dashboard instruments. He exuded strength. Would he help her? Could he? But what about the gun she'd seen? He wouldn't tell her why he had it. He avoided answering her questions about how he ended up on the board of directors.

She sat up a little straighter. Actually, now that she thought about it, he'd avoided answering most of her questions tonight. She had only a vague sense of anything about him—other than the fact she saw him at the hotel, with a gun, hours after a woman was found shot to death on a beach beside the same hotel—and he played a great Conrad Birdie. Questions spun around her in a dizzying array until the throbbing in her head would no longer allow her to contemplate any more.

"Do you want me to drop you at the theater to pick up your car?"

An idea struck her. She glanced at the clock. It wouldn't take that long.

"Would you mind dropping me off at Mystical Musings? It's actually closer."

"This late at night?"

"It'll be fine. Bee and Stephanie are meeting me there." *Even though they don't know it yet.*

"No problem. I'll take you wherever you want to go."

"Thank you."

"Sure."

He walked her up the cobblestone walkway with his arm around her shoulders. When they reached the front porch, he climbed the steps with her and stopped at the front door.

She thought briefly of taking him home. If she could get him undressed, she'd know for sure if he carried a weapon. She giggled out loud at the thought. *Jeez . . . stop yourself.*

He tucked a strand of windblown hair behind her ear. "What's so funny?"

"Trust me, you don't want to know." *And I definitely do not want to tell you.* "Thank you for dinner. I had a great time."

"Me, too." He turned on the charm. "Promise you're going to behave yourself?"

She met his gaze. "I'm immune to your southern boy charms, you know."

His eyes held only amusement. "Oh, really?"

"Yes, really." *Okay, that was a little too breathless.*

His gaze fell to her neck, where her frantically fluttering pulse surely gave her away. He ran a finger down her neck. "I think you're lying." He pressed his lips to hers, gently, the touch featherlight, leaving her longing for more. "Good night."

What? "Uh . . . good night."

A smirk played at the corners of his mouth just before he turned to walk away. He walked to the car. *I sure do hope he's not guilty.*

Cass locked the door, flipped on the light, grabbed the phone, and dialed Bee's number as she weaved between the cases and into the back room.

Ring.

I know it's here somewhere.

Ring.

"Hey, sugar. How was your date?"

"It was great, and if you pick Stephanie up and meet me at the shop, I'll give you all the sordid details."

"On my way, sweetie." Bee disconnected, and Cass laughed out loud. Hopefully, he'd forgive her when he found out the details weren't all that sordid.

She rummaged through boxes of old merchandise. *It has to be here somewhere.* Bee might forgive her for not having anything juicy to share, but getting over this might be a little harder. Oh well. Desperate times and all that.

Aha . . . She pulled the Ouija board from the very bottom of a box, right where she'd buried it after the last time she'd used it. A chill raced up her spine. She'd never really considered herself psychic, just very intuitive. And yet, the last time she used the Ouija board, she'd definitely felt . . . something. Besides, she wasn't getting anywhere any other way. What could it hurt?

She turned off the light in the back room, dimmed the lights in the shop, and placed the box on the table. After lighting several candles and placing them throughout the room, she dragged three chairs to the center of the floor.

A soft knock at the door caught her attention, and she sucked in a deep breath before she went to open it.

Bee strolled in with Stephanie on his heels. "Okay, spill it." He looked around the dimly lit room. "Oooh, candlelight. Very romantic. I want to hear every last—" His gaze fell on the box with the Ouija board. "Oh. Oh no. No way, Cass. What are you doing with that thing?" Bee stumbled back, almost falling off his platform shoes.

"Okay. Just hear me out."

"Are you crazy?" His voice had reached a nearly hysterical pitch. "What do you plan on doing with that thing?"

Stephanie simply stood staring at her as if she'd lost her mind completely. Who knew? Maybe she had.

Cass massaged the bridge of her nose between her thumb and forefinger but gave up and dropped her hand to her side when her tension wasn't relieved. "Listen. I have to figure out who killed Marge and the other woman. Sherriff Langdon is determined to pin both murders on me. Since no one alive can seem to tell me who killed them, I thought maybe . . ." She shrugged and heat crept up her cheeks. "It couldn't hurt to try."

Bee groaned. "Please don't make me do this, Cass. You know I don't believe in this drivel."

Cass bit back any retort. No sense contradicting him when she needed his help. But he'd turned awfully pale for someone who didn't believe in anything otherworldly.

Stephanie huffed out a breath. "What the heck. I'll give it a try."

Bee clutched his chest, his breath coming in shallow gasps.

"Oh, stop yourself, Bee." Stephanie grabbed his arm and pulled him toward the seats Cass had arranged in a small circle.

He frantically fanned himself as he continued to wheeze.

Cass couldn't restrain the laugh that bubbled out.

He pinned her with his harshest stare, the one he reserved for people he disliked immensely. "I'm so"—he sucked in a breath—"glad"—and another—"you're amused."

"Come on, Bee. It'll be okay." She couldn't resist a small jab. "Besides, you don't believe in this mumbo jumbo, so what's the problem?"

He glared daggers at her but didn't say anything else.

"Okay. Pull the chairs a little closer together." When they did as she asked, she took the board from the box, sat in the circle with them, and placed it on their knees.

Bee shivered. "I'm telling you now. You better contact the other woman, not . . ." He looked around the room, leaned closer and lowered his voice. "Marge."

Cass bit the inside of her cheek. "Sure. I'll do my best."

She stared at the board for another few seconds: each letter of the alphabet, zero, the numbers one through nine, and the words *yes*, *no*, *hello*, and *goodbye*. Her heart raced. Last time she'd used the board with a small group of friends, she'd ended up with a welt down her arm. No one seemed to know how it had gotten there, and Cass didn't remember scratching it on anything. Of course, she must have.

She pushed her fear aside and placed the planchette on the board. "Place your fingers very lightly on the planchette."

Bee squeaked quietly.

Stephanie did as instructed. "Oh, Bee. Come on. It's not going to bite."

"Fine." He lowered his shaking hands.

"Okay." Cass took a deep breath. She tried to envision the blond woman who'd come into the shop. Was that even the woman who was killed? She blew out a breath. *Okay, Marge it is. Sorry, Bee.*

She struggled to concentrate. Unfortunately, every time she tried to focus on an image of Marge, the sight from the theater popped into her mind. Not a picture she wanted to hold on to.

She placed the tips of her fingers on the planchette and closed her eyes, willing her body to relax. The chimes tinkled, startling her. She glanced toward them, but no one had come through the locked door.

Sweat sprang out on Bee's forehead. If possible, he'd paled even further.

Stephanie's gaze darted to Cass.

Cass turned back to the board and shrugged.

Keeping her fingers firmly in place, she rolled her shoulders and tilted her head from side to side. There had to be a way to relieve some of her tension.

The door rattled.

Cass jumped and turned toward the sound, lifting her

hands from the planchette. Nothing. Her gaze shot to Bee, whose hands fluttered to his chest, and Stephanie, who sat biting a thumbnail.

She lowered her gaze back to the board. She stared at the planchette, now resting on the word *hello*.

Bee's scream tore through the small space. He jumped from the chair, tumbling the board and planchette to the floor. "Did you see that?" He pointed at the board, his finger trembling wildly. "It said hello."

"Calm down, Bee." Cass stood and held her hands out toward him. "It probably moved when we all jumped at the wind hitting the door."

Bee harrumphed indignantly. "Yeah, and just happened to land on *hello*, right?"

Cass glanced at Stephanie for support.

"Don't look at her. I'm telling you right now, I'm done. Put that thing away, and let's get out of here." His gaze darted back and forth as if trying to take in every corner of the room at once.

Stephanie bent to retrieve the board. She put it back in the box, then used the top of the box to shove the planchette into the bottom of the box on top of the board. She shot Cass a sheepish grin. "What? Bee screaming like a banshee probably scared all the spirits away anyway. No sense trying again now."

Cass huffed out a breath. "Okay. I guess it's back to trying to solve this the old-fashioned way."

24

Bee and Stephanie sat in the car and watched Cass until she opened the front door and went inside. She waved before she closed and locked the door. Exhaustion overtook her. She thought briefly about pouring a glass of wine to take in the bath with her but dismissed the thought just as quickly. All she wanted was a hot bath and a soft bed.

"*Ruff!*"

Beast. She should probably let him out again if she didn't want a repeat of the last time she'd forgotten. She sighed and headed toward the kitchen.

"*Ruff!*"

"*Shhh!*"

Cass's heart stuttered in her chest and stopped. Someone was in the house. The sound of someone hushing Beast was unmistakable.

Indecision held her frozen in place. Hide? Turn and run?

But where? Her car was still at the theater. She forced air into her lungs. *A weapon.* She needed a weapon.

Had whoever it was heard her come in? Maybe they didn't even know she was home yet. She tiptoed backward across the living room, keeping her eyes glued to the kitchen door. Thankfully, she had to keep it closed so Beast didn't tear the house a—

Beast. Would he have let someone in? He'd never acted weird toward strangers and was friendly to everyone who came into the shop. Except Jay. Which made it highly unlikely it was Jay in her kitchen.

Okay. She couldn't stand there all night. She was going to have to do something. Could she call for help? What if whoever it was heard her? She crept quietly into the living room, searching desperately for some sort of weapon. Anything. She wished desperately she'd brought an umbrella with her. At least that would be something.

She eased open the small drawer on the table where the answering machine sat. The red light blinked rapidly. Two messages. She searched the drawer in the pulsing red light, terrified to turn on any lamps. *Aha* . . . She pulled the letter opener triumphantly from the drawer.

"It's about time you got home."

Cass sucked in a breath and spun toward the voice. Her heart lurched into her throat.

The overhead light flipped on, forcing Cass to squint against the brightness. Ellie stood in the doorway.

"What are you doing here?"

"I'm sorry. I didn't know what else to do. I need to talk to you."

"How did you get in here?" Cass pressed her hand to her chest in an effort to get her heart lodged back in there.

Ellie wrung her hands. "The back door."

She was going to have to start locking the door. If Ellie could walk right in, so could anyone else. With the initial fright over, Cass studied the young woman more closely. The stress of the last week had taken its toll. Dark circles ringed her eyes. Her cheekbones appeared more prominent, and she seemed to have lost weight, if that was even possible. Her usually mousy brown hair hung greasy and limp down her back. "I thought you were afraid of the dog."

She nodded. "I am, but not as afraid as I am of . . . other things out there." Her gaze shot nervously toward the window.

Cass gave up all hope of a hot bath and a good night's sleep. She moved to close the curtains over the big picture window. "Do you want a cup of tea? Or a glass of wine, maybe?"

Ellie shook her head.

"All right. Why don't you have a seat?"

Ellie eyed the cushionless couch, then moved to sit in the chair.

Cass slid a small stack of books aside and perched on the edge of the coffee table, facing her. Now that she was past the shock of finding Ellie in her living room, a barrage of questions assailed her. Her tired brain worked to sort through and make sense of them all. She squeezed the bridge of her nose between her thumb and forefinger, shook her head, then dropped her hand into her lap and looked directly at Ellie. "Where have you been? I've been worried sick."

"I'm sorry. I didn't mean to scare anyone." She covered her mouth and choked back a sob.

"It's okay. Don't worry about it. Are you all right?"

Ellie hugged herself and rocked back and forth. She didn't say anything, so Cass simply waited. She watched the other woman closely but didn't say a word.

Ellie lowered her head and put a hand across her eyes. Her shoulders shook softly.

Cass went to the bedroom and grabbed a box of tissues from the nightstand. She brought them back and handed them to Ellie.

Ellie finally looked up. "Thank you." She grabbed a tissue from the box and wiped her face, then took a few more to blow her nose.

Cass moved a wastebasket to the side of the chair, then returned to sit on the table. "Can you tell me what happened? Are you hurt?"

Ellie shook her head and spoke so softly Cass had to lean forward and close the two-foot gap between them to hear her. "No. Not really, just scared."

"Scared of whom?"

The look in Ellie's eyes was feral, panicked prey running from a predator. "Jay."

"What happened?"

She heaved in a deep breath and blew her nose once more. "Jay's always been a little . . . nasty . . . maybe even a bit controlling."

No. Really?

"He never hurt me, physically. But he'd make me feel so bad about myself, and there were a few times he scared me pretty bad." Ellie's hands flew up to cover her face, the memories obviously traumatic.

Cass's heart ached.

"He'd yell at me for everything. No matter what I did or how hard I tried, I never seemed to get things the way he wanted them. I never told anyone, not even my mother, though she suspected."

Did Ellie really think no one knew she was being emotionally abused by that bully? She was even more naïve than Cass realized. Her anger toward Jay grew into rage.

"Why didn't you file for divorce?"

Ellie's eyes widened. "My mother said the same thing, but how could I do that? He's my husband. I love him. Besides, it's my own fault. If I made sure everything was just the way he liked it when he was around, he left me alone."

Cass pushed her fingers through her hair and squeezed. She counted slowly to ten. *This girl has been abused her whole life. She doesn't know any other way.* Cass blew out her breath slowly, choking back the reprimand that sat on the tip of her tongue. She'd worked with too many women like Ellie over the years in her practice. Insecure women were targets for men like Jay.

"Anyway, the reason I came to you for that reading after my mother specifically ordered me not to was because . . ." Ellie sat up straighter, determination hardening her eyes. "My mother told me Jay was cheating on me. She said he had girlfriends all over the place and that was why he was sending me to the city with his sister. We argued about it, and my mother told me to smarten up.

"After I saw you, I went home and confronted Jay. I told

him what my mother told me, but I told him you said it was going to be okay."

A wave of guilt tore through Cass, but at least that explained why Jay thought he could trust her. He probably thought she was just as gullible as Ellie.

"He asked if I believed my mother, and I told him I didn't know. He was working on his car, and he had a screwdriver in his hand. He came at me so fast I didn't know what to do. I put my hand up, and he accidently swung the screwdriver and cut my hand."

Accidentally? Was this girl out of her mind?

"Then he took off out of the house in a blind rage." Terror filled Ellie's eyes. "I've never seen him that mad." She broke down into sobs, covering her face with her hands.

Cass got up and went to her. She crouched beside her and rubbed circles on her back. "It's all right, Ellie." Her psychiatrist instincts warred with her friendship instincts. "You're going to have to call the police. You know that, right?"

She lifted her head, and the pain etched in her face was heartbreaking. "I can't."

"Even if he did hurt you by accident, you should still have it on record." Cass had seen too many emotional abuse cases escalate over the years to be comfortable letting Ellie return home to Jay. "You can get an order of protection, and he'll have to stay away from you. I have a friend. Stephanie's husband, Tank. He'll be very kind."

"No. You don't understand. He'll kill me if I go to the police."

Cass sat up, startled at the vehemence in her words.

"Don't you get it? He left that night . . . irate . . . and he never came home. The next morning, my mother was . . ."

Cass sucked in a breath. "Oh crap." She hadn't put the timeline together.

"Exactly."

"All right." Her mind raced. Jay killed Marge. If he killed Marge, he probably wouldn't hesitate to kill anyone else. "What about the other woman? Did he kill her, too?"

Ellie's eyebrows drew together. "What other woman?"

Ah jeez . . . All right. Think, think, think. She had to do something. "Will you talk to the police and tell them what you suspect?"

Ellie shook her head wildly and launched herself from the chair.

"Calm down, Ellie. Sit down. We'll think of something else."

Ellie barely perched on the edge of the seat, ready to bolt at the least provocation.

Cass took a breath. She had to calm down. *What if Jay followed Ellie here?* She ran through the kitchen to lock the back door. Beast greeted her wildly, prancing in circles in front of the door. Cass glanced out into the dark. She scanned the section of the yard lit by the floodlight on the back deck. "Sorry, boy. You're gonna have to hold it."

She ran back to the living room and knelt on the floor in front of Ellie. Her heart raced, her pulse pounding erratically. She took Ellie's hands. "Listen to me. You're not going to be safe unless Jay is in jail. You know that, right?"

She nodded absently.

"If you won't talk to the police, I will."

Ellie stiffened, but Cass held firmly to her hands. "I can have Bee or Stephanie come stay with you here, and I'll go to the police station and tell Tank what you've told me."

Ellie looked at Cass—though it seemed her mind was a million miles away—bit her lower lip, and nodded.

"All right. Stay put. I'm going to see whom I can get ahold of."

Ellie slid back on the chair, obviously resigned. She tucked her legs beneath her, curled into a ball, and lowered her head.

Cass grabbed an afghan from the love seat and covered her. Her mind raced. Bee was probably still up. He didn't usually go to bed until early in the morning. She dialed his cell phone.

He picked up on the first ring. "I'm not talking to you until you've sufficiently groveled for forgiveness."

"Bee. I need help." Her voice shook, but she couldn't help it.

He sobered instantly. "Where are you?"

"I'm home. Ellie's here. I have to go to the police station, but I can't leave Ellie alone, and my car's at the theater."

"I'm already walking out the door."

Cass disconnected. A flicker of guilt licked at her consciousness. How could she have suspected Bee of killing anyone?

Cass stood in the foyer, peering through a gap in the curtains on the window beside the front door. Her heart thundered. Was Jay out there right now? Was he watching? She scanned the dark yard, the pools of light beneath the streetlights . . . The deep shadows tormented her. The darkness was too complete. Anything could be crouched there. Waiting.

Twin beams of light rounded the curve. Headlights. Relief battled sheer terror. Help, or danger? She jumped back from the window. *All right, now you're just being dramatic.*

She took a few shaky breaths, then peeked through the curtains. Bee.

Relief surged over her like a tidal wave. She flung the door open, met him at the bottom of the porch steps, and threw herself into his arms.

He didn't say a word. She hugged him tightly until she got a grip on herself, released him, and stepped back. "Come in, hurry." She led him up the stairs and into the house, slammed the door behind her, and breathed a sigh of relief.

"Are you all right?"

She shook her head. "Honestly? I have no idea." She double-checked the lock and led Bee to the living room, where Ellie slept, curled in the armchair.

"Oh, the poor thing." Bee pressed a hand to his chest. "My heart just breaks for her."

Cass put a finger to her lips to shush him. She gestured for him to follow her into the kitchen. With Bee there, the sense of urgency receded a little. She popped a cup in the Keurig and pulled out two mugs. Despite everything that was going on and the adrenaline pumping through her system, her eyes burned with exhaustion.

Bee pulled out a chair and sat at the table. "What's going on?"

"After you dropped me off . . ." Her thoughts faltered. If Jay was the killer, Luke was innocent. A small smile formed.

"Mmm . . . Looks like there's a story there, but unless you're going to share it, can you go on?"

"Oh, sorry." Heat crept into her cheeks, and she turned to get the first cup of coffee and start the second one. She placed Bee's cup in front of him, along with a carton of milk. "Anyway, she admitted Jay's been emotionally abusive."

Bee rolled his eyes as he stirred milk into his coffee.

"I know, I know. But at least she's finally admitted it." Cass grabbed her coffee and sat at the table across from Bee. "She said on the night Marge was killed, Jay left the house in a rage and didn't come home."

Bee's eyes shot up and coffee sloshed onto the table. "Are you serious?"

Cass nodded and sipped her coffee. "She's terrified, but she won't go to the police. Would you stay here with her while I go to the sheriff's office and talk to Tank?"

Bee grabbed napkins and mopped up the spill. "Of course."

Beast whined at the door. Cass got up and went to him. She peered out the window and studied the yard. Nothing. At least, nothing she could see. "Okay, boy. I'm going to open the door. You run out, do your business, and get back here. Got it?"

Beast whined again and danced around.

Cass whipped the door open long enough for him to dart through, then slammed it shut and turned the dead bolt. "Make sure you keep the doors locked. He shouldn't have to go out again until after I get back."

Scratching against the outside of the door interrupted them, and Cass's heart skipped a beat. She scolded herself as she peeked out and opened the door to let Beast back in. She picked up her coffee and paced the kitchen.

Bee ran a finger around the rim of his cup. "I can't blame her for being scared. If he killed her mother, and she's the only one who knows he was gone that whole night . . ."

Cass hadn't thought of that. Ellie was in more danger than she'd first realized. "Do you think maybe I should drop you guys off at your house? Jay's already contacted me once. He assumes Ellie will come to me for help."

"Nah. Don't worry about it. Beast will protect us. Right, boy?" He rubbed the big dog's head.

"Marge must have known."

Bee looked up. "Known what?"

"When she decided to tell Ellie about Jay, she must have known he might try to hurt her. It's the only thing that makes sense. Why else would Marge have gotten this giant dog?"

Bee delicately sipped his coffee. "You could be right. But where does the second body come in?"

Cass shrugged and massaged her temples. "Who knows? Maybe she found out what he did, and he had to eliminate her, too."

"Could be."

Cass dumped the remainder of her coffee down the sink and set the mug on the counter. "I'm going." She glanced at the clock. *Ugh . . .* "Do you know what time Tank gets off?"

"I'm pretty sure Stephanie said seven. They were going to meet at the diner for breakfast, and she asked if I wanted to go before I went to bed."

"I don't think I'll be back by then."

Bee waved her off. "Actually, I'm kinda beat. I think I'll take Beast and go lie on the couch . . . uh . . . maybe I can curl up on the love seat."

Cass laughed. "Good idea—at least that one has cushions. For now."

Bee tossed her his keys, walked her to the front door, and stood on the porch until she reached the car, climbed in, and shut the door. She glanced in the backseat to make sure it was empty, swallowed a sigh of relief that it was, and hit the lock button. Then she waved. He went back inside before she pulled out.

Cass hit the button for the radio but turned it right back off. Her head ached too badly to have even the slightest noise. Besides, she needed the quiet to order her thoughts. How could she have been stupid enough to meet Jay alone in the middle of the night? She was lucky he hadn't added her to his list of casualties.

Bright light reflected from the rearview mirror, momentarily blinding her. She squinted and looked away. Her heart hammered against her ribs. She glanced in the side mirror. The headlights came closer, inched their way forward until they were only an inch from her bumper. "Oh jeez." She fumbled in her purse for her phone.

25

Cass hit the brakes, hoping whoever it was—*oh please, not Jay*—would back off. Her bag tumbled off the seat, spilling its contents across the floor. *Ugh . . .*

The car stayed on her bumper. Tears threatened, but she forced them back, scared they would impair her vision. She kept her eyes glued to the road. *Okay. Think.* She was only a few miles from the police station. She could keep going and hope for the best. Or . . . maybe she was just being paranoid. It was probably just some jerk trying to pass her.

"All right . . ." There was no shoulder where she was now, but in a minute the road would widen a bit, and there would be room for her to pull to the side and let him pass. She prayed fervently as the residential neighborhood opened up into farmland and the road widened. She eased to the side of the road, only slowing a little to allow the other car to pass—not that he couldn't have used the deserted oncoming lane to go around—but, whatever.

He inched out past her, and the pressure on her chest eased a bit. He pulled around to the side of her. She held her breath but didn't dare take her eyes from the road ahead. Her tires skimmed along the dirt at the edge of the road, kicking up trails of what looked like smoke. Bee was going to kill her when he saw how filthy the car was. Maybe she could run through the car wash on her way home.

The other car kept pace at her flank, and she risked a quick glance to the side. She recognized Jay's truck instantly. He rode beside her for only a brief moment, then started to angle in front of her. He cut it too short. Too late, she realized he wasn't cutting in front of her to pass. He was angling toward her to stop her.

Cass pulled the wheel hard to the right, sending her car careening into the field.

Jay's truck easily kept pace.

She finally came to a stop, slammed the shifter into park, and struggled desperately to control her breathing.

Jay stopped, his truck angled to block her path.

Her heart slammed against her ribs. Pressure sat like an anvil on her chest.

Jay jumped out of the truck and ran around to her door.

Even with her head reeling, she quickly hit the lock button.

"You have to listen to me, Cass. I don't know what she's telling you, but it's not true. Open the window." He grabbed the door handle and rattled it, kicking the door in frustration when it wouldn't open. "Can you hear me through the window?"

She stared dumbly at him and nodded. The sound was muffled, but she could pretty much make out the words.

"Okay." He pressed his palms to the window and leaned close. "I'm going to step back from the car a minute. I want you to crack the window a little bit. Just enough that you can hear me but not enough for me to get my fingers in. Okay? Can you do that?"

She held his gaze, terrified to turn away.

He backed away with his hands in the air in an *I surrender* gesture.

She did what he asked. She opened the window the slightest bit, then waited for him to return. Tears streaked down her cheeks. There was no stopping them now. Terror gripped her throat. Did he have the gun with him? His hands were empty, but that didn't mean anything.

He approached the car. Leaned close to the window. "I didn't kill anyone, Cass. I'm telling you. I'm being framed. I think Ellie killed them, and she's trying to throw the blame on me."

Yeah, right.

"You have to believe me. I'm the victim here, Cass." His eyes were wild with something. Fear?

The harsh whisper blurted out before she could stop it. "Where were you, then?"

"What?" He pressed his ear to the crack. "I couldn't hear you."

She took a deep breath, searching for calm. "Where were you when Marge was killed?"

She studied his profile. It didn't seem as if his expression changed. "I was with my lady friend at the hotel. Ellie and

I had a huge blowout. I needed comfort, someone who understood it wasn't my fault. You know?"

Sure. It made perfect sense. Nothing was ever Jay's fault.

She nodded and tried to paste an understanding, compassionate look on her face. It probably looked more like a grimace, since that was how it felt. "Okay. Then, why not talk to the sheriff about it? Explain what happened?"

"Are you kidding me? What are you, stupid? Haven't you heard anything I've said?" His semi-calm façade exploded in a fit of rage. He pounded on the window, kicked the door . . . "My mother-in-law is dead, my wife thinks I killed her, and my alibi turned up on the beach with a bullet in her head."

Even Cass had to concede, it didn't look good.

With one last kick to the headlight on his way past, Jay stormed to the back of his truck. He flung open the hatchback and reached inside.

Cass pulled in a deep breath. Held it. She stepped on the brake and eased the car gently into reverse. *Please, don't be stuck. Please, don't be stuck.*

Jay pulled a crowbar from the back of the truck and ran back toward her. She waited until he was almost on her, then hit the accelerator. The car lurched and shot backward across the field and onto the road. Thankfully, no one was coming. Jay ran after her. She shifted into drive and hit the gas. The tires chirped but caught and launched her forward. Jay threw the crowbar, hitting the back window. It shattered.

In her rearview mirror, he bent over to grab the crowbar and ran to the truck. He'd never make it in time. She floored it, flying past the farms as the darkness began to creep toward a sickly gray.

Cass struggled to breathe. Pain radiated through her head, tunneling her vision. She fought the urge to pass out. If she didn't stop hyperventilating, she was going to lose the battle. She tried desperately to control her breathing. When her vision got hazy, she swiped at the tears she hadn't realized were falling.

She glanced in the mirror. Nothing. *Where is he?* Was he back there? Following her? Would he give up and go back to the house after Ellie? She had to warn Bee. She eased off the gas for a second and glanced down to the floor. Still too dark.

She flipped on the overhead light, casting enough light to see her cell phone. The air rushed out of her lungs in a whoosh of relief. She looked all around her. Nothing. No sign of Jay or anyone else. She quickly hit the brake, without pulling over, and reached for the phone.

Holding it in her hand brought instant relief. A lifeline. She dialed Bee's number as she drove. When he answered groggily, obviously half-asleep, the pressure on her chest relaxed a little.

"Bee. You and Ellie have to get out of there."

"What's wrong now?"

"I just had a run-in with Jay, and I'm afraid he's on his way back there."

Dead silence greeted her.

"Bee?" She pulled the phone away from her ear to check the connection. "Bee, are you there?"

"Yes. I'm here. Don't worry about it. If Jay shows up here, I'll take care of it."

"What are you going to do? Please, just get out of there. And don't forget to take Beast."

"Look, Cass. I didn't want to worry you, but when you called and said there was a problem I brought protection."

She frowned at the thought of what a condom was going to do against Jay Callahan. "What are you talking about?"

"I brought my gun."

She swallowed any further argument. Bee had a gun? Since when?

"See. I knew you'd bug out."

Cass pulled into the police station parking lot, shifted into park, and turned the car off. She forced her grip from the wheel and bent to gather the contents of her purse. What was Bee doing with a gun? Sure, lots of people owned guns, and it sort of made sense he'd bring it with him if he thought there might be danger. *Ugh* . . . Frustration pounded through her chest and her head. Even if he did own a gun, Bee was no killer. Right? It had to be Jay.

The stress was getting to be too much. She stared at the building a moment longer before climbing out of the car and starting forward with a determined stride. She scanned the parking lot as she walked, with an occasional glance back over her shoulder. No sign of Jay. She jogged up the front steps. Maybe she should have called Tank? Had him come to the house?

No. She couldn't do that. Ellie would bolt for sure, and then Jay might get her. She opened the door and strode purposely toward the receptionist.

The tired-looking woman looked up from whatever she was writing. "May I help you?"

"Yes." Cass's hands shook as she clutched her bag in front of her. "I need to see Officer Lawrence. It's urgent."

"Name?"

"Cass Donovan."

"Have a seat." She gestured toward a row of molded plastic chairs bolted to the floor across the room.

Cass sat while the woman spoke quietly into the phone. She'd simply tell Tank everything she'd learned so far and let him take it from there. He could pick up Jay and question him. Ellie would have to talk to them at some point, but Tank would be gentle with her. Hopefully she'd have calmed down by then.

"Miss Donovan?"

Cass looked up. The receptionist was staring at her.

"Oh. Sorry."

She offered a weak smile. "Would you follow me, please?"

"Sure. Thanks." Cass stood and followed the woman down a long corridor.

They stopped in front of an office door with an opaque window. The plaque on the front read SHERIFF OTIS LANGDON.

"No. You don't understand. I have to talk to Officer Lawrence."

The woman shoved open the door. Chief Langdon sat back in his desk chair. "Well, well, well. Come to confess?"

Cass bit her lip and resisted the urge to turn and run. She thanked the receptionist and stepped calmly into the office. The door closed behind her with a very final-sounding thump. She stood, rooted to the ground, unable to move forward—or any other direction, for that matter.

Chief Langdon sighed. "What is it, Ms. Donovan? I don't have all day." He tapped his pen repeatedly against the desk, the pounding in her head keeping time with the rhythm.

"I . . . um . . ."

"Spit it out already. What's the problem?"

She wiped her sweaty palms on her jeans. "I know who killed Ms. Hawkins."

Now she had his full attention. He looked at her and stilled. "So do I."

"No. You're wrong. It wasn't me."

He lifted a brow but remained quiet.

Cass moved to sit in one of the chairs in front of his desk. It was either that or her legs were going to give out, leaving her sprawled on the floor. "I didn't kill anyone."

"Okay. Enlighten me. Who was it?" He wiped a hand across the back of his neck.

"Jay Callahan."

Langdon relaxed. He rested his elbows on the desk, clasped his hands together, and leaned his chin on them. "Talk."

She relayed the entire story. Jay's midnight phone call, meeting him at the lighthouse, the visit from Ellie saying she was sure he did it. The abuse Ellie had suffered at his hands for years.

At that, Chief Langdon clenched his teeth and lowered his hands. Of course, everyone knew, but hearing the details was difficult.

She told him about Jay's affair with the woman who ended up dead, the only chance he had at an alibi.

Chief Langdon slowly nodded.

"Then, when I was on my way here, he ran me off the road." Relief washed through her. It was almost over. She could see the acceptance slowly creeping into the chief's eyes. "He tried to convince me it wasn't him, then shattered my back window with a crowbar."

Chief Langdon chewed on the inside of his cheek for a minute. "Where is he now?"

Cass blew out a breath. He believed her. Her shoulders slumped with relief. "I don't know. Bee's at my house with Ellie, but I have no idea where Jay went."

He studied her for another long moment, pursed his lips, and stood. "All right. Wait here. I'll issue an APB on Jay. I'll have him picked up before he can leave the island." He stood, hiked up his belt, and strode from the room.

Relief washed over her. It was done. Maybe she should insist on an apology. She peered out the open door at the chief talking to someone, face red with anger, hands gesturing wildly. *Then again . . . maybe not.*

Cass stood and stretched her back. She paced the room, waiting for him to return. Books lined a wall of shelves, and she scanned the titles. From what she could tell, they were all law books of one sort or another. A black-and-white photo in a silver frame sat in one corner of a shelf. She looked closer. Her dad? The shock of seeing him there stole her breath for a minute. Then she remembered he'd been friends with Otis Langdon at one time. She studied the picture more closely.

They were at the beach. Her father stood to one side. A much younger Chief Langdon stood with his arm casually draped around a smiling woman. A young woman who looked surprisingly like Ellie Callahan, but with more steel in her spine.

Cass's breath caught in her throat. *Oh . . . oh no.* It was the smile that threw her. She'd never once seen Marge Hawkins smile. Cass glanced over her shoulder toward the door, then leaned closer to the photo. Marge looked up at Langdon, adoration in her eyes and her smile.

Fear ratcheted up Cass's heart rate. An image flashed into her mind. Chief Langdon standing next to her car, left hand poised over his ticket pad, gold pen hovering . . .

The breath shot from her lungs. *It was him.*

She squeezed her eyes shut. She had to get out of there. She opened her eyes and turned to flee. Fear slammed through her and held her immobilized.

Langdon stood blocking the door. One look at her face was all it would have taken him to know she'd figured it out. He eased the door closed gently behind him without turning around.

26

"It was you." Cass slapped her hand over her mouth, but it was too late.

Chief Langdon stood, stony faced. "I thought it was Jay Callahan. Which is it, Cass?"

She shook her head and snapped her mouth closed. "How could you kill her . . . and then pin it on me?" Her voice was nearing a hysterical pitch, and she fought to get a grip on her emotions.

A pained look crossed his face. "I'm sorry, Cass. I'm sorry you got caught up in this."

Sorry. Is he kidding? "Caught up?" Indignation beat out some of the fear. "I didn't get caught up. You tried to frame me."

"Yeah, well. It was nothing personal. You just happened to be convenient."

"Nothing personal? You've hated me since I came back here."

Langdon shook his head. "I don't hate you. I simply got tired of listening to Marge complain about you. *'Cass is harassing my Ellie. She won't leave her alone. Cass is telling my Ellie to stay with that low-life husband of hers.'* And on, and on, and on . . . A man can only listen to so much."

Cass frowned. The gravity of her situation started to settle in. She opened her mouth to ask *Now what?* but clamped it shut before anything came out. Why push the issue?

Chief Langdon rubbed a hand across the back of his neck. "The way I figure it, Jay is an even better scapegoat than you. Bee knows Jay went after you on your way here." He chewed on the inside of his cheek, seeming more lost in thought than in the here and now. "If your body turns up on the beach by the hotel with a bullet from the same gun, I can pin the whole thing on Jay Callahan." He lifted his gaze to look at Cass. "That was the one problem I ran into using you as the killer. Not enough people believed you did it. Jay, on the other hand, well . . . not only will everyone believe it, but a bully who's basically abusing his wife will end up in jail, where he should be."

Langdon smiled at her, a sick, but surprisingly and frighteningly sane smile. "Don't worry. I'll issue a public statement clearing you so at least your memory won't be tarnished."

"Uh . . . thank you?" Cass searched for a way out. There were no windows, except for the one in the only door, and he was standing in front of it. Besides, no one could see through the opaque film anyway. Maybe she could stall. "Umm . . . Why was Marge holding my business card?" Oh. Actually, she really did want to know that.

"A stroke of genius on my part."

"Huh?"

"I put it in her hand when you called me to the theater."
His sick laughter crawled up her spine. "The fact the other
woman had your business card with an appointment for the
day she was killed in her pocket when she was found just
added another nail to your coffin."

So it *had* been the blonde who came into the shop. A
pang of sorrow shot through her. If she had taken the time
to do the reading, could she have warned her? Maybe pre-
vented her from being killed?

"We're going to walk out of here now," Langdon said. "I
want you to walk right in front of me and get into your car.
Understand?"

Sweat dripped steadily down her back and pooled at the
bottom of her spine. "Yeah . . . um . . . I don't think so."

Langdon frowned. "What do you mean, you don't think so?"

"Well, I was thinking, and I don't really feel like going
anywhere just yet."

"Really." He pulled out his gun and held it steadily aimed
at her chest. "Can I change your mind?"

Cass's mouth went dry. She tried to swallow, but it felt
sort of like swallowing paste. She licked her lips. The hustle
and bustle of the police station was starting to increase.
Muffled sounds of laughter and people talking drifted by as
they arrived for the workday. Soon the whole station would
be buzzing with the usual chaos. Surely someone would
come in looking for the chief and find them. If she could stall
long enough, maybe she'd have a chance.

"I don't understand." She worked to keep her voice somewhat steady but allowed the slightest tremor to let him know
he had the upper hand—in case he didn't already realize it.
"Why would you kill Ms. Hawkins?"

Rage contorted his face. A vein throbbed at the side of his forehead.

Maybe that was the wrong question to ask.

"Do you know how many years I kept our affair secret, settling for twice weekly visits to the local hotel for an afternoon tryst with the woman I've loved my whole adult life? When she married someone else, I accepted it and tried to move on." He pressed a hand to his forehead and shook his head. "I couldn't get over her. When her husband died, I waited an acceptable amount of time before approaching her. She thought it was too soon and was afraid she'd appear callous about her husband's death, so I accepted her terms." He paused.

Cass wasn't sure if he'd continue and was contemplating what to say when he spoke quietly.

"I knew something was going on with her. She'd been acting strange, canceled a few of our . . . dates. When I followed her to the theater that night, I had a feeling she was cheating on me, but I had no idea . . ." He shook his head.

Cass almost felt sorry for him. What must it be like to be that much in love with a woman like Marge Hawkins?

"I walked in and found her with Kyle Benedict, from the theater board."

Cass's eyebrows shot up. Marge had not one lover but two?

"I know. Can you even believe she would cheat on me with him?"

Cass shook her head. She was having a hard time believing any of this.

"Well, imagine my surprise when I walked in and found her in that little weasel's arms. I was furious, but I wouldn't have killed her. Honest." He lifted his free hand, palm toward her. "I would have walked out right then and there if she hadn't sent him away."

A tear slid from the corner of his eye to run down his cheek. "She sent him home, and I thought she was going to apologize, beg my forgiveness, tell me we could be together . . ."

"What happened?" Cass couldn't help herself. She was completely engrossed in the story and had to know how it ended. Oh . . . wait . . . She did know how it ended. She blew out a slow breath.

"She told me she was going to marry Kyle. That dorky little rat . . ." Something like a growl erupted. "I snuck around with that woman for years, only for her to sit there with that smug attitude and tell me she was marrying someone else. Again." He swiped at the tear dripping off his chin with more force than necessary. "I lost it."

Cass had to admit, he seemed to sincerely regret killing her. Of course, that didn't help anyone now. "Do you think if you explained what happened and told them you were really sorry, the court might be lenient?"

Langdon chuckled, not an amused chuckle, but an *I'm going to kill you* chuckle.

The blood in Cass's veins turned to ice.

"Let's go," he said. "It's getting too crowded out there. I don't want to hear another word."

She tried to project a sense of bravado, while her insides quivered. "What are you going to do if I don't come with you? Shoot me right here in the middle of the police station?" There. She had him. As long as she didn't leave the office with him, she was fairly safe. Probably.

"That's exactly what I'm going to do."

She sucked in a breath.

"Hands up, Cass."

She lifted her hands. Blood rushed in her ears.

He moved closer, gun held steady.

This was it. She held her breath.

He reached behind him.

She squeezed her eyes shut, then . . . nothing. She slitted one eye and peeked out.

He stood in front of her, holding something that looked like a gun wrapped in a handkerchief. "Do you know what this is, Cass?"

She shook her head, unable to force words past the fear lodged in her throat.

"The weapon that killed Marge and that other woman. Right now, there are no prints on it. Three seconds after I shoot you, your prints will be all over it. About two seconds before the first of my officers breaks down that door. I'll act like you pulled a gun on me and I shot you before you could shoot me." He grinned. "It's a no-win situation for you."

"How will you explain why I killed Carmen?"

He lifted a brow, perhaps surprised she knew the woman's name. "Maybe she saw you kill Marge. Who knows? It doesn't really matter. I guess that's a secret you took to the grave with you." He smiled. "Makes for wonderful speculation for the gossipmongers, though. Don't you think?"

"Is that why you killed her?"

He laughed. "Nothing quite that dramatic. But she did see me with Marge a time or two, and after the murder, she kept looking at me suspiciously."

He killed a woman because she looked at him wrong? Panic raced through Cass's every nerve ending, prickling her skin with goose bumps.

He slipped the gun in her jacket pocket and took a step back.

"Don't get any ideas. I'm not stupid enough to put a loaded gun in your pocket . . . Of course, that'll be part of the tragedy. The weapon wasn't even loaded, but how could I have known that? Now. Walk out that door and straight to your car. Get in and turn it on. Do you understand?"

She nodded dumbly.

"And, Cass. If anyone speaks to you, say hello and you're sorry but you're in a hurry. That's it. And whatever you do, don't pull that weapon out of your pocket, because mine probably wouldn't be the first bullet to slam through you."

She exhaled slowly, struggling to keep her legs from collapsing, and followed his orders.

"Turn here." Langdon used the gun to gesture to a dirt road on her right.

She glanced in her rearview mirror one last time, praying for someone to see her. Very few cars traveled the mostly deserted road at that time of the morning. And none of the drivers appeared to pay any attention to her.

She bumped along the rutted path, keeping one eye on the road and the other on the weapon trained at her side. "Could you point that thing somewhere else before it goes off by accident?"

He stared at her for a minute. "I'd prefer to shoot you on the beach, but if you try anything, I can just as easily shoot you in the car." He lowered the gun but didn't put it away. Instead, he held it against his leg, barrel pointed at the floor.

Could she open the door and jump out before he could

lift the weapon and shoot? Maybe. But then what? It was full daylight now, so she couldn't hope to disappear into darkness. She blew out a frustrated breath. Better to go along with him for now. The immediate sense of danger began to dim as her mind raced to find a way to escape.

"All right. That's far enough. Pull into that clear area over there."

The clear area he pointed to was a small clearing of sorts, covered in low brush and bushes. She winced as the branches scraped loudly along the undercarriage. If she managed to get away from this lunatic, Bee would kill her for sure.

"Stop the car."

She did as instructed.

"Now get out."

Cass turned off the car and climbed out. Her insides had pretty much liquefied. Her hands shook so badly she fumbled the keys and dropped them on the floor, trying to pull them out of the ignition. She started to reach down for them.

"Don't worry about it—you won't need them again."

A jolt of fear pierced her heart. She climbed from the car, mind racing, heart hammering wildly against her ribs. No sign of a weapon. No one in sight. *Stay calm. Breathe. In and out, in and out.*

There had to be a way out of this if she could stay calm enough to think. He led her through the woods. Tangles of thorns tore at her clothes, but she pushed her way through. They emerged from the woods a few yards from a rusted storage shed behind the Bay Side Hotel.

"Where are you taking me?"

"I can't very well shoot you in broad daylight, now, can I? I also can't risk being seen with you. At least all those

years of passing this piece of garbage shed as I snuck in and
out of the hotel will come in handy." He opened the door—
which screeched loudly in protest—looked around, and
propelled her through.

"Sit down."

It was now or never.

"I said sit down. Now."

Wait. He'd said he couldn't shoot her in broad daylight.
Did that mean he was going to leave her alone there? A flare
of hope burned through her. "You're not going to leave me
in this place, are you?" *Please, say yes. Please, say yes.*

He squinted as if trying to figure out what game she was
playing.

She swallowed hard. With a tremor in her voice and tears
in her eyes, she tried to show real fear. It wasn't hard. "There
might be . . . rats . . . in here." She whispered, as if afraid
the rodents might hear her.

A smile played at the corner of his mouth. "You'll have
plenty of time to find out. Now, sit down."

She sat.

"Lean against the leg of the workbench and put your arms
behind your back."

She did as he said.

He pulled her hands together on the far side of the bench
leg and taped her wrists together, then secured them to the
leg. He taped her ankles and wound a strip around her head
to cover her mouth. Since the workbench was securely fas-
tened to the floor, she wasn't going anywhere. All thoughts
of pounding against the thin walls until help came
vanished.

"Sorry to run, but I have to be at the station when the

missing person's report comes in. Bee being . . . well . . . Bee, I'm sure it won't take long for him to panic."

Violent tremors shook her as he closed the door behind him.

She worked desperately to remove the tape. The sweat pouring down her face and arms should have made it easier to work the tape off, but it held tight. *This stuff really does hold anything.*

She tried to envision what was happening now. Bee would have surely tried to call her cell phone at some point. Wait. Where was her cell phone? In her bag on the seat of Bee's car. Of course, Langdon must have taken the car back to town, or at least dumped it somewhere closer to the station.

Cass sighed and returned her attention to freeing herself. When she was completely exhausted, after not having slept at all the night before, she gave up trying to escape and started searching for a weapon.

There wasn't much in the dilapidated shed. A few old, rusted paint cans—one of those might make a good weapon if it was full . . . and if she could reach it. But her chances of reaching them without getting free were nonexistent. They were just too far away.

Real fear gripped her. It might be time to face the reality she might die tonight.

What would Bee do when she didn't answer her phone? Would he assume she was with Tank? Would he look for her? He'd probably stay with Ellie.

All right. She was going to have to get out of this on her own. Something caught her eye. Half-buried in the dirt floor. The handle of a screwdriver. She remembered the damage

Jay had done to Ellie's hand. It wasn't much, but it was better than nothing, which was what she had now.

Could she reach it with her feet? She stretched her feet as far as they would go toward the screwdriver. Well, the handle anyway. It was only a distant hope that the pointy part was still attached.

She scooted her bottom away from the workbench as far as she could and stretched her legs again. Almost. Sweat sprang out on her forehead. She toed off her shoes and reached as far as she could, pointed her toes and rotated her legs in as best she could with her ankles taped.

She gripped the edge of the handle between her toes. Pulled it toward her. It slipped out of her grasp. *Ugh* . . .

She scooted back against the workbench and dropped her head back to rest. Exhaustion beat at her. The stress of the past week sat like a weight on her shoulders. She closed her eyes and gave in to the pressure. Deep sobs racked her body.

She was going to die.

An eddy of blackness swirled in her periphery, tunneling her vision until there was nothing left but merciful darkness. Escape.

27

The first thing Cass became vaguely aware of was pain. Excruciating pain in her—well, pretty much everywhere. She tried to ease her position, to alleviate the worst of the stiffness in her joints. The memory of being tied up surged through her like a bucket of ice water being thrown in her face.

She jerked to sit up and was rewarded with a wrenching in her shoulder. She ignored the stabbing pain. Through slim cracks in the shed walls, the sunlight was fading. It was almost dark. Panic clawed its way up her throat.

She had to reach the screwdriver.

Cass scooted away from the workbench, and her shoulder screamed in protest. She stretched her legs as far as she could and pointed her toes. A deep breath in. Hold it. She gripped the handle between her feet and inched it painstakingly slowly toward her. As she pulled it closer, she unearthed the pointy end—intact but rusted. *Yes!* If she couldn't incapacitate him, she could at least give him tetanus. When she was finally able to sit up straight, she took a breath.

But how could she get it to her hands? They were taped securely behind her back. Twenty years of dance lessons were about to pay off. She twisted her legs beneath her, pushing the screwdriver toward her hands.

She grabbed the wrong end, turned it around, and grabbed the handle. Relief left her weak, but she didn't dare take a moment to rest. Langdon could be back at any moment. She flipped the screwdriver around again and held it close to the tip. If she could just work the point through the tape, she'd be out of there.

A noise by the door killed her hope. The door was flung open, and a bright light seared her eyes, temporarily blinding her. She squinted against the attack and worked frantically to shove the screwdriver into the back of her pants. It slid easily into her pocket. No good. He'd see it when he cut the tape . . . if he cut the tape. If not, she was dead anyway. She jammed the screwdriver into her waistband and pulled her shirt over it.

Langdon crossed the room without a word, cut the tape from her wrists, and pulled her to her feet.

He turned her around and cut the tape from her ankles. "Don't say a word. Understand?"

Cass nodded, and he cut the tape around her mouth and ripped it off, taking a handful of hair with it. She rubbed at her head. Every part of her body had stiffened and she tried to work out the sore muscles, but there was no time.

"Walk." He shoved her forward and she stepped into her shoes and walked in the direction he propelled her.

Sheer terror clutched her throat, threatening to strangle her. Nausea turned her stomach and forced bile up her throat. She swallowed it back down.

They walked in silence, trampling through the underbrush by the light of his flashlight. Clouds sat overhead, blocking Cass's vision of the moon and the stars. Also blocking any light they might provide. She contemplated the gun in her pocket. Should she keep it? Her prints weren't on it now, but they would be once he killed her. What good would it do to drop it? It was wiped clean, so it didn't have his prints on it. It wouldn't prove anything. No sense risking his anger to drop it, she decided.

"Stop right there."

They'd come to the edge of the woods. Langdon halted their progress just inside the tree line. He stepped in front of her, poked his head out, and looked up and down the beach.

It was now or never. She reached behind her and grabbed the screwdriver. Her palms were sweating so badly it almost slid from her grasp. She gripped it tighter. Sucked in a breath. *Please, God, help me.*

She plunged the screwdriver into his right shoulder.

His scream tore through the night.

She launched herself into the woods, running blindly, tripping over roots and branches. He'd have to drop the light or the gun to pull the screwdriver from his shoulder. She desperately hoped it was the gun.

He fired.

Crap. The bullet ricocheted off a tree way too close to her.

Cass's lungs burned. She tried to weave as she ran. Another bullet whizzed by. She went down. Hard. She lay in the tangle of bushes and thorns, sucking air and dirt into her straining lungs. Blackness pressed down on her and threatened to suffocate her.

The sound of Langdon crashing through the woods came closer. She held her breath and wished herself invisible. He tore past her, not five feet away, cursing up a storm.

She obviously hadn't hurt him as badly as she'd hoped, but he must have dropped the light because he was stumbling around in the darkness. She belly-crawled forward, inch by inch, staying as silent as possible. She strained her ears to keep track of him. When he moved off toward her right, she risked scooting herself forward a little quicker.

The dried leaves crunched beneath her with every twitch. It *would* have to be autumn. She started to creep forward again when she noticed the silence. *Uh . . . oh.* Where was he? Her labored breathing was incredibly loud. She struggled to hear past it. Nothing but deafening silence.

A deadly game of cat and mouse. The hunter and the prey. But sometimes the prey got away. She clung to that thought.

She focused her gaze straight ahead to where the forest was brightly lit. Too brightly lit. What was going on?

Okay . . . You can do this. She eased herself forward another inch. No sound of a maniac crashing through the woods. Thorns scratched her face, grabbed at her clothes, and tore her hands and arms as she used them to drag herself forward. Drag. Stop. Listen. Nothing. Drag . . .

Her efforts continued to be met only with silence. Had he given up? Run away? Hidden? Set a trap a little farther up? Her shoulder screamed in protest with each pull forward. She ignored it.

She stared at the light dancing through the trees, teasing her. She was almost there. Was Langdon lying in wait?

She'd gotten so turned around she wasn't sure where she was. She scrambled forward the last few feet, barely resisting the urge to get up and run. The woods opened up. Bright, portable floodlights bathed the entire hotel parking lot with something near full daylight. Cars sat haphazardly scattered throughout the area she could see. People rushed to and fro. *What the . . .*

A familiar form backlit by a floodlight crossed the lot. All caution fled the instant recognition came. She scrambled to her feet and lurched into the parking lot.

"Luke!" The scream tore from her lungs.

The form stopped. It moved toward her quickly. "Get down."

What? She stumbled toward him, had to reach him. Her heart hammered painfully. Blood roared in her ears.

He waved at her with one hand, but the other hand stayed in front of him. A gun was pointed straight at her. Luke?

"Get down, Cass."

Down?

"Freeze. Police. Drop it, Langdon."

Langdon?

She glanced over her shoulder.

Langdon had emerged from the woods about twenty feet farther down than Cass and stood aiming his weapon straight at her.

Time slowed. She hurled herself to the ground. She tried to use her hands to break the fall, but her already-damaged chin took the brunt of the impact.

Chaos erupted around her. People running and yelling. Sirens pierced the night.

"Don't move, Langdon."

Tank? Cass rolled onto her side in time to see Tank remove the gun from Chief Langdon's hand and put handcuffs on him. From the number of guns aimed at him, she didn't figure he would even flinch, never mind move. He turned his head, and his stare bored straight through her.

She held his gaze and started to climb to her feet, but Luke pressed a hand to her shoulder. "Stay still. The ambulance is here."

"I can't, Luke. Please. Let me up."

He followed her gaze and stepped back. He held up a hand to halt the two men running toward her with a stretcher.

Her vision tunneled until her whole world came down to her and Langdon. Cass stood. Tank read the chief his rights and put him in the back of a police car. Pain hammered at her, but still she stood. Waited. The car pulled out of the lot.

"Good?"

"Yeah."

Luke lifted her off her feet and put her on the stretcher. Her eyes fell shut.

"Ouch!" Cass winced as she shifted her weight to allow Beast to drop his head in her lap. She raked her fingers through the big dog's fur.

"Hey, be careful. The doctor was nice enough not to admit you, after all the whining you did about wanting to go home, but he said no exerting yourself for a day or two."

Bee pushed the coffee table over to the love seat so she could prop her feet up. He held out a mug of hot chocolate, and she reluctantly removed her hand from Beast's fur to take it.

She smiled at him. "Thanks, Bee."

"Yeah, well, don't get too used to it. You have one week to recover before the final preparations for the fashion show." He arranged a pillow beneath her arm, which was in a sling, then patted her arm affectionately. If it hadn't been for his frantic phone call to Tank, the outcome might have been much different.

The doorbell rang, and Bee went to answer.

Tank looked after him. "You know. He's really not such a bad guy." He turned his gaze back to Cass. "He was hysterical when he called. It took almost five minutes for me to figure out who it was and what he was talking about. He's a good friend." He lifted his and Stephanie's entwined hands, kissed her knuckles, and stood. "I gotta run. I'll stop back and check on you guys again later. If you want, I'll bring Chinese." He leaned over and dropped a kiss on Cass's head. "Stay out of trouble."

She laughed.

Stephanie moved to sit next to her. "Are you really all right?"

Cass shrugged. "Yeah. I'm still a little nervous, but I'm okay."

"You sure you don't want me to stay tonight?"

She hugged Beast's neck. "Nah. I'll be all right."

She squeezed Cass's hand. "I'll be right back. I'm just gonna walk Tank out."

Luke poked his head around the corner. "Hey. How are you feeling?" He walked in and held out a huge bouquet, which Bee promptly took and headed toward the kitchen.

"I'm doing okay, thank you. I've been mostly sleeping the past few hours, but I feel a little better now." She frowned. "Tank said Bee called him and said I disappeared, but I don't understand what was going on at the hotel. What were all the lights about, and why did you say you were the police? I asked Tank, but he said you'd come by later and explain everything."

"I asked him not to say anything until I had a chance to talk to you." He shoved a hand through his hair. "I'm with the state police on the mainland. I was here investigating an art theft ring when my boss got a call from Kyle Benedict. He suspected Otis Langdon killed Marge Hawkins. He also told them there was no way the sweet, young girl he was pinning it on could have done it." Luke grinned.

Cass lowered her gaze as heat crept up her neck into her cheeks. "Sweet, young girl? Then why did he give me such a hard time about keeping the dates for Bee's show?"

"It wasn't anything personal against you. When I spoke to him privately about letting you continue production, he said the only reason he was so adamant against it was that Marge begged them to halt production. It obviously meant a lot to her, and . . . well . . . you know how he felt about her."

Cass shrugged. "I guess I can understand that."

"Anyway, my boss called and told me what was going on. He didn't really believe Mr. Benedict, but it did have to be checked out. Since I was already here, and it wouldn't raise any questions, he asked me to look into it." Luke sat across from her on the coffee table. He lifted the mug from her hand, placed it on the coffee table, and took her hand in his. "I'm sorry I couldn't tell you the truth." He rubbed a thumb over her knuckles. "When I found out you were missing . . ." He shook his head. "We were setting up a search party when you stumbled out of the woods."

"I've never been so happy to see anyone." She squeezed his hand. "Thank you."

"Does that mean we're okay?"

She smiled. "Yeah. We're good."

He grinned, and her heart stirred in ways she wasn't yet ready to examine too closely. "Whatever happened with the theft ring?"

"Actually, we inadvertently solved the art thefts when we talked to Bee and confiscated Jay Callahan's truck." He laughed and shook his head. "Turns out Jay's love interest, Carmen, was smuggling artwork stolen from the Hamptons onto the island. She'd take it to Jay, rolled in carpets, then he'd take it across on the ferry to the North Shore and on to Connecticut. You didn't witness him carrying a carpet from the hotel but from a truck parked out front."

"Does that mean he'll go to jail?" Cass asked.

Luke's expression turned sober. "He will if we find him. Unfortunately, we found his truck abandoned at the marina with the carpet still in the back, but no sign of Jay. A boat's missing."

Cass contemplated the implications. "Do you think he'll come back?"

Luke shrugged. "There's no way to tell. He'd be foolish to return to such a small island where everyone knows him, but who knows?" His expression hardened. "You should have stayed out of it, Cass. You had no business investigating on your own. I wish you would have trusted me enough to ask for help."

She squirmed. "I really had no clue it was Langdon. I thought it was Jay." *Or maybe you . . .*

Luke nodded. "In all honesty, he would have gotten away with pinning it on Callahan if it wasn't for you. Without him confessing to you and kidnapping you, we had no proof against him."

"What made you search by the hotel?"

"When Bee wasn't getting anywhere with officially reporting you missing—especially with Langdon running the investigation most of the day—he reported the car stolen." Luke smiled and shook his head, and she could only imagine the hissy fit Bee had pitched in the sheriff's office. "A patrol officer found it in the woods and broadcast it over the radio. So, we had a general idea of where to look for you, and Langdon couldn't control that aspect of the investigation." His mood brightened, and that sexy dimple returned. "Now that these cases are pretty much wrapped up, I have a week's vacation time coming, so I thought I'd hang around. Maybe we could take a ride and visit some farm stands."

"I'd like that."

Luke stood, and Cass's stomach flip-flopped. He bent to kiss her cheek. "I'll see you soon." The thick southern drawl sent a shiver down her spine.

"Mmm . . . hmm . . ."

His smooth, rich laughter slid over her as he left. She was going to have to develop some sort of resistance to that good ol' boy charm. Or she just might be in trouble.

Bee walked back in and set the vase of flowers on top of the mantle. He fussed with them for a minute before propping himself daintily on the edge of the chair. "So . . . did you hear?"

Cass resisted the urge to roll her eyes at his theatrics. If she didn't check the urge, he wouldn't share whatever good gossip he was about to dish. "No. What?"

"Hey. You promised you'd wait for me." Stephanie perched on the arm of the chair beside Bee.

"Remember how strange Emmett was acting the night of the group reading?" Bee fluffed his scarf and waited.

Cass grinned at Stephanie. She couldn't help it. "Yeah."

"Well . . . Ellie told me Jay told her—before this whole . . . incident, of course—that Emmett has the biggest crush on Sara Ryan, Jess's mom."

Cass sucked in a breath. "Are you serious?"

He slid back into the chair and crossed one leg over the other. "Can you even imagine those two . . ." Warm laughter filled the room.

Cass shifted in an effort to settle herself more comfortably. Bee got up and tucked the afghan tighter around her legs. "Are you okay, dear?"

"I am now." She smiled at him. "Thank you, Bee."

He waved her off, but his eyes glistened. He leaned down to hug her.

"Don't forget me." Stephanie wiggled between them to join the pile.

A surge of love washed over Cass. These were her two best friends, the two people in the world who had taught her that it was okay to begin to trust again.

"**S**top the car!"

Bee Maxwell slammed on the brakes, skidding to a stop on the sand-covered shoulder. Without loosening his white-knuckled grip on the steering wheel, he turned and glared at Cass. "Are you crazy? What's the matter?"

Cass released her hold on the dashboard and shot him a grin. "We're here."

A hand the size of a baseball mitt fluttered to Bee's chest, with all the drama of a true diva. "You nearly gave me a heart attack because we've arrived at our secret destination?" Gritting his teeth, he shifted gently into park. No way would he jam the shifter into gear, even though she could tell he badly wanted to. The black Trans Am was his baby, always to be treated tenderly. Cass, on the other hand, was a different story. Bee looked about ready to throttle her. "Wouldn't it have been easier to tell me where we were going?"

Stephanie Lawrence poked her head between the seats to stare at Cass. "Not that I want to agree with Bee, but really, Cass, you could have just told him where to go. Then maybe this maniac wouldn't have nearly put us through the windshield."

She shrugged. "I didn't think he'd agree to take us if I told him where we were going."

Bee waved a hand in dismissal and glanced out the window as if realizing for the first time where they were.

The old—supposedly haunted—Madison Estate crouched in the center of the highest ground on the island, amid dried-up beach grass, trees long devoid of leaves, and garbage from kids that were brave—or stupid—enough to ignore their parents' warnings. Thick, gray clouds gathered overhead, lending credence to the haunted house stories Cass had heard since childhood.

A dainty shiver ran through Bee's bulky frame. "Well, if your destination has anything to do with that house, you can just count me out."

"But it's perfect." She opened the door and shot him a quick grin over her shoulder.

"Hey. Where are you going?"

Ignoring Bee's protest, Cass climbed from the car. She closed the door behind her, effectively cutting off any further argument. Bee happened to be deathly afraid of ghosts. Not that he believed in them.

As she stared up at the abandoned mansion, ideas ran around in her head.

During the summer months, tourists flocked to the small island that sat nestled between Long Island's north and south forks. They rented cottages, swarmed the beaches, hung out until all hours in the beach bars, climbed to the tops of light-houses, and swamped Mystical Musings—Cass's small psychic shop on the boardwalk.

But with winter in full force, the island was less than thriving. The murky waters of Gardiner's Bay were rough and choppy, and the piercing wind was a bitter enemy that made the ferry ride to the island less than comfortable. As much as Cass loved living on the tiny island, if she couldn't drive business into Mystical Musings during the harsh season, she wouldn't be able to stay. She'd have to go back to New York City and her once-thriving psychiatric practice.

An icy gust of wind tore through Cass, chasing the thoughts away. Something touched her shoulder, and she almost jumped out of her skin.

"Sorry, didn't mean to scare you." Stephanie laughed.

"Jeez, you could at least say something before you grab me." Bee glared at them from inside the car.

"What are we doing here?" Stephanie zipped up her thick down coat, tucked her wild mane of frizzy brown hair inside it, and tried to pull the collar farther up around her ears.

"Come on. I'll show you." Cass shoved open the rusty wrought iron gate.

Screeeeeech!

Bee's muffled protests followed her through the gate and up the cracked cobblestone walkway.

She smiled.

Bee was one of her best friends, but he was also the biggest drama queen she'd ever met.

It was a house; nothing more and nothing less. At one time, people lived in it . . . and died in it. She swallowed hard.

A seagull shrieked as it dove toward the dark, churning waters of the bay behind the mansion.

A shiver raced through her, and she pulled her long coat tighter around her, failing to ward off a chill that had little to do with the near-freezing temperatures. Although Cass didn't consider herself psychic in any traditional sense—despite the fact that she made her living reading people and "talking" to the dead—she had to admit the house gave her the creeps. *Perfect!*

The stone had long since weathered and cracked. Many of the shingles, which once might have been brown, were now a dull gray and hung precariously, if they weren't missing altogether. The front porch sagged, but the steps looked sturdy enough. She tested each one before putting her full weight on it. They creaked, but held. She tiptoed across, her heart hammered erratically, and she cupped her hands around her eyes to peek into the large front window. Nothing. Dirt, grime, and salt made it impossible to see the dark interior. A chill crept up her spine.

This is ridiculous. No one has lived in this house for longer than I can remember.

Using a crumpled tissue from her coat pocket, she rubbed a circle of dirt away and leaned closer.

"Cass Donovan!"

She jumped, whacked the back of her head against Stephanie's chin, and spun around, startled by Bee's booming voice from behind her. "Ouch." She rubbed the back of her head. "What's the matter with you?"

He stood just outside the gate, his gaze darting around frantically. "You get back in the car right this minute, missy, or I'm leaving you here. You and your sidekick." He gestured toward Stephanie, who was moving her jaw from side to side and rubbing her chin.

Cass pressed a hand to her chest, hoping to keep her heart from jumping out, and laughed. "You wouldn't dare."

At better than six feet tall—even without his platform shoes—Bee could have been an imposing figure, if not for the hand resting on his cocked hip and the look of sheer terror marring his pale face. "Try me, sugar."

She started back toward the gate. A flicker of something, movement from the corner of her eye caught her attention, and she stopped short and turned. *What the . . . ?* A reflection? She squinted, but the sun was hidden behind the thick cloud cover. Her imagination?

"Oh, come on." Bee's whine followed her as she started around the side of the house.

The screech of the opening gate told her Bee had given up his threat to abandon them and decided to join them, or at least come closer to argue his point. He muttered to himself as he stalked toward Stephanie, probably figuring she was the more reasonable of the two. He was probably right.

Cass glanced up at the huge house. She'd never been inside, but from the number of wings and windows, she guessed it had a lot of rooms. Her gaze caught on the huge stone chimney running up between two Quarter Round windows, giving the impression of a face staring back at her. Another flicker of movement grabbed her attention as a curtain rippled in the rounded cupola that sat slightly off-center on the roof.

Her heart stuttered, and she tore her gaze from the house and jogged back to the porch, where Bee and Stephanie stood arguing.

Ignoring them, she headed for the front door.

"What are you doing now?" The fear in Bee's voice made her pause, but only for a moment.

She'd been planning this for over a month and had already gotten permission and cooperation from the owners. Her idea might be nuts, but she was pretty sure it would be a big hit. *If* she could convince her two best friends to help her out. She forced a smile, waggled her eyebrows, and held the front door key up between them. A puff of condensation enveloped the shiny new key each time she exhaled.

"Are you crazy?" Bee's voice only hit that high note when he was completely shocked or extremely upset. In this case, it was probably a little of both.

"Look, Bee. I have to find a way to generate income during the winter."

He offered a quick look of sympathy. Before his designer dress shop, Dreamweaver Designs, had gotten so big, he'd had the same problem. Now that his designs were becoming more popular, and big names in the fashion industry had started attending his annual fashion shows, he had a steady stream of orders pretty much year round.

Good, maybe he'd help her.

"You know how we do the group readings in the shop?"

He eyed her suspiciously. "Yeah."

Although Bee didn't believe in psychic powers or talking to the dead, he stayed as far away from it as possible, just in case. Cass had cajoled him into helping with the group readings since there were no dead people involved. She'd also convinced him it was all done very scientifically.

She shrugged, hoping to appear casual. "Well, I want to do a group reading."

He stuffed his hands into his coat pockets and rocked back and forth. The thought of him falling through the old boards of the rotting porch ran fleetingly through her mind. "In addition to the once-a-month readings you usually do?"

"Sort of?" She caught her bottom lip between her teeth and peered at him from beneath her lashes.

It only took a moment for him to figure it out. "No. Oh no. Not happening, sugar."

"But—"

"Not on your life, sweetie. There is no way I'm going into that house while you"—he shook his head and waved his hand wildly—"do whatever it is you do."

"It's just a reading, Bee. I'll do it the same way I do in the shop." Knowing she was perilously close to whining, she rushed on. "I need your help. You have a background in theater, plus you put on the best fashion shows." No need to remind him how much Cass had helped with those shows. *All right, now I'm getting catty.* She sucked in a deep breath of the frigid air. "How about you just help with the setup? You don't have to stay for the reading."

Bee sighed.

Yes!

"I don't know." He glanced toward the front door, shaking his head. "We'll see. Okay?"

"Bu—"

He held up a hand to stop her. "Be happy with it, honey. It's the best you're going to get."

"I'm telling you, it'll work. A group reading at a haunted house? Are you kidding me? People will line up for that." Cass pushed the mansion's front door open and held it for Stephanie, who followed her into the foyer.

Bee caught the door, held it open, and lodged himself firmly between the door and the jamb without actually crossing the threshold.

"I rented the space fairly cheap, and I'll charge more for the tickets than a regular reading. If I've figured it right, I should be able to make a decent profit." She moved through the foyer and peeked into the large living room, weaving between several ladders, drop cloths, cans of paint, and paint trays with remnants of several different colors splattered in them. The inside of the house was in considerably better condition than the outside.

Bee swallowed hard, his Adam's apple bobbing noticeably. "How did you manage to rent it cheap?"

She shrugged. "It's owned by Wellington, Wellington, and Wellington." The same investment company her ex-husband and ex-best friend both worked for. She tamped down the flare of anger that always accompanied thoughts of her exes.

She'd met Priscilla Wellington at a few holiday parties, when the staff was invited to bring their spouses. Though they'd never shared more than a few words, Priscilla always seemed warm and approachable. "I called Priscilla Wellington last month and she loved the idea. They've been having work done on the house anyway, to turn it into a bed-and-breakfast–style hotel, so they allowed me to do the reading next Friday, a few weeks before their official grand opening is scheduled. They're hoping the guests will stay the weekend."

Bee lifted a skeptical brow. "Why would they open a hotel on Bay Island in the dead of winter?" A cold gust of wind blasted through the open door, hammering home Bee's point.

Cass couldn't help but frown. She'd wondered the same thing, but shrugged off any misgivings. She needed this to work. Whatever ulterior motives the Wellingtons might have were of no concern to her. "Who knows? Some people love stuff like this, Bee."

He scowled and remained in the doorway while she and Stephanie moved farther into the room. It obviously had not been cleaned yet. Cobwebs marred the corners, as she'd expected, and dust floated in the dim light filtering in from the front door. It could definitely use a few coats of paint. Priscilla had said the guest rooms were already finished, so apparently this room was next up on the agenda. She shuddered upon seeing the cracks running down several walls, hoping they were only cosmetic. Having the house tumble down around them was the last thing she needed.

The sound of car doors slamming pulled her from her reverie, and she and Stephanie moved back toward the front door.

Bee stood blocking the doorway, his arms folded across his massive chest. "It's a crazy idea. For all you know, this house is falling apart. It's dangerous. Right, Stephanie?"

Stephanie bit her lip and stared at Bee, excitement lighting her eyes.

"Oh, don't even tell me. Not you, too." Bee slouched against the doorjamb, dropped his arms to his sides, and sulked.

"Why not make it a weekend? You could do a bunch of stuff. There are a gazillion rooms in this house. Do a psychic weekend. You said the Wellingtons were hoping guests would spend the weekend anyway, so they've probably worked that out already. You could offer individual readings, a large group reading, sell crystals . . ." Although Stephanie offered Bee a sympathetic smile, her enthusiasm grew the more she spoke. "And maybe on Saturday night, you could have a masquerade ball or something."

"I don't know." But ideas were already barreling through Cass's mind. It was brilliant. An entire weekend devoted to psychic events.

The voice of reason intruded in the form of Bee's whine. "Do you have any idea what something like that would cost? You'd have to have everyone stay over, have inventory to sell, feed everyone . . ." Bee ticked off the list on his fingers.

Stephanie waved off his concerns. "We can get Isabella Trapani to cater it. Her shop is dead in the winter, too. She'll probably give you a really good deal. As far as the guests, it's only going to make the Wellingtons money. Let them worry about it."

"Let the Wellingtons worry about what?"

Bee jumped, startled, and squealed as he closed the door on the man standing on the porch behind him and launched himself toward Cass.

She held her breath, waiting for all two hundred or so pounds of him to jump into her arms like a frightened child. Thankfully, he stopped just short of her.

"Will you calm down, Bee?" Stephanie stepped around him toward the man who'd pushed the door open and was now entering the house, eyeing Bee with suspicion. "Can I help you?"

"Are you Cass Donovan?"

"No." Shooting Bee a warning glare, Cass sidestepped him and held out her hand. "I'm Cass, and you are?" He had to be one of the Wellington brothers—with his neatly creased and pleated slacks, cashmere sweater, and short blond hair—but she had no idea which one.

"Conrad Wellington the third, Ms. Donovan." He gripped the tips of her fingers in a tentative hold, quickly releasing them to wipe his hand on his perfectly pressed pants. "And, in case my sister hasn't mentioned it, I'm completely opposed to this absurd idea."

Ooookay. "Uhh . . ."

"Marring our pre–grand opening weekend with a bunch of psychic drivel . . . " His face reddened as he glanced around the room. "Well, let's just say anyone with even the slightest amount of intelligence knows there's no such thing as ghosts, and having a so-called psychic"—his gaze crawled up and down Cass, lingering on her chest—"feed into the reputation this house has for being haunted can't possibly bring us the type of clientele we are hoping to attract."

Cass resisted the urge to pull her coat closed around her.

Bee stepped forward, chin lifted, broad shoulders squared, and tossed one end of his silk scarf over his shoulder.

Uh . . . oh.

Ignoring Cass's warning glare, he stood toe to toe with Conrad Wellington. "I actually agree with you about the whole no-such-thing-as-ghosts idea, but what exactly do you mean by *so-called* psychic?"

Conrad's upper lip curled, and he looked down his nose as if Bee was something disgusting stuck to the bottom of his shoe.

Bee wasn't deterred. If anything, his haughtiness increased to match Conrad Wellington the third's. "And just what sort of clientele were you hoping to attract?" He tilted his head and lifted one bushy brow. "A bunch of snooty, stick-up-their—"

"Hi, all." A woman breezed through the still open front door. "I'm Priscilla Wellington." Although she had to be in her fifties, she appeared much younger at first glance. Her long blond hair was pulled back into a high ponytail, and she wore jeans, a gray pullover sweatshirt, and black boots—a stark contrast to her straight-laced brother. Ignoring the tension, she strode through the room as if she owned the place.

Oh, right. She does own the place.

"Ms. Donovan." She approached Cass immediately and gripped the hand Cass managed to extend between both of hers. "It's a pleasure to see you again."

"It's . . . uh . . . nice to see you, too, Ms. Wellington."

She released Cass and waved a hand dismissively. "Please, call me Priscilla. Now . . ." She paused and glanced around, seeming to notice the tension for the first time. Pursing her lips, she turned her attention to her brother. "Do I even need to ask what this is all about?"

Twin spots of color blossomed on his pale cheeks. "Nothing, Prissy, just having a discussion with . . ." He gestured at Bee. "Seems he agrees with me about the psychic babble."

Bee harrumphed, folded his arms across his chest, and pouted.

"Now, dear." She patted Conrad's cheek as if speaking to a small, rebellious child. "I thought we'd already settled all of this." Her voice hardened. "We are launching the pre–grand opening celebration with a psychic reading on Friday night."

"Actually, you and *James* settled this." He spat the name with more contempt than Cass could ever muster. "I've disagreed from the beginning."

"Yes, dear, but Joan is so excited and looking forward to the opening. Do you really want to disappoint your wife?"

Conrad scowled, but offered no further argument.

Ignoring him, Priscilla returned her attention to the others. "Why don't I give you a tour of the mansion while you tell me about the reading. Turning the old Madison Estate into a bed-and-breakfast was a fabulous idea, if I do say so, but opening with a psychic reading was sheer genius, Cass. I'm just thrilled about it."

Cass stood with her mouth open, not sure what to say or do.

Thankfully, Stephanie found her voice . . . sort of. "Um . . . " Her gaze shot to Cass, who simply stared at Priscilla.

Even though she'd dismissed her brother so rudely, Cass liked the woman. She had a fresh, no-nonsense way about her that Cass appreciated. "Just before you got here, we were discussing the possibility of doing some additional events throughout the weekend," Cass said.

Bee sighed.

Conrad balked.

Stephanie smiled encouragingly.

Ugh . . .

Priscilla wove her arm through Cass's and started toward the stairs. "Come, dear, I can't wait to show you the guest rooms. They're all finished, and they look gorgeous." She crossed the room slowly, as if she had all the time in the world. A different person than the whirlwind that had first blown through the door. "Tell me about your plans while we walk."

Stephanie fell into place at Cass's other side, while Bee and Conrad jostled for a position directly behind them.

"Well, I thought maybe we could make a weekend out of it."

The elaborate, curved stairway gave way to the second-floor rotunda, which overlooked the living room and a ballroom behind it.

Cass's breath shot out. Stunning. She tried to imagine how it would look once it was fully restored. Would the Wellingtons eventually invest the money necessary to completely renovate the old place? Maybe, if the hotel was successful. "I'd like to move the group reading to Saturday." It would be easier to do a group reading after she'd gotten to know some of the guests. "Maybe have individual readings throughout the day, followed by the group reading that night."

Priscilla frowned. "What about Friday night?"

What had Stephanie said? A masquerade ball?

"A séance." With a quick wink at Cass, Stephanie continued. "She wants to do a séance on Friday."

Priscilla stopped walking and turned to face Cass.

Elbowing Bee aside, Conrad stepped between them and confronted his sister. "No way."

Bee leaned over and whispered urgently in Cass's ear, "Are you out of your mind?"

"What? It's a great idea." Stephanie pushed past Cass to get to Bee.

The sounds of their bickering faded as Cass tried to focus on the confrontation between the Wellington siblings, their silent stare-off left Cass completely lost, until Priscilla stepped around Conrad to study her.

Cass held her breath.

Bee and Stephanie must have stopped arguing, because the hum of silence echoed loudly.

Cass waited.

Nothing.

The silence ate at her until she couldn't take it anymore. *What about Sunday? Hmm . . .* "Then maybe Sunday we could have a brunch with the opportunity for guests to buy crystals and essential oils." Lame? Too much info? She had no idea, but if Priscilla didn't say something soon, she was just going to give up. "You know the house is supposed to be haunted, right?" *All right, just shut up now.*

Priscilla cleared her throat. "It's brilliant."

"Huh?"

"It's brilliant. I love the entire concept."

Conrad huffed out a breath.

"This could be just the publicity we need to make this all work. Have you sold any tickets yet?"

"Uh . . . no, actually. I just came up with the idea, but I've sold tickets to the Friday night event, and if most of the guests are planning to stay the weekend anyway, it shouldn't be a problem."

"Do you think you can still pull it all together by next weekend, even with the additional events?"

Cass shrugged. Could she? Getting together some inventory to sell would only take a few hours. She'd already touched base with most of the people invited for Friday night's reading. She knew they planned to attend, and Isabella was a miracle worker. This time of year, she'd definitely be able to put something together at the last minute. The only thing that would take some work would be the séance, and she could probably talk Bee into helping her set that up. "Sure. I can do it by next weekend." *I hope.* She crossed her fingers behind her back.

"Well, I'm quite intrigued. I'll tell you what, fax me a proposal listing the itinerary, the cost, and the number of tickets available, and I'll let you know how many I want."

"Excuse me?"

"I'll let you know how many tickets to put aside for me."

"Um . . . great. Thank you so much." Cass's heart raced. *What have I gotten myself into?*

1844